# THE DUALITY OF SWANS

Lilly Atlas

Copyright © 2024  Lilly Atlas

ISBN-13:978-1-946068-56-9

As has now become tradition, the first in the series is dedicated to my husband, who has not only supported me every step of this crazy writing journey but jumped in to help in immeasurable ways. Were it not for him, this would all still be a pipe dream.

## Content Warning

This book contains scenes and discussions of homophobia, which may be difficult for some readers.

Swan, Oklahoma, is a fictional town. Any places mentioned have all been created in my crazy head.

# Table of Contents

# *Prologue*

"Will you hurry up already?" Randy hollered as he kicked a spray of dusty rocks down the dirt path. He spun, cupping his hands over his mouth and shouting, "Next time, I'll bring that broken-down stroller in front of Old Man Hinkle's trailer so I can roll your slow ass. At least we'd get there faster."

Randy back-walked along the dirt road a good thirty feet in front of Tate with a forty of Budweiser sticking out from his back pocket. His hair, the same dark blond as Tate's, was buzzed short as always. He constantly teased Tate for leaving it a bit longer and shaggier, calling him a girl and asking if he wanted pink bows for his birthday.

Tate rolled his eyes. His damn brother wasn't breathing if he wasn't acting dramatic or ragging on someone. "Where's the damn fire?" he yelled back. "Pretty sure you've never given a shit about the county fair before. It ain't going nowhere for five days. Why you gotta rush me? It's too hot to walk fast."

"The fire's in my fucking pants," Randy said, jiggling his crotch as he waggled his eyebrows. "Whit's gonna be there. She told Ginger if I find her 'fore Daryl, she'll blow me, but if he gets there first, he's gonna get his cock sucked insteada me. So fucking move it."

Oh, for fuck's sake. Tate slowed his pace, shooting his

1

brother a smirk. "Has Whit seen those pubes on your face? Cuz if she has, it won't matter what time you show up. She ain't gonna blow you if she sees you looking like a walking ball sac."

"Fuck you," Randy said, stroking his new, patchy goatee. It grew darker than the rest of his hair, making him look stupid as hell. "Ma said it makes me look like a movie star."

Snorting, Tate slowed to a snail's pace. "Should probably do the opposite of what Ma recommends. In case you haven't noticed, she's strung out ninety percent of the time. Probably can't see shit right."

Randy flipped him the double bird. "Shut up. I look good. And can you just walk faster, loser? You're doing this shit on purpose cuz you're jealous. No chick wants your knob."

Tate rolled his eyes again. Annoyance, not jealousy, had him messing with Randy. He didn't give two shits about having some chick slobbering over his dick. Two years ago, Randy started calling him all sorts of names for not showing much interest in girls, so he talked the talk, but he'd yet to walk the walk. Not that Randy knew. Tate could spin a tale like nobody's business, and he'd let Randy think he was getting some.

"Run ahead! What the hell do you need me with you for? Need me to cheer you on so you can get hard for Whit?"

"Fuck no." Randy blinked, then laughed. "But, shit, you're right. What am I doing waiting on your stupid ass? Later, loser." He took off at a jog, shaking up that warm Bud hugging his ass. There'd be an unpleasant surprise if he offered the beer to Whitney after the poor girl blew him. At least something would erupt for her, though it'd be the last blowie she offered up. His brother needed a few more brain cells. Tate didn't hold out much hope of him finding any.

He took his sweet time, strolling past cornfield after cornfield on his way to the county fair. Carnivals weren't his scene, but he had a few extra bucks from the tile job he'd helped his neighbor, Jim, with last weekend. Jim gave him a hundred fucking bucks for two days' work. Tate hadn't ever had his hands on that much cash at once. He spent eighty of it on groceries and saved twenty. The good groceries too. Frozen peas instead of the kind that came in a can and some bacon. Spending that last twenty on some funnel cake and a few rides at the fair would make this the most exciting night he'd had in ages.

By the time he reached the event, the sun had dipped into the horizon, leaving the whole fairground shadowed in twilight. Tate didn't bother looking for his brother. The last thing he wanted was to walk behind some booth and find him getting blown by Whitney, the easiest girl in their high school. She was cool, though. She was always nice to Tate, which he couldn't say of all of Randy's dipshit friends.

At eighteen, she and Randy would graduate in a few weeks, while Tate had a few more years to go. Fifteen, but some days, he felt like forty. Guess that's what happened when your old man was a damn deadbeat, and your mother couldn't make it through the day without pumping something into her bloodstream. Some days she made it to her job waiting tables at the local truck stop diner, but it was a crap shoot. The only reason she hadn't been fired was pity. The owner had known his mother since childhood and felt fucking sorry for her.

Someone bumped his shoulder, jostling him from his thoughts. Tate blinked the fair into focus with a muttered apology. He glanced around at the bright, blinking lights and the crowds of townsfolk. Shit, he'd wandered halfway through the fairgrounds without paying a lick of attention to where he was walking.

Where was the damn funnel cake booth? He'd had a craving for the stuff since he'd seen the first fair flyer a few weeks ago. There was not much better than some warm, fried, sugary goodness.

As he glanced around, movement from a stage to his left caught his attention. Performers moved all over the stage, but what had him walking closer was the music that seemed so out of place for a state fair. Behind him, obnoxious carnival music blared from the rickety Ferris wheel, while in front of him, something slow and elegant played for the performers he now realized were ballet dancers.

What an odd thing to have at the fair. Last year, the main event was pig races, and this year a ballet? Maybe someone was trying to class up the place. Tate snorted. They'd have had better luck getting lipstick on those racing pigs.

Still, he took another step closer to the show out of what he'd later call morbid curiosity.

The stage, like everything else at this hick fair, had seen better days, made of rusted metal with what looked like plywood layered on top. Rows of folding chairs held maybe fifteen scattered audience members despite the crowds at the fair. It seemed like most people were as confused as he was to see a ballet performance at the county carnival. Either that, or they were too busy puking their guts out on rides.

Or getting blown like Randy.

Girls who seemed to be around his age danced across the stage in pink tutus with flowers in their hair. They pranced and leaped on the tips of their toes with identical smiles plastered on their faces. Tate watched for a minute before boredom set in. As he was about to resume his search for a fried treat, a new dancer practically floated onto the stage.

Tate froze.

His skin prickled, starting at the nape of his neck and spreading through to the tips of his fingers.

Air whooshed out of his lungs like it did when Randy socked him in the gut.

The guy on stage danced with a fluidity that almost seemed fake like a person shouldn't be able to move with such grace.

*Grace?* When the hell had he ever used the word *grace*?

When the male dancer leaped, his long legs extended as straight as an arrow. When he twirled, Tate held his breath, sure no one could possibly spin that fast and that many times without toppling over.

This was the first ballet Tate had seen, and his brother and friends would rib him to no end if they saw him gawking like a fool, but he couldn't turn away. He couldn't even blink for fear of missing a second of the guy's routine.

Sweat broke out across Tate's brow as he watched the play of muscles in the guy's bare chest while performing a move that required a flexibility Tate couldn't fathom. The dancer's lower half was covered by a pair of light gray tights that were so fucking snug he could make out each individual ass muscle as the guy danced.

Or he could have if he was looking.

But he wasn't.

He especially wasn't looking at the way those tights cupped the guy's crotch.

No fucking way.

Tate swallowed.

*Fuck, I'm looking.*

*Staring.*

His heart raced.

Completely transfixed.

The dancer held a final pose, and the sparse crowd cheered. Tate should have clapped, but he still couldn't move. If it wasn't for the fact he stood seventy feet from the stage, he'd have sworn the dancer's gaze met his.

His gut tightened.

God, he couldn't fucking breathe. Nothing in the world

had captured his attention the way this dancer had. The entire fair could erupt in flames, and he'd never notice. It felt like live wires were popping and crackling under his skin, making him crave *something* he couldn't put his finger on.

He swallowed a painful lump down his arid throat.

The guy's body was like marble, crafted to perfection— smooth, hairless planes, rippling abs, sculpted arms, and that muscular ass. Were he closer, Tate wouldn't be able to keep from reaching out and touching—

*Oh fuck.*

*No. No, no, no.*

His stomach cramped. Forget the funnel cake. He couldn't eat to save his life right then.

*I can't be. It's not possible.*

The weird feelings were nothing more than admiration for someone who worked hard at their impressive skillset. A skillset Tate would never have but could appreciate the sacrifices it would take to get there.

No way in hell was he attracted to the guy on stage. This was probably from all the girls in their tight costumes. He tried to shift his attention to one of the perky ballerinas, but his damn eyes wouldn't cooperate.

*No.*

His stomach lurched.

A heavy weight slammed into his back, making him stagger forward with a grunt.

"Here you are, you fucking slowpoke." Daryl, Randy's best friend since they popped out of the womb, hopped on Tate, piggyback-style. "What the fuck are you watching this shit for?"

Tate tore his gaze from the stage where the ballet troop bowed for their meager applause. He forced himself to turn toward the rest of his friends.

Randy laughed. "Look at that. One dude dancing with all

those bitches."

Still hanging off Tate, Daryl snorted. "That ain't a dude. It's a fairy. That why you are watching them, Tatey boy? You got a thing for fairies?" He ruffled Tate's hair.

A crushing pain bore down on his chest, making it impossible to speak.

Randy's laughter increased. "You better not be a fucking fairy, Tate. I ain't living with a homo."

"Fuck off," he grumbled, bucking backward.

Daryl yelped as he flew off Tate's back. His ass hit the dusty ground. "What the fuck, Tate? Rude."

Whitney, standing under Randy's arm, giggled. "Maybe you're the fairy, Daryl. Always jumping on Tate's back and rubbing his head."

Randy's eyes widened. "Oh shit, you two fucking?"

Was this what a heart attack felt like?

Tate's face burned hotter than the damn sun.

"Fuck off," he mumbled again.

"I ain't no fucking fairy," Daryl said, all humor gone. "I'll fuck you right here right now, Whit."

"I'd rather die," she said with a smirk.

"C'mon." Randy kicked Daryl's leg.

"Ow! What the hell, Whit? You'da blown me if I got here first, right?"

She shrugged.

"Quit it, you two. I want some fucking funnel cake," Randy announced.

"Oh, me, too," Whitney cooed, running her hand up Randy's torso.

Daryl hopped up. "Let's do it."

The three of them started for the food tent. Tate still couldn't move. Chances were high he'd need CPR in the next few minutes.

"You coming, asshole?" Daryl shouted, walking backward

n`ext to the others.

Tate risked a final glance at the stage. It stood empty and quiet, and any onlookers had disappeared into the crowded fair.

He shuddered and blew out a breath. "Yeah. I'm fucking coming," he said as he forced himself to jog after the group. Whatever had happened a few moments ago had been a damn fluke. Maybe he'd had a mini-stroke or needed some damn water.

Dehydration fucked people up, right?

Whatever. It didn't matter. All that mattered was that he knew for certain he hadn't been attracted to that dancer.

No way, no how.

They passed the next few hours laughing, eating, riding rides, and making general fools of themselves, not attempting to leave until they were stuffed and a little nauseated.

"I gotta take a leak before we walk home," Tate said as they approached a restroom.

"Hurry," Randy said. "I hate waiting."

"What do you care? Didn't you already get blown?"

Whitney, Daryl, and a few of their other friends snickered.

"I'm young," Randy said with a shrug. "Time to go again." He slung an arm around Whitney's shoulders.

"Poor Whitney," he muttered as he strode into the restroom.

Not more than a minute later, he emerged a few ounces lighter. Of course, his loser friends were nowhere to be seen.

"Jackoffs," he muttered, starting for the fair's exit. Whatever. It wasn't as though he needed them to find his way home. As he reached the edge of the building that housed the bathrooms, jeering and a familiar laugh caught his attention.

"The fuck? Randy?" he called as he followed the sound around to the back of the building. His brother had a unique laugh, and Tate loved to bust his balls over it. When he really got going, his laugh sounded like a six-year-old girl, high-pitched and giggly.

"Dude," Randy called, waving him over. "Look at this shit."

He pointed, and Tate craned his neck to see past his friends. What he saw had his stomach twisting.

Two guys with dark hoodies and bandanas over their faces huddled over someone curled in the fetal position on the ground. They whaled on him, kicking, shouting homophobic slurs, and laughing. The sight made him sick. Tate could hold his own and had been in a crap load of fights in his fifteen years, mostly with his brother, but he didn't enjoy it, and he'd never go after anyone for shits and giggles.

"What the fuck?" Tate said. "Why are you standing around watching this shit?"

Daryl jumped up and down, practically giddy. "It's that guy. The sissy from the ballet."

"What?" Tate whispered, blood turning to ice.

"They're teaching him a fucking lesson," Randy said.

"Damn straight," Daryl agreed. "Bet he'll think twice before prancing around on a stage in this town again. We do not need his kind spreading their fairy dust all around."

Tate didn't hear what else was said. His feet acted of their own accord, propelling him toward the fray. "Hey!" he shouted.

Randy caught his arm. "What the fuck are you doing?"

Tate whipped around while still walking. He jerked his arm from Randy's hold. "They're gonna kill him," he shouted, gesturing toward the beating.

Scoffing, Daryl shook his head. "Who the fuck cares?"

Jesus. He spun back. "Get the fuck off him!" he screamed, charging forward.

The assailants were big, and two-on-one odds were never

good, but Randy and Daryl would have his back. They might not be eager to save a gay guy's life, but they wouldn't let Tate get his ass kicked.

"I said, get the fuck off him." He reached one of the guys, grabbing the back of his sweaty shirt.

The guy stopped kicking the dancer and whirled on Tate. "What the fuck?" he shouted in a lethal growl

"Tate!" Randy hollered.

"Fuck this," Daryl yelled. "I'm out of here."

"Let's go."

Randy's voice.

Guess Tate was on his own. He cocked his arm and rammed it into the attacker's face. Blood spurted beneath the bandana, but he didn't go down. His buddy stopped kicking the dancer and spun toward Tate.

*Shit, I'm so fucked.*

He fought as hard as he could, but the dudes were huge, and before long, he was bruised and bloodied, but so were the attackers.

The dancer lay curled up on the ground, twitching every so often but unable to get up and run away.

Tate dodged a fist coming at his nose and kicked out, but his foot only met air. Another fist collided with his stomach, making him double over and nearly tossing his funnel cake.

"Hey! What the fuck is going on back here?" The new voice came from twenty or so feet away.

The fight stopped instantly, and all three of them faced the voice. A rent-a-cop rounded the corner of the building and jogged their way.

Without another word, the two attackers took off in opposite directions.

"Stop!" the guard shouted as he raced after one of them. He grabbed his radio. "I need an ambulance behind the bathrooms. Cops too!"

He had to get the hell out of there before he was arrested. An ambulance was coming. The dancer would be taken care of.

*Go, go. Run.*

But he didn't move. Instead, he gave into the driving urge to peer back at the dancer on the ground. He'd managed to sit himself up. Blood trickled from his nose and mouth, and his dark hair had twigs and dust throughout the strands. He cradled his arm against his chest and trembled. He seemed to be struggling to breathe.

"T-thank you," he whispered.

Tate froze, unable to speak. Even battered, the guy captured his attention in a way no one had before. He wanted to rush forward, wrap his arms around the dancer, and promise no one would hurt him ever again. He wanted to chase after his brother and beat the shit out of him for watching and laughing.

He wanted to kiss the tears right off that devastated face.

*No.*

A siren sounded, closer than was comfortable. Red lights flashed, providing the electric jolt he needed. Help was on the way. Instead of responding, he fled.

He ran until his legs burned, and his lungs screamed at him to stop. He ran straight through the cornfields, ignoring the stinging cuts from the coarse leaves slicing his skin. He ignored the blood and bruises on his face and body.

He had no idea how much time or distance passed before he tripped and landed hard on all fours, panting like an exhausted dog.

*Fuck.*

He couldn't be gay. He could not be gay.

*I'm not gay.*

He'd be next. The next guy on the ground protecting his vital organs as giant feet slammed into him again and again.

*I'm not gay.*

A flash of the dancer holding a beautiful pose flitted through his mind, and his heart skipped a damn beat.

*Oh God.*

*I'm not gay.*

He vomited all over fallen ears of corn.

# Chapter One

"This better be the call where you tell me you came to your senses and decided to move back home."

Liam chuckled at the blunt greeting from one of his sassiest friends. "Hello to you, too, Erin." A shock of longing washed over him. He'd known he'd miss his best friend and former roommate, but hearing her voice after seven days apart drove home how difficult this transition would be.

"Sweetie…" The silence that followed conveyed her continued confusion with his decision to move from their swanky Manhattan apartment to the middle of nowhere, Oklahoma, to open a dance studio.

He sighed as he glanced around the room that needed work he had no idea how to complete. Floors needed buffing, the barre needed replacing, and the floors in the locker rooms were straight out of the nineteen seventies.

Hideous.

"This isn't some flight of fancy, Er. You know I've been planning this for a long time. Years before we met." As brand-new students at Julliard, it seemed like they met as two eighteen-year-olds a lifetime ago, wide-eyed and terrified but bursting with excited ambition. It had taken them two-point-two seconds to become friends, and they'd stayed that way for the past seven years.

"I know," she said, and he could hear the pout in her voice. Her long, graceful neck led to a slender face with high cheekbones and thin lips that didn't pout well. Nine times out of ten, Erin kept her long, blonde hair in a high bun, making her the picture-perfect ballerina. "I know, Liam, but why now?"

He shrugged even though she couldn't see him through the phone. The familiar ache and stiffness in his right shoulder reminded him he hadn't stretched that morning. "I'm getting old, Er. It's time."

Her inelegant snort made him grin. "You're twenty-five, which also happens to be my age, so don't think I didn't notice the insult there. Twenty-five is not old, Liam, even in the dance world."

"It's not young." Fresh, new *young* dancers joined the company all the time, hungry for the lead roles and ready to usurp the twenty-five-year-old geezers.

"Okay, I'll give you that, but it's not old enough to throw away an incredible career where you travel the world and do the thing you not only love but are amazing at." Her frustration came through the phone loud and clear. "I just don't get it."

Of course she didn't. Who would? He barely got it himself. Yes, he was twenty-five, and he had an old shoulder injury that drove him bananas, but it hadn't slowed him down. He never let it. He didn't have to leave New York. No one had even hinted that he'd reached the downslide in his career. His instructors, fans, and company members loved him and had been flabbergasted at his decision to end his career so early.

But, as he'd mentioned to Erin, this had been his plan for a decade. He wanted to bring world-class dance lessons to a place that never had it before. And he'd chosen Swan, Oklahoma, as that place. Swan was a small Midwest town surrounded by cornfields. The closest dance studio was an hour away in Tulsa. The children of Swan didn't have the opportunities he and Erin had growing up for many reasons. Access to studios and teachers, financial hardships, and stigmas were a few reasons the studio he'd purchased had closed its doors and remained vacant for over fifteen years.

Liam planned to change all that.

A hefty inheritance from his grandmother and a successful career as a premier ballet dancer had given him the means to bring his dream to life. In exactly one month, Dance For All would open its doors to the rural town of Swan. He'd provide expert dance classes for toddlers to adults at affordable prices. Bringing his passion to rural communities was the dream he'd harbored for more than a decade.

*Liar.*

"Li?"

He blinked. "Sorry, my mind wandered to my six-foot-long to-do list." Blowing out a breath, he strode to the center of the empty studio room. Staring at himself in the wall mirror, he said, "I know you don't get it, Erin. But this is what I want. This is what makes me happy."

"Hmm."

His eyebrows winged up. Maybe he should have FaceTimed her instead of calling. It was always easier to pick up on subtleties when he could see someone's face. "What?"

"Nothing."

He scoffed. "Nothing? Since when do you hold back?"

"Since never," she said with a laugh. "I just know this is a sensitive topic for you."

"Erin…"

He could practically feel her rolling her eyes. "Fine, I'll say it. I think your burning desire to move to Bumfuck Oklahoma is less about your passion for teaching and more about you having something to prove to the world."

Her words were sharp arrows pinging off his non-existent

emotional armor.

"That's ridiculous." He might not have armor, but he had denial. And nervous laughter.

"Is it? If you were here right now, could you look me in the eye and tell me you're not out there in the middle of nowhere trying to prove something to yourself and the hillbillies who live there?"

"Don't call them hillbillies. It's rude," he muttered.

What were the chances she wouldn't notice he avoided her question?

Slim to none, most likely.

"You're saying it wasn't hillbillies who—"

*Oh no. No, no, no.* "Don't go there, Erin. Please don't go there."

His shoulder throbbed.

Erin sighed, and a heavy silence fell between them.

Damn her for calling him on his bullshit. Weren't besties supposed to turn a blind eye to their friend's shortcomings? Not that he and Erin had ever rolled that way, but he just couldn't do this today. Or ever. "Er…"

"Okay. I get it. I'll stop."

He could practically see her lifting her hands in surrender. "Thank you."

"So," she said after another silence. "What are you planning to do on your first Friday night in Swan, Oklahoma? A hay ride? Maybe some cow tipping? Oh, I know. You're gonna go pick some corn and eat it fresh from the stalk or whatever it's called."

Liam laughed, and the tension dissolved. "You know cow tipping isn't actually a thing, right?"

"Pfft, don't ruin my city-girl stereotypes of rural America."

"Actually, I think I'm going to drive to Tulsa and check out this club called Stardust."

"Ooh, Stardust. Might this be a gay club?"

He rolled his eyes. "Yes, Erin, there are gay clubs west of Manhattan."

She sniffed. "Sure, but I bet they're not as good as ours."

"I'll be sure to call and give you a full report tomorrow."

"You better. Especially if you meet a sexy farmer in overalls and a John Deere ball cap. Oh, do you think guys out there drive their tractors to the clubs?"

"Oh my God," he said, laughing. "Could you typecast the people who live here anymore?"

"If someone brings a chicken, I want you to text me a pic."

"A chicken? In a club? You should be ashamed of yourself." He shook his head but couldn't keep from smiling.

"Remember, Li, it's not the size of his farm that matters, but what he can grow on it."

"I'm hanging up now."

"Wait, wait! Don't hang up."

He pinched the bridge of his nose. "What?"

"I've got a great pickup line for you. Is that an ear of corn in your pocket, or are you just happy to see me?" She rushed the words out, knowing he'd make good on his threat.

"Goodbye, Erin." He hit 'end call' at the sound of her loud laughter. Shaking his head, he pocketed the phone in his jeans but had to admit she'd lifted his mood. She'd also made him nostalgic for the life he'd left behind.

Two weeks ago, he and Erin, along with the rest of their friend group, mostly dancers in their company, hit up a brand-new swanky club on the Lower Eastside. They'd danced the night away surrounded by other trendy twenty-somethings in the glitz and glamor of New York.

He lied when he told her he planned to go to a club in Tulsa tonight. He'd found one, that was true, but he planned on binge-watching something mindless while eating a tub of ice cream and contemplating how big of a mistake he had made with his life. If he'd admitted that, she might get on a plane and drag him back to New York.

Maybe he should go out. Perhaps he should start this new phase of life by being social and exploring instead of hiding away in his shoebox apartment.

He stared at his reflection in the mirror, seeing the fear he refused to acknowledge aloud. But eyes never lied, and his held a world of trepidation. How was he supposed to create a life in this town if he was too scared to venture to the one place where he'd be accepted for who he was?

"Damn you, Erin," he muttered. "Something to prove, my ass."

But he did have something to prove, didn't he? It was the whole reason for uprooting his life and moving to Swan.

"No!" he snapped at his reflection. "I'm here to teach. To bring the New York Ballet to a rural town."

He swore his reflection snickered and rolled its eyes.

"Fuck it." Liam marched out of the studio and up the back stairs to the small apartment that came with the lease. The prior owner used it as storage, but he needed a place to live, so he decided to make it his home.

A few hours later, he stood beyond the club doorway, having received his admittance stamp and a serious once-over from the massive bouncer. The good news was Erin had been way off base.

Not a chicken or overalls in sight.

The bad news—the place was tacky as hell, cringeworthy, even. A rainbow disco ball hung over the center of the dance floor, spinning and bouncing dizzying rainbow lights throughout the room. Colorful streamers dangled from the ceiling as though someone had hit up Party City before coming to work at the club.

But the place was full of men and a few women drinking, dancing, and groping like any other club. He blew out a breath and a ton of tension with it. So far, Swan seemed to have a gay population of one courtesy of his moving to town. He'd been too stubborn to admit it, even to himself, but for the past three days, he'd felt like Alice falling down that damn rabbit hole. Going from New York to Swan was a culture shock he'd been less prepared for than he'd thought.

At least in the tacky Stardust Club, he could be himself. This place could become a refuge when he grew tired of being stoic. When the whispers and stares grew too much or the bigots too loud.

Tulsa wasn't Manhattan, but it would do.

"What can I get you, hot stuff?" A bartender wearing a black fishnet tank top leaned across the bar. A silver nipple ring peeked through his netting, catching the disco lights. He was only an inch or two taller than Liam's five-nine but had a platinum-blond fauxhawk that added two inches.

"Gin and tonic. Two limes, please."

"Sure thing." The bartender set about concocting his drink of choice. "Haven't seen you around here before, cutie. You visiting?"

"Uh, no, I just moved here. Well, to Swan."

The bartender grimaced and poured an extra splash of gin into the drink. "You're gonna need that. Why the hell would you move there?" He deposited the drink in front of Liam, who snorted a laugh.

"Maybe I'll figure it out after a few of these. Thanks." He dropped cash on the bar, lifted the drink, and took a healthy swig.

The bartender gathered up the payment. "Well, have fun tonight, man. I have a feeling we'll be seeing a lot of you around here."

Liam saluted him with his drink, then turned and faced the crowd. Since he didn't have any friends to chat with, he finished his drink in record time. The alcohol hit his bloodstream, chasing away his inhibition. With a smile, he set his empty glass on the bar and strode out into the throng of gyrating men to do what he did best—dance.

# Chapter Two

Secrets sucked—literally.

They reached inside a body, found whatever soul a person possessed, and sucked it out like a fucking Hoover on turbo until nothing remained but a walking, talking husk of a human.

Still, that was preferable to having someone rip your actual guts out, which would have happened had Tate not held on to his secret tighter than a virgin asshole.

His secret began long before he understood he'd need to keep it for his whole goddamn shitty life. It began early in his childhood when he'd been a sponge absorbing the toxicity his parents poured on him. *Parents* was a loose term. Sperm and egg donors turned roommates painted a more accurate picture.

By thirteen, he'd long been caring for himself and his needs. Hell, he'd been more responsible than his damn brother, who was older by three years. Randy came out of the womb a damn fuck-up, feet first, and not even smart enough to take a breath until the doctor whacked him on his ass.

Food? Tate had shopped for it, begged it from friends, and even stole it if he got hungry enough.

Clothes? Goodwill for the win.

Shelter? Their shitty trailer was about the only thing his

old man had ever paid for. To this day, they have never paid a lot fee. His mother had been banging the trailer park's manager for as long as he could remember.

Slutty mom for the win.

That left love and affection, but he didn't think someone in their trailer park had experience with either. Even Letti and Jack, the newlyweds in the trailer diagonal from his, hated each other's fucking guts. Oh, they'd devour each other's faces for all the world to see and profess their undying love at the top of their lungs, but their fights could wake the dead, and Letti slashed the tires on Jack's bike last week. New ones were expensive as hell, and Jack worked at a damn junkyard. She wouldn't have pulled that shit if she loved him for real. He had a sneaking suspicion Letti was banging Daryl on the side too.

They lived in a fucked-up town with fucked-up people.

Last week, he heard Old Man Richards, who lived in the first lot in their park, say nothing could shock him after living in Swan for over fifty years.

*I could shock him. I could shock the shit outta him.*

*God, I'm in a mood.*

It had been a long, frustrating day, and traffic to Tulsa sucked, turning the sixty-minute trip into almost ninety. Randy gave him shit for not hanging out tonight too. He and Whitney got in a fight—big fucking surprise—and he needed someone to listen to him bitch while he drank half a case of beer.

But Tate had needs, too, and he hadn't had his needs met in six months.

Tonight, that was going to change. He'd needed a nameless man with stellar sucking skills to swallow his cock and drain his balls. Fuck, it had been so damn long. He'd been a surly bastard this past week. Even his mother asked what crawled up his ass, and she barely knew what year it was on a good day.

His hand wasn't cutting it anymore. He needed to get off with another person, and to do that, he had to go out of town. Way out of town to Tulsa, the only place with a gay bar, and was far enough from home that he didn't have to look over his shoulder every two seconds.

But he did anyway.

Some habits were unbreakable, especially when they kept him breathing.

He got half-hard on the walk from his car to the club, imagining the sea of men grinding all over each other beyond the entrance. His brother would stroke out if he got a peek inside, but not before beating the shit out of Tate.

As he strode to the entrance, he rolled his shoulders and tried to shake off the unease that always cropped up when he went there. No matter how many years he'd been playing this game, he couldn't shake the fear he'd return home, and somehow, they'd all know. Maybe someone would smell lingering cum on his breath. Maybe Daryl would take one look at his sated smile and shout, "Holy fuck, you got off with a dude." Or he'd show up at a job site on Monday, and Randy would be waiting to pound him into the ground because someone saw him fucking a twink's throat behind the club.

It hadn't happened yet, but it could.

The possibility of discovery always hovered, dampening the experience. It was hard to fully let go when he had to keep one eye on alert.

"Hey there," a giant bouncer said as he approached. The guy gave him a suggestive once-over that screamed of sex, but he wasn't Tate's type. At six-foot-two with a fairly solid build, Tate preferred men smaller and slimmer than he was. This mountain of a man didn't do much for him. "Ten dollar cover waived if you give me your ass after my shift."

Fuck no.

Never going to happen. He did not bottom. Ever. But knowing someone wanted him never failed to boost his ego. "Sorry, man, not my thing." Tate wasn't one to beat around the bush or play coy. He didn't have time for that shit. He needed to get in, get off, and get out before he made too much of an impression. Anonymity was the name of the game.

The bouncer pouted and held out his hand. "Cover's fifteen."

Snorting, Tate raised an eyebrow. What a fucking hustler.

"Inflation sucks," the bouncer said with a shrug.

"Fine." Instead of telling this guy where he could shove the extra five bucks, he fished two bills out of his wallet and slapped them in the bouncer's palm.

Just went to show how badly he needed another man's hand on his cock.

After accepting the stamp, which the bouncer dug into his skin like he was trying to brand him, Tate wandered into the club. His heart rate immediately thumped in time with the EDM pulsing through the building.

Clubs weren't his typical scene. Most weekend nights, he could be found sitting in a lawn chair, drinking beer with his friends and Randy around a shitty bonfire in the center of the trailer park, or drag racing behind the abandoned factory on the outside of town. Sometimes, they hit up a sports bar, but dance clubs?

Fuck no.

But he did what he had to do when the loneliness crept in, and his mask felt too heavy to wear another day.

Christ, he sounded like a damn sad sack.

After grabbing a beer from the bar, he took his usual spot propped against a wall to search for his conquest. When he found him, Tate would dance. One dance. No more. He couldn't dance to save his life, but he could grind against a hot ass for a few moments before taking them out back for a quick suck or fuck.

Bodies moved all around, flowing with the heavy beat. Most were men, but a few women were sprinkled throughout the mix. The thing that stuck with Tate the most every time he went there was the variety of people.

Big and small.

Old and young.

Black and white.

Flashy and subdued.

They represented all walks of life with one main commonality.

They were all queer.

And no one blinked an eye. Hell, it was fucking celebrated with the cheesy rainbow streamers and blowjob shots given out like water. Inside these four walls represented a world in which Tate belonged.

But he also belonged where he came from, and the two universes did not mix. Maybe someday someone would be brave enough to bridge the gap, but Tate couldn't be that man. He'd seen firsthand what happened to people like him in Swan, and he knew to the very depths of his soul he'd lose every single person in his life if he came out.

Was it wrong?

Fuck yes.

But it was his reality.

The song changed, though they all sounded the same to him, and a flash of bright pink caught his eye. He craned his neck to see past a couple making out and groping each other in his line of sight. The taller guy broke off the kiss, whispered something to his partner, then dragged him off the dance floor.

"Be safe, kids," Tate muttered, lifting his beer in salute.

The second they moved away, the dancer in pink came into view.

Tate's blood rushed south. He was so hard-up that a glimpse of a sexy man made him chub right up.

"Jesus," he whispered as he straightened off the wall.

Like all the others, the guy danced to the music, but that's where the similarities ended. This guy moved on another level entirely. He danced like he was one with the music, flowing, spinning, and twisting in perfect time to the beat. He wore dark jeans and a skin-tight hot pink T-shirt that showcased sleek muscles every time he shifted.

Tate swallowed a painful gulp of beer. His cock filled so fast that he needed to reach for the wall to steady himself. The guy's eyes were closed, and a blissed-out smile curled his full lips, lips that would look unreal wrapped around Tate's dick. Sweat ran down the side of his face, tempting Tate's tongue and teasing his cock. His short, dark hair had been artfully styled in gelled spikes.

Tate wanted, needed to mess it the fuck up while he choked the guy on his dick.

He was fucking beautiful.

He stared for a few more minutes before setting his empty beer bottle on the floor against the wall. As though in a trance, he closed the distance to his prey. Each step brought him closer to all that beauty and grace. That's what it was. Somehow, while vibing to club music, the guy managed to convey grace and elegance.

Randy would drop dead on the spot if he had a front-row seat to Tate's thoughts. But Tate couldn't stop them, just as he couldn't keep himself from tucking up behind the dancer in pink.

The guy sensed his presence and opened his eyes before Tate got close enough to touch. But he could smell him, and, damn, did he smell intoxicating. The man shook his head and opened his mouth, probably to tell Tate to fuck off, but then his gaze went hot and dark as it took a slow journey up and down Tate's body. He couldn't help but puff out his chest and didn't bother hiding the tent in his jeans. Everywhere that heated gaze touched, fire licked across his skin. Tate was burning up, and all they'd done was stare at each other.

If they touched, he might turn to ash and blow away.

His heart pounded harder than the time he'd chased after Whitney, who tried to run down Randy with his brother's own car. That day, he'd thought he needed to drive himself to the hospital once he caught up to Whitney. His heart nearly shot out of his chest.

If he went into cardiac arrest now, there'd be no shortage of sexy men willing to blow air into his lungs.

But only one had his dick hard as a fucking railroad spike.

The dancer's chest rose and fell, showcasing strong but not bulky pecs. If Tate could have given God a list of characteristics for the man he wanted crafted for his personal pleasure, this guy was it. A body made for moving.

He raised an eyebrow. An invitation.

The guy licked his lips, and Tate grunted as his damn dick twitched, which earned him a smirk.

"Liam," the guy said, still moving in the most seductive way imaginable. "And yes, I'd love to dance with you." His voice fit him well—smooth like honey, confident and strong. His honey-colored eyes sparkled with interest.

Without knowing a damn thing about the man, he knew Liam didn't live a life hiding his identity as Tate did.

Envy twisted low in his gut, but he shoved it aside. Tomorrow, when he wove a fake fucking tale about the woman he fucked on this trip to Tulsa, he could feel that envy. Tonight, he just wanted to feel Liam.

He hooked his finger in one of Liam's belt loops and tugged the smaller man to him. Liam's eyes flared as their bodies collided. "Tate," he whispered in Liam's ear.

He rolled his hips into Liam's, grinding his erection against the man in time with the music.

"Shit," Liam mumbled. He looped an arm around Tate's neck, bringing their chests flush.

His skin was damp from dancing. All he wanted was to lean in and lick the salt off Liam's neck. He came close, inhaling the intoxicating fragrance of the man's cologne. It had a beachy undertone, perfect for a steamy summer night.

"You didn't come to play," his dance partner said as he began to rock them to the music.

Tate chuckled. He could feel Liam's cock growing against his own, and he let the other man lead, following wherever his hips went. "That's exactly what I came to do."

Liam groaned. "I wasn't looking for anything more than dancing tonight, but I have a feeling I'd regret turning you down for the rest of my life."

"Fuck yeah, you would."

They didn't speak after that. The music took over, and Tate lost himself in Liam's perfect body. Zaps of electricity coursed through his veins, bringing him to life in a way he hadn't experienced in ages. Where Liam moved, Tate followed, and before long, they found a rhythm that worked despite Tate's two left feet. Every time their cocks bumped, Liam breathed out a little puff of air that tickled Tate's neck and tightened his balls.

The song changed, and neither noticed, continuing straight into the next one, rolling, grinding, and breathing each other in. For all he knew or cared, the rest of the clubgoers had gone home, and only he and Liam remained dancing.

Sweat, the beachy cologne, and desire all rolled into one, invading his senses. As Liam's scent overwhelmed his brain, Tate's ability to think disappeared, and all he could do was feel.

And want.

He couldn't keep his mouth off the man any longer.

He dragged his tongue up the side of Liam's neck, gathering the trail of sweat that had been torturing him for the past thirty seconds. The move drew a long groan from his dance partner.

Liam turned his face a fraction of an inch. Their lips lined up. Liam's curved in a hint of a smile before he struck, nipping Tate's lower lip.

He growled. The sting fired up his blood and drove him to act. He grabbed the back of Liam's neck with one hand and a firm ass cheek in the other—God, that ass was a handful of perfection—and yanked him even closer. He covered Liam's mouth with his own in a deep kiss.

*Finally.*

Liam tasted of gin and freedom. Within seconds, Tate grew drunk on both.

Fireworks went off behind his closed eyelids as Liam's tongue slid against his own. The guy wasn't shy. He kissed like a dream and wasn't afraid to take what he wanted, which seemed to be Tate's tongue dancing with his the same way their bodies had moved seconds ago.

Soft but sure hands landed at the nape of his neck, playing with the shaggy hair he should have cut weeks ago. A rumble built in his chest like a cat seeking affection. Those hands felt so good, and they were only on his damn scalp.

He had to get himself under control, or he'd fucking die the second Liam got those hands on his skin.

Though, if he was going to go out, that was the way to do it.

It sure beat the bloody attack if his brother and friends found out about this night.

## Chapter Three

*He's hungry.*

It was Liam's first thought when Tate kissed him like a man starving, and Liam was there for it.

He'd felt Tate's presence before he saw him and prepared to reject the guy right off. Of course, he could use a strings-free hookup, but he'd meant it when he'd said he hadn't come to the club for that. But when he opened his eyes to find the other man close and staring, he lost his ability to speak.

Sporting a plain charcoal T-shirt and worn jeans, Tate hadn't dressed to impress, but it worked on him. Boy, did it work on him. So did the height, shaggy, dark blond hair, deep blue eyes, and slight scowl. Combined with his general don't-fuck-with-me vibe and impressive muscles, Tate made Liam's stomach flutter. So much for not wanting a hookup. In his defense, it'd been a long time since he had such an instant and powerful physical reaction to a man. And if the hard-on grinding all over him was any indication, Tate wanted him too.

He tasted of beer and the faintest hint of cigarettes, which did nothing to negate his bad-boy image. The men Liam typically dated or hooked up with were from a similar walk of life, New York City twenty-somethings clambering up the ladder of success. Tate didn't seem like the type to give a fuck about his social media presence or financial portfolio. Something about him felt exciting, daring, and different, and it woke Liam's desire.

Tate squeezed his ass, and Liam moaned into his mouth. The guy knew how to use his tongue. Within minutes, Liam was a quivering mess of lust and need. They broke away, gasping for breath.

Tate's dirty blond hair stuck out in all directions from Liam's wandering hands, and his deep blue eyes had darkened to match the ocean just before a storm. Panting, they stared at each other, no longer dancing.

Liam's cock was so hard it ached, testing the strength of his jeans zipper. He'd gone beyond the point where it could be ignored. An orgasm was a must, and soon. There was always the option of taking care of it himself, but why on earth would he go that route when he had a sexy-as-fuck man with an equally hard dick watching him with a ravenous gaze.

The tiny part of his brain that remained rational screamed that going home with a man he didn't know in a city he didn't know had disaster written all over it. But his brain didn't have enough blood for a majority vote.

"Wanna take this somewhere else?" he asked, rising on his toes to reach Tate's ear. God, yes, he loved a bigger man. He loved feeling engulfed and overpowered under the right circumstances. "I live too far to head to my place. You close?"

"No." The word was clipped as though the thought of going to his house seemed ridiculous. "Bathroom?"

Then again, maybe he was merely as desperate as Liam.

It'd been years since he'd had a quicky in a club's bathroom—not since his college days. With a nice apartment within walking distance from many of New York's trendiest clubs, bathroom hookups hadn't been necessary.

*You're not in Kansas anymore, Dorothy.*

Nope. He was in Oklahoma, and things were different

here. Was he really going to do this? Head to the bathroom in this tacky club to tug some random guy's dick?

Tate met his gaze. The raw hunger nearly brought him to his knees right there. He pressed the heel of his hand over his cock with a hiss.

Tate raised one of those light eyebrows.

Fuck it.

He grabbed Tate's rough hand—those calluses would do amazing things to his skin. And on his cock? They would feel unbelievable. "Let's go."

Together, they weaved through the throngs of clubgoers to the back hallway where four single-user bathrooms resided. A short, barrel-chested man walked out of one as Liam reached the mouth of the hallway.

"Hell yes," Liam muttered. He tugged Tate along straight to the vacant restroom. The second Tate followed Liam into the stall, he slammed the door shut so hard it rattled the thin walls. The snick of the lock sent a shiver racing down Liam's spine.

Crazy things were about to happen in there.

As much as he wanted to get off, the idea of driving Tate out of his mind set Liam's blood boiling. He spun and slapped his palms to Tate's chest, shoving the bigger man against the closed door.

Tate's eyes widened, and his nostrils flared. "So, it's like that, huh?"

Meeting his gaze, Liam nodded once. "Yeah." He ripped the button on Tate's jeans open and lowered the zipper in one smooth move.

Life had been crazy lately. Leaving his ballet company and moving from New York, where he knew he was loved and accepted, to a potentially hostile town where he didn't have friends had his head spinning. Add to it starting a business that had the potential to fail, and Liam felt out of control. He needed to take some power back, and what better way to do that than by turning a rougher, bigger man into a needy mess?

Before he reached into Tate's black boxer briefs, he raised an eyebrow. "Any objection to me giving you the blowjob of your life?"

Tate's nostrils flared. "Christ, you're not what I expected."

Liam smirked. This wasn't what anyone would have expected of him.

"Do your worst, Luxe."

He slid his hand down the waistband of Tate's underwear and wrapped his hand around the hot steel trying to escape. God, the skin was soft and sleek over all that stiffness. "Luxe?" he asked, already breathless.

Tate hissed out a curse. "Damn, your hand feels nice." His eyes fluttered as though wanting to close, but he fought it. "The way you move, it's elegant, graceful." He shrugged. "Luxe."

Liam blinked. His throat thickened. From childhood, his entire life had been spent honing those exact skills. What was a professional ballet dancer without elegance and grace? Tate's comment expanded a warm feeling in his chest. His last boyfriend hated the way Liam carried his training into his everyday movements.

*Don't be an emotional fool.*

This was a down-and-dirty hookup in a damn bathroom stall, nothing more, and he'd be an idiot if he pretended it was anything else.

The man was gorgeous in a down-to-earth kind of way, not the polished type of guy Liam typically went for, but stunning, nonetheless. He had a raw magnetism about him that drew Liam in the most primal way. Whatever it was— chemistry, pheromones, or black magic— he wanted to devour this man with an instant passion he wasn't used to.

Liam wanted to tear off his clothes, shove his nose in Tate's armpit, inhale his masculine scent, bite him, and leave teeth marks to show where he'd been.

But he'd settle for swallowing what promised to be a stellar cock and hearing Tate shout his release.

He tightened his grip, shoving aside all those pesky feelings that always caused him trouble, and smirked.

"Shit." Tate reached for him, but he dropped to his knees out of the man's grasp.

He'd regret kneeling on the hard floor in the morning when he couldn't perform a simple plié, but that was tomorrow's problem. One hard yank had Tate's pants and boxer briefs down around his knees.

His cock sprang forward, long, hard, and mouthwateringly thick. Liam would love to spend hours worshiping all that flesh, but this was a race against the clock. Someone would come banging on that door before long, so he needed to act.

He cupped Tate's heavy balls, drawing another of those tortured hisses from the man.

"My fucking favorite," Tate rasped.

*Good to know.*

He licked the head of Tate's cock, catching a large drop of precum before it fell to the floor, wasted. The flavors of heat and sin hit his tongue and invaded his senses. His own cock throbbed, trapped behind his jeans. He was dying to free it and tug himself to completion, but the fantasy of Tate doing it for him kept him in check.

He opened his mouth and engulfed Tate down to the root as he gave a gentle tug to his balls. Tate shouted. The sound of his palms smacking against the wall to stabilize himself made Liam smile despite his full mouth.

He cast his gaze upward to find Tate staring down at him with a near snarl on his face and fire in his eyes.

It was the hottest look anyone had ever given him.

After that, it was game on. He sucked like his damn life depended on it while playing with Tate's balls and occasionally his taint. Wicked curses flew from Tate's mouth over and over.

He loved the feel of Tate's heavy cock on his tongue. Loved everything about this experience. The scent, the taste, the way with each passing second, Tate's shouts became more unhinged and desperate. All of it made him feel powerful and sexy as hell.

Tate's cock hit the back of his throat, and Liam swallowed once, then a second time. He'd long ago learned to dominate his gag reflex.

"Jesus fucking Christ, you can suck a cock." Tate grabbed his hair and held him in place as he thrust forward. The ability to breathe disappeared for a few seconds, making his eyes water.

He swallowed again.

"Yes. Shit, yes. Fuck, Luxe, you're amazing."

Was it possible to preen with a mouth full of cock?

He sure gave it his best try.

He moved his mouth to Tate's balls, licking over the taut sack. Tate groaned when Liam sucked one into his mouth.

"Shit, I'm not gonna last much longer."

After a final lick, he moved back to Tate's cock. He sucked the head hard before sliding his lips down.

"Shit! Coming." Tate held Liam's head and thrust once before unloading down Liam's throat. The salty, bitty flavor coated his tongue as he swallowed every last drop.

"Fuck, too sensitive." Tate jolted as Liam stuck with him, laving his softening cock with his tongue.

If there were a chance this would happen again, Liam would have filed that information away for the future, along with how much the guy loved ball play, but it never would, so he let it go. Fun as this was, he wouldn't get the chance to tease Tate's oversensitive cock after future orgasms.

When Tate stopped trembling, he hauled Liam to his feet. His head spun from lack of blood flow, but before he could catch his balance, Tate slammed their mouths together. The man wasted no time invading Liam's mouth with his tongue.

God, he loved a man who wanted to taste himself after a blowjob. Not much ranked hotter on the scale.

He ground his hips against Tate, still harder than steel and desperate for release.

"Can I return the favor?" Tate's voice was growly after all that shouting. He nudged his thigh between Liam's legs, pressing against his needy cock, and Liam nearly blew right there.

"No time," he said, panting and fighting his body's need for release. "I'm too damn close already. Just jerk me. Now!"

Tate smirked. "Someone liked sucking my cock, huh?" he asked as he worked Liam's pants open.

"So much." Tate's callused hand slid into his Andrew Christians and wrapped around his cock. "Oh, fuck." That hand was big, rough, and able to hold so much at once.

His head dropped back. Pleasure zinged through his bloodstream at warp speed.

He hadn't even thought of lube. The first few tugs were hot and dry, but his cock leaked, and within seconds, Tate had gathered enough precum to ease the glide. The man knew just what to do. When to squeeze, when to tug, when to back off enough to have Liam whimpering with need. He was a master at his craft, and Liam reaped the benefits of his skill.

*Damn, I could get used to this.*

Twice? Three times a day? If Tate could be at his beck and call, ready to jack him off at a moment's notice, Liam could die a happy man.

"You're making a damn mess. So fucking needy," Tate whispered in his ear. "It's hot as fuck."

One more tug was all it took. "Oh shit," he whispered, digging his nails into Tate's shoulders. His stomach contracted as his balls started to empty into Tate's hand.

"Watch me," Tate barked.

Liam fought to keep his heavy eyes open, and damn, it was worth the effort.

Tate's hungry gaze captured every shudder and facial expression Liam made.

His legs felt like Jell-O. If only there were somewhere to sit besides a nasty club toilet. A bed would be great, one where they could catch a power nap and start all over again in a few hours.

Tate kissed him once, quickly and efficiently, before releasing Liam's softening dick. With blazing eyes, he brought his hand to his mouth and cleaned each finger of Liam's spunk with his tongue.

"Damn, that was hot," Liam said as Tate pulled up his pants.

Liam followed suit. His briefs were wet and gross, but he was too sated to care. Much. The drive home would be uncomfortable.

Tate stared at him, and it looked like some emotion flickered in his eyes.

Was he going to ask for more? A date? Another round?

*Do it. Ask me.*

Liam would take either. This had been incredible.

But whatever it was disappeared with one blink, replaced by a hard mask. "Thanks, Luxe. That was epic." Tate turned, unlocked the door, and left, practically running.

Liam frowned.

*Uh, what just happened?*

Sure, he'd expected this to end when it was over, but at the very least, Tate could have walked out of the bathroom instead of sprinting. Maybe held the door and let Liam walk out too.

Rolling his eyes, he jerked the door open and stepped out into the hallway. Tate was nowhere to be seen. Vanished in the time it took Liam to walk five feet out of the stall.

The amazing feeling from two seconds ago gave way to confusion and embarrassment.

This was why he didn't do hookups. They always left him second-guessing himself and feeling used in the end, even if he'd used his partner just as thoroughly. Well, at least he'd gotten off, though it would have been nice to have said goodbye.

He might as well go home for the night. There was no way he could go out there and dance with another guy while smelling like cum and wondering about the man who'd fled the scene of their crime.

*I'm too emotional for this crap.*

# Chapter Four

"Yo, T, you 'bout ready to go, man?" Randy pounded his fist on Tate's bedroom door.

Tate rolled over with a groan as the morning sun seared his eyeballs. Damn, the light hit right through his window at this time of year.

If Tate had thought his brother moving to his own trailer with Whitney two years ago would have given him more privacy and space, he'd have been dead wrong. The asshole still acted like he lived there, coming and going whenever he damn well pleased.

"Ma, why the hell do you let this loser in?" Tate shouted.

"She ain't here, Sleeping Beauty."

Right. Mondays, she got up at the ass crack of dawn to head out and blow whatever tips she'd earned over the weekend at the diner on the damn ponies.

"Give me five minutes. Meet you outside." He rolled flat on his back, arms and legs starfished in the double bed he'd slept in since childhood.

"Your lazy ass better not still be in bed."

"It's not. I'm up. Give me five fucking minutes, Jesus." The one time Randy was ready before him, he was acting like Tate lounged around all day, every day. They'd been working together for years, and ninety-nine times out of a hundred,

Randy was the fuck-up. Of course, his brother had to be on top of his shit today when Tate had been balls-deep in Dream Liam and about to blow his load. Maybe it was a good thing Randy woke him before Dream Tate could bust a nut. With his luck, he'd have jizzed himself in his sleep like a damn horny teenager.

"Four minutes," Randy grumbled. "And you're buying coffee."

He scrubbed a hand over his scruffy face. He always bought the damn coffee. For a dollar at the closest gas station, the crap shouldn't even be called coffee. It was one drip away from sludge. But they rarely had any at home, and it had caffeine, so they bought some almost every day.

He lifted an arm and turned his head, taking a quick sniff. Not terrible or good, but nothing a little deodorant couldn't cover. He hopped out of bed while stripping off his T-shirt. Shit, he must have been tired if he'd slept in the thing. Typically, he slept in as little as possible. Clothes bothered the hell out of him while he was trying to sleep. A red, grout-stained tee stuck out from his dresser drawer. Tate grabbed it and tugged it over his head. The stains didn't matter, he'd earn a dozen more before lunch.

He changed his boxer briefs and then shrugged on a ratty pair of jeans. They were old, torn, and easy to work in. After taking a leak and a thirty-second tooth brushing, he was out the door and ready for the day.

"Nice hair," Randy said with a snort as Tate jogged to his car.

"Shut the fuck up." He really needed a haircut.

As he raked his fingers through it in a wasted attempt to tame the mess, a flash of someone else's hands playing with the strands at the nape of his neck ran through his mind. Liam had soft hands, unlike Tate's, which were beaten to hell but still strong. He'd wanted Liam to tug so he could feel the sting, but there hadn't been time for that. They'd both been too focused on getting off.

And then Tate had been focused on getting the fuck out of there. Being with Liam was good. Too damn good. The kind of good that threatened everything in his carefully constructed life. He'd seen the question in the other man's eyes. He'd been about to ask for a repeat, or a date, or even a phone number, and despite knowing it could never happen, Tate would have been tempted. He avoided that temptation at all costs because he knew himself, and one day, he'd give into the temptation and fuck up everything.

So, before he'd lost his brain to his cock, Tate had gotten the fuck out of there. Unfortunately, the last thing he'd seen before he'd turned tail and fled like a pussy was the disappointment and confusion on Liam's gorgeous face. Those eyes were the color of warm honey. They'd haunted Tate's dreams for the past few nights.

"Uh, we going, or you just gonna stare at the car?"

"We're going. Unwad your fucking panties." He unlocked the car and climbed into the driver's seat, immediately rolling the window down. His car might be a heap of crap, but he'd die before letting Randy drive it. Not that he could drive it if he wanted to right now. He'd managed to get his license suspended after having five fender-benders in the past year. The man drove like a damn fool, yet somehow, he could drag race and win his lot fee in one night.

It didn't make any sense. Then again, the shit Randy did rarely made sense.

Randy dropped into the passenger seat. He shifted Tate's way and pulled a rumpled pack of cigarettes out of his back pocket. Tate raised an eyebrow as his brother took one out, stuck it between his lips, and then depressed the car's lighter.

Shaking his head, Tate ripped the cigarette from his brother's mouth and tossed it out the window.

"What the fuck?" Randy socked his arm.

"You know I hate you smoking in my car."

"You smoke, jackass." Randy whined as Tate rubbed his arm where his brother whacked him. "Probably more than me." He started to take another cigarette out, but Tate's raised eyebrow had him shoving it back into the pack.

"First off, you know that shit's not true. I smoke a fucking quarter of what you do. And two, I never smoke in my car." He started the engine and pulled toward the park's exit, honking at Letti as he passed her house. She waved from a lawn chair while drinking coffee straight out of the carafe and eating dry cereal from a box.

"Classy," he shouted, earning a middle finger.

Randy chuckled and then fiddled with the radio. After he found his favorite rock station, he asked, "So, what's up with you this morning? Shouldn't you be all loose and relaxed from seeing your super-secret girlfriend this weekend?"

"The fuck are you talking about?" Tate navigated the car out of the trailer park and onto the highway.

"Please." Randy rolled his eyes. "Like I don't know. You think you're so much smarter than the rest of us."

Tate snorted. He took his eyes off the road to glare at his brother. "I am smarter than you. Way fucking smarter. Fat lotta good it does for me, though. Did you see where I woke up this morning? Alone in a double bed in our cracked Ma's trailer I pay for because she can't. I'm living the dream, brother."

"Every couple of months, you head over to Tulsa to get you some city pussy. You hiding a rich bitch out there or something? I get being embarrassed by our shit and not wanting to bring her to the craphole we call home, but you don't gotta be all sneaky about it."

Heat prickled his skin. He laughed, but it sounded so fake that he couldn't believe Randy didn't question him. "Well, shit," he said, clearing his throat. "Thought I had you fooled." The lie soured in his mouth.

"She's good, huh?" Randy asked, grinning like a loon. "Gotta be some prime pussy to drive your ass all the way to Tulsa."

Tate's stomach lurched. If Randy kept talking, he would vomit all over the steering wheel. "Yeah, real good pussy."

"So, you like 'em, classy, huh? And I guess your girl likes slummin' it." He elbowed Tate, chuckling.

Slumming it. Randy's comment hit too close to home. Beyond his name and the fact that he sucked cock like a damn god, Tate knew squat about Liam. But his clothes had been nice, and he'd reeked of class, so the guy must have been slumming it last night.

For some reason, that twisted his insides to knots.

"Hey…" Randy elbowed him again. "Ain't nothing to be embarrassed of. You like what you like. No need to hide it. You like classy pussy. You go and get you all the classy pussy you can handle."

If he only knew.

"How's Whit?" If this conversation dragged on any longer, he'd steer them into oncoming traffic.

Randy snorted. "Fuck if I know. Thought she was pissed at me, but you know what that crazy ass woman said yesterday?"

He took the bait. Thank God.

"What?" They passed the fairgrounds, and Tate shuddered. It was ten years since he witnessed a gay kid take a horrifying beating, and he still hadn't been back. He begged off every year with some lame excuse Randy bought because he was too stupid to realize something was up.

"She told me she thinks we should have a fucking baby." He snorted, shaking his head. "You believe that shit?"

He did believe it. He loved his sister-in-law, but Whitney

was crazier than Randy, and together, they were a volcano of insanity. No one knew when they would erupt, but they were active and exploded frequently and without warning.

Tate zoned out as Randy rambled on about his dysfunctional marriage. Keeping up with their drama was a full-time job, and Tate didn't need or want a second one. Randy could talk, and he did while they stopped for their crappy coffee, filled up on gas, and all the way to their job site. Finally, he shut the hell up when they parked.

"Okay…" Tate searched for his boss's email explaining the details of the job estimate. Their boss was lazy as a damn slug and should have handled his own estimates, but he threw Tate an extra hundred bucks each time he handled an estimate that led to a job booking, so he sucked it up and did them. Maybe someday he'd be the one in charge, and he could forget about having to bow down to a boss who didn't care about him.

"What do we got today?" Randy asked.

"We're finishing the job at the McMillian's ranch at ten, but first, we have an estimate for this new dance studio. They're looking to have the locker rooms and bathrooms retiled. The business owner apparently has some pretty detailed ideas, so let's go on in and see what's up."

"Oh, fuck no," Randy said. "I ain't goin' in there. No fucking way."

"What?" Tate glanced up from his phone to see Randy staring at the dance studio through the windshield, shaking his head. "What's the problem?"

"Look." Randy tipped his chin in the direction of the studio. The sign read Dance For All Studio. Through the windows, he made out the outline of a man walking through the lobby with a clipboard in his hand.

"I don't get it. You got a problem with dancers?"

Randy snorted. "Some of 'em, yeah. Look what's in the

damn window."

It took a moment, but Tate finally found what had Randy freaking out. An icy wave washed over him, leaving him cold and empty. In the bottom left corner of the storefront windows gleamed a rainbow sticker with the words LGBTQIA+ Owned and Operated Business.

"You see it, right? You know what it means?"

*Of course, I fucking know what it means.*

Goddammit, why did he have to be the one assigned to this job?

"I know what it means, Randy."

"It means this place is owned by a fag," he plowed on as though Tate hadn't spoken.

"It's owned by someone who wants to pay us money. Get the fuck over it."

"Ain't going in there." Randy was still shaking his head. You'd think Tate had asked him to climb in a coffin and shut the lid.

Tate clenched his teeth so hard his jaw spasmed. "You know it can't rub off on you, right?" He turned to face his ignorant brother. "You're not gonna walk in there wanting pussy and come out with a thing for dick because you spent ten minutes measuring the guy's bathroom for tiles."

"Ain't worth the risk, T. I ain't doin' it."

"For fuck's sake." Tate shoved his door open, stepped out of the car, and tromped toward the dance studio's entrance.

*Don't let them see your legs wobble.*

His insides churned like the wall of a hurricane, fierce and destructive. He clenched his fists at his side to keep his hands from trembling.

*Don't vomit.*

A door slammed behind him, and Randy called, "Fine. But I'm not shaking his hand. Got it?"

Tate plowed on toward the door. He wrenched it open too

hard, making the overhead bells smack against the glass with a harsh clatter. "Shit, sorry," he mumbled.

The man with the clipboard whirled around at the same time Randy came through the door, looking as excited as he'd be if he'd been there for a colonoscopy.

Tate froze. His blood stopped pumping, and his lungs seized. Alarm bells blared in his brain louder than a parade of firetruck sirens.

*No.*

*This cannot be happening.*

Liam met his gaze, and his expression went from neutral to surprised to excited in the blink of an eye. "Oh, my God," he whispered, leaving his mouth dangling.

"Uh..." Leave it to Randy to capture the moment with eloquent words.

Liam crossed the room with a smile stretching the lips that had wrapped around his cock and made him come harder than ever before. "I can't believe it's y—"

*Fuck.*

He worked to keep his face blank despite the riot in his chest. "Mr. Brady? William Brady?"

"Wha... uh, yeah?" Liam shook his head as he wrinkled his nose. "But it's Liam, reme—"

Tate thrust his right hand out. "Good morning, Mr. Brady. I'm with Expert Flooring and Tile. Thanks for meeting with us this morning."

His heart hammered so loud it threatened to drown out Liam's response. As he waited for Liam to shake his hand, he speared him with the most imploring look he could muster. His entire life came down to this one moment. Liam could either make or break him—literally. If Liam outed him, Randy would tear him in two, brothers or not.

A fucking dance teacher, of course. It jived perfectly with everything he'd learned about the man on Saturday.

"Uh, sure." Liam pressed his lips together as he assessed Tate. Finally, after Tate's arm started to cramp, Liam grasped his hand. "Thanks for coming."

Randy's eyes bugged out as their hands met.

Tate cleared his throat, drawing Liam's attention away from his idiot brother. "I'm Tate, and this is Randy. If you can show us the space and tell us your vision, we'll get started on measurements and get you a quote so we can get out of your hair."

A flash of sadness crossed Liam's face, but he cleared it before saying, "Sure, follow me."

Nothing remained of the open, hungry man Tate had met —*touched, tasted*—Saturday night. He kept his face neutral as he walked them toward the first locker room area.

His nerves hadn't eased even though it seemed, for now, Liam wouldn't spill his secret. Keeping his eyes off Liam's ass as he followed him through the studio proved a near-impossible task. Could his damn shorts be any tighter or shorter? And that shirt? For fuck's sake, the workout tank might as well have been painted on his sleek body.

The definition in those arms…

Tate couldn't help but wonder how it'd feel to run his tongue over the satiny skin housing those muscles.

A sharp elbow to his side had him stumbling. "What the fuck?" he mouthed to Randy.

Randy jerked his head in Liam's direction before rubbing his hands together as though cleaning them. "Wash your hands," he mouthed without making a sound.

*For fuck's sake.*

He flipped Randy off.

Wash his hands? This was his older brother. The person he'd grown up with his entire life. The person he was closest to despite how often Randy pissed him off. And the person who couldn't shake a gay man's hand and worried Tate should wash his hands after touching Liam.

This was his life.

Was it any wonder he lived in the deepest, darkest closet?

"Hey, Rand, I think I left my tape measure in the car. Could you grab it for me?"

Randy frowned. The outline of the tape measure was obvious as hell in Tate's back pocket. "I think it's right th—"

"In the trunk? Yeah, I think so." He slapped Randy's shoulder—hard. "Thanks, man."

Randy's eyes narrowed, then popped wide. A grin crossed his face. "Oh, shit, yeah, you're right. It is in the trunk. I'll just, uh, go get it," he said as he walked backward toward the door. Before leaving, the idiot turned. "Thanks, bro."

Tate shut his eyes.

"Smooth." Liam leaned against the locker room door, folding his arms across his smooth chest. "Let me guess, he's relieved to get the hell out of here so he doesn't catch the gay." He fluttered his hands up by his head.

Sick as he felt, Tate couldn't help but snort a laugh. "Something like that."

Liam grunted. "Lovely. Who doesn't love a little homophobia first thing in the morning?"

"Listen, Lux… Liam, I, uh…"

"So, I take it you're not out."

Tate pressed his lips together. Not out. Those words made it sound so simple when the reality was much more complicated.

"Okay." Liam pushed off the wall. "I get it." He walked like a panther, with smooth, shifting muscles and animal heat. Without a flicker of unease or nerves, he stepped into Tate's personal space. They were practically chest to chest.

Tate stiffened. His heart rate skyrocketed, and he flicked a reflexive glance out the window. Randy stood at the car, smoking and staring into the distance, facing away from the studio.

"Hey."

He looked back at Liam. The man stood too close. He was too hot, too sexy, too *everything*. Tate's dick thickened.

Shit.

He thought of the dead possum he'd seen outside his trailer last night. It'd smelled of rot and had maggots crawling all over it.

Even that wasn't enough to keep his cock from getting excited. Liam stood too damn close.

"Hey," Liam said again. "You're really freaked out."

Scowling, Tate shook his head. "I'm not. I'm good."

The studio owner frowned. "I won't out you, Tate. I would never out you or anyone."

He met Liam's gaze, and the empathy reflected on him had him swallowing a hard lump in his throat. "This town…"

A sad smile crossed Liam's face. "I know."

"No, you don't. My boss told me you had just moved here. This town is not friendly to people like… *us, say us…* you." He couldn't even claim his sexuality in front of another gay man.

"I'm not scared." Liam straightened to his full height, maybe five inches shorter than Tate.

If he only knew. This wasn't a place where someone would spray paint a few slurs on his studio windows. In this town, someone would jump him out back and leave him broken and bleeding in the dirt. "Maybe you should be. If you're gonna do this…" he said, waving a hand around the studio, "… you need to be aware of what could happen."

Liam gave him another of those sad smiles. "And by *this*, you mean something so obviously gay, like being a guy opening a dance studio?"

Tate shut his mouth.

Sadness entered Liam's eyes. "Tate, I came out when I was

twelve. I'm twenty-five now. I have a lot of experience doing *this*. You don't need to worry about me. I can handle myself."

Frustration clawed at him. Couldn't Liam understand the severity of the situation? Didn't he get Tate was trying to protect him? "You don't understand—"

"I understand more than you think, Tate." Liam stepped back. "Now, Randy just tossed his cancer stick on the ground, so I assume he's on his way back in. Your secret is safe with me. Always. From here on out, you're nothing more than a guy coming to retile my very outdated locker rooms."

The words should have sent relief coursing through him. Why did they bring an odd sense of disappointment? Maybe he should have grabbed some breakfast to go with his coffee.

He cleared his throat. "Thanks... Luxe."

A look of surprise crossed Liam's face, but it disappeared the second Randy walked back in. "Uh, sorry, Tate. Not sure what's going on, but I didn't see the hammer, er, tape measure in the trunk."

Liam snorted.

Christ, Randy was a fuck-up.

"Thanks for looking, Randy." He dug into his back pocket. "Sorry, looks like I sent you out there for nothing. I had it all along."

"Well, huh, funny how that worked out."

Liam pressed his lips together as though trying not to laugh. Or maybe sneer.

Randy hovered by the door, eyeing Liam like he had the plague. Tate rolled his eyes.

"C'mon," Liam said, waving for them to follow. "I'll take you to the locker room."

Tate fell in step behind him. Randy could tag along if he wanted, and if he didn't? No skin off Tate's back.

"Oh, and straight boy?" Liam whirled around with a fancy ballet spin, spearing Randy with a flirty look. "Two things.

First, you can come closer. I promise you all this fabulousness is not contagious." He struck a pose, and Randy's eyes practically fell out of his head.

Tate grinned. The man had balls along with all his elegance.

"And two, you're not my type. I prefer my men strong and sexy." With that, he turned and walked, no strutted, into the locker room, leaving Tate and Randy to trail behind him.

Randy stood at the door, mouth hanging open. "Did he just say I'm not sexy?"

Tate burst out laughing. His admiration for Liam grew tenfold. He was brave, fiery, and proud in a way Tate could never be.

But would all that bravery serve him well or get him hurt?

## Chapter Five

"Come on, stay closed already," Liam muttered as he jumped up and used his body weight to help close his full trunk. His car was busting at the seams with everything from cleaning supplies to promotional materials to DIY repair materials—all things he'd need for the grand opening, which would happen in exactly fourteen days.

Work on the locker rooms was scheduled to begin tomorrow. He had no idea if Tate and that Randy guy would show up to complete the work or if a different crew would, but they planned to demolish the old tiles while they waited for the order of new tiles to arrive. When all was said and done, the locker rooms would be comfortable, modern, and spacious—exactly what he wanted.

Of course, nothing would happen if he got stuck in the parking lot of the Tulsa Office Max because his trunk wouldn't close.

"Freaking close already," he shouted with a growl as he jumped again. This time, when he came down, practically sitting on the trunk lid, it clicked as the latch caught. "Ha!" He brushed his hands off, then waved to a woman, giving him some serious side-eye. "Good morning."

She smiled but didn't return the greeting. Not that he blamed her. He probably looked crazy, talking to himself and slamming on his car.

Liam had gotten an early start that morning, hitting up every store on his list before noon. Now that those tasks were completed, the rest of the day was his to do with as he pleased. He planned to head back to Swan to start setting up the studio's lobby and merchandise display, but first, he deserved to treat himself to a snack.

About a mile back, he'd passed a trendy coffee shop and had been dreaming of an iced caramel latte ever since. He hopped in his overstuffed Jetta and zipped down the road toward the delicious promise of icy sugar and caffeine.

He pulled in around ten thirty, which seemed to be the ideal time. It was too early for the lunch rush and too late for breakfast, so the parking lot only had a few cars. The silence would give him time to sit in peace, review his lengthy to-do list, and plan the week's social media marketing posts.

He strode in and straight to the ordering counter. Only a few customers sat at tables, and one ordered in line before him. Other than that, the place was empty and quiet. As he perused the overhead menu, waiting for his turn to order, the hairs on his nape rose to attention. He rubbed a hand across the back of his neck, but it did nothing to dull the sensation of being watched. Not in a threatening way, but he'd bet his first client's class fee that someone was staring at him.

Shifting, he rolled his shoulders and tried to relax. Turning now would be too obvious, so he tried to ignore the awareness and focus on the menu.

"Hi, welcome to Brewed Awakening. What can I get for you today?" The barista had a flirty tone and a suggestive smile as he batted his eyes at Liam. "You can have anything you'd like." He leaned in and whispered, "Anything."

Liam chuckled. The guy was cute in his black polo and pants, with a dark purple apron boasting the shop's logo. He had dark eyes framed by thick black lashes and artfully styled hair to match. He was a few inches shorter than Liam and slender. Cute, but not Liam's type, especially since he couldn't shake the memory of one tall, sexy, closeted man. "I'm flattered, but just a large, iced caramel latte with almond milk and a blueberry muffin for today."

Pouting, the barista put the order into the computer. "Your loss."

"No doubt." He winked. No reason to make the guy feel bad about himself.

"Name for the order?"

"Liam."

The ego boost seemed to be the trick, and the barista bounced off with a smile to make his coffee. Liam moved down the counter to the designated pick-up area. He leaned against the wall and scanned the room while waiting for his order. About halfway through his sweep, his gaze snagged on the one man he hadn't been able to stop thinking about.

Tate sat at a table against a wall with a to-go cup of hot coffee and a bagel. A backward ballcap concealed his shaggy hair, and stubble covered his strong jaw. He wore ripped jeans and a plain black T-shirt with tan work boots. The look fit him—hot, scruffy working man.

Forget his muffin. Liam found his snack right there.

Guess that explained the feeling of being watched, though Tate hadn't even glanced in Liam's direction. His attention and deep scowl remained directed at the cute, flirty barista.

*Interesting.*

"Here's your order, Liam." The barista didn't set it on the counter but held a plate with the muffin and iced coffee out for him to take.

"Thank you." He accepted the food, but the barista didn't release it just yet. Liam raised an eyebrow.

The cute barista shrugged with a sheepish grin. "Figured I'd give it one more shot. I left you my number on the napkin.

Shoot me a text sometime." He winked and sashayed away, leaving Liam smiling. Who wouldn't like attention from a cute guy?

He spun back around and—*eek*. Tate looked ready to rip the barista's head off.

Tate shot lasers at the back of the poor guy's head for another few seconds before shifting his annoyed gaze to Liam. What was it about him that just did it for Liam and made his blood heat with a single stare?

Tate's facial expression didn't change, but he lifted a booted foot and pushed the chair opposite him out a few inches.

A non-verbal invitation to sit? More like a command to sit.

How hot was that?

He forced himself to stroll instead of sprinting over to the table like the overeager single man he was.

"Tulsa seems to be our place, huh, hot stuff?" he said as he reached the table.

Discomfort flickered in Tate's eyes for half a second before he cleared it and nodded. How sad. Liam had gotten so damn lucky with his family and the dance community. No one ever made an issue of him being gay. Everyone he knew accepted him. Now, he'd met plenty of closed-minded and hateful individuals, but the people who mattered had always loved and supported him. But it didn't seem the same for Tate, which broke Liam's heart.

Darkness tried to invade his excitement and put a raincloud over his entire day. There had been one time where being an out gay guy had cost him dearly. Once, he'd run into bigots he couldn't defeat with sass and snark, his usual weapons of choice. Their hatred had nearly cost Liam his life. Recovering from shattered ribs and a broken shoulder had been an uphill battle that almost cost him his dance career. The deep, gruesome bruises had hurt almost as much as the broken bones and left him looking like a victim for months.

Old, traumatic memories tried to worm their way into his consciousness. Things he'd put to bed years ago with the help of rehab and therapy threatened to return and steal his happiness.

He imagined swiping them away as one did an undesirable Grindr date. The visual had worked for him in the past and worked again now.

"So, uh, what are you doing all the way out here in Tulsa this morning?" he asked instead of sitting in tense silence as Tate seemed happy to do.

The man across the table shrugged. "Picking up some tile from our supplier."

Excitement surged through him. "My tiles?" He couldn't keep the enthusiasm out of his voice. Opening a studio had been his dream for years, and modernizing the locker rooms was a huge step toward making that dream come true.

Tate tore a chunk off his bagel and popped it in his mouth. "Yep," he answered around the bite.

"Yay!" Liam threw his hands in the air as he cheered, drawing curious stares from other patrons, but within a second, they lost interest. "Gah, I'm so freaking excited." He did a little shimmy in his seat. What could he say? When he was happy, he danced.

Tate stiffened and glanced around. When he realized no one cared about two men sitting at a table together, even with Liam's shout, he relaxed again.

Baby steps.

"So, Tate, what's your story?"

The man across the table raised an eyebrow. "My story."

"Yeah." He took a bite of his muffin and groaned. "Oh, my God, this is so good. Wanna bite?" he asked, pointing to his plate.

Tate shook his head. "I'm good."

"More for me." After shrugging, Liam ripped off another piece of the incredible muffin and stuffed it in his mouth. The buttery, cakey dough combined with the sweet and tart bite of blueberry made his taste buds sing. "Mmm, seriously, this is so good." After one more taste, he set the muffin down. "Okay, sorry, I'm done making love to the muffin. Your story. You know, where you're from, what you like to do for fun, what's your family like."

*Why aren't you out?*

Tate glanced toward the counter where the barista was laughing loudly, having found a new customer to flirt with. This one seemed ready and willing to banter right back.

Once the laughter stopped, Tate glanced down at his bagel and then up at Liam. He stared him straight in the eye when he said, "I'm from here. I've lived in the same shitty trailer park my entire life. Never traveled out of Oklahoma. My family sucks. Mom's a drug addict who doesn't give a shit about anything but her next fix, and my old man split when I was two. He comes around from time to time fucking up our lives and putting my mom through the wringer. I've got one brother, Randy, who you met the other day. He's a bigot and an idiot like everyone else I know."

A swallow of muffin dried up halfway down his throat, scratching the entire way to his stomach. Pain and longing, which Tate would probably never admit to, bled through his story loud and clear, but he'd still left so much unsaid. Those words seemed to brush over years of fear and hiding so many young men like Tate suffered. Liam wanted to weep for this man who lived his life in hiding. Who didn't feel safe showing the world his true self. The way he ran from the club the other night practically before he finished coming made sense now.

Liam grabbed his coffee to keep from rubbing a hand over his aching heart. Instead of taking a sip, he traced his finger over the lines of condensation running down the chilly cup. Based on the way both Tate and Randy reacted to him in the studio, he had a feeling Tate didn't have a lot of queer role models in his life, if any.

A thought struck Liam. One he had to have answered right then. "Am I the first gay man you've ever known?" Even though the café wasn't crowded, and no one paid them any attention, he kept his voice down in deference to Tate's skittishness. It felt as though if Liam said the wrong thing, the other man would flee at any time.

Snorting, Tate shook his head. "You know where we met," he whispered back. "That wasn't my first time there, Luxe. Lots of gay guys there."

A sly smile curved Liam's lips. "Oh yes, I remember that night very well," he crooned, unable to keep the desire out of his voice. "In fact, I've relived it quite a few times, if you catch my meaning." Relived it with his hand wrapped around his cock and Tate's name on his lips.

Tate didn't glance around this time to see if anyone was eavesdropping. Instead, his eyes darkened, and he shifted as though he needed to relieve an uncomfortable stiffening in those jeans.

"Let me ask it this way. Am I the first gay man you've sat at a table with and shared coffee?"

Tate didn't need to answer. The flattening of this expression and how he averted his gaze told Liam all he needed to know. This man needed a tribe. He needed others who understood him and supported the real Tate.

Lucky for him, Liam also needed friends. "Well, Tate, I am proud to be your first queer friend."

"We friends?"

"We are," he said with a nod as he ripped another chunk off his muffin and popped it into his mouth. "Mmm, as your new friend, I insist you try this. It's heavenly." He pulled a piece off for Tate and held it up. In his mind, Tate opened his mouth and allowed Liam to place it on his tongue. He even closed his lips too fast, capturing Liam's finger and teasing it with his tongue.

God, that would be hot.

In the real world, Tate reached out and plucked the bite from his fingers before tossing it in his mouth. "You're right," he said after he chewed and swallowed. "That's a damn good muffin."

Liam beamed. "Told you."

The conversation flowed after that. They chatted without missing a beat. Tate filled him in on the main things he needed to know about Swan—places to check out, restaurants to hit, and ones to avoid. Unfortunately, there seemed to be more of the latter, but he hadn't expected to be moving to a culinary mecca. Liam avoided further questions about Tate's family, which served him well. They didn't hit an awkward moment.

Tate relaxed with each passing minute. His shoulders loosened, he talked more, and he didn't spare a glance for anyone else in the room. He also smiled, which transformed his looks from handsome to breathtaking.

Liam couldn't stop smiling either. He hadn't realized how much he needed to hang out with someone his own age. For a social creature like himself, moving to a town where he didn't know a single person had been a challenge.

And now he had a friend.

A very hot friend who knew his way around a cock.

"You know," Liam said when they finally hit a lull in the conversation. "I'm pretty sure you forgot a spot when taking measurements at my studio the other day."

Tate had just polished off his bagel. He brushed his hands together with a frown. "Really?"

"Yep," he replied, popping the *p* at the end of the word.

"Huh, I don't think so, Luxe. I was pretty thorough."

*Yes, thorough is exactly what I'm looking for.*

"No, there's one spot I'm pretty sure I forgot to show you." He shrugged and let his desire show on his face. "Maybe you should come to the studio with me so I can show you. Up close and personal."

Tate froze. His nostrils flared. For some reason, Liam found that extremely sexy. It made Tate seem like an animal scenting Liam's arousal.

He shivered under Tate's dark, heated gaze. "I have to be at a job in an hour and forty-five minutes."

God, the man had a stellar sex voice. Deep, smokey, raspy. The perfect octave to whisper filthy promises in Liam's ear.

He tilted his head. "It'll be tight, but I have no doubt we can finish before you have to be at work." It wasn't a flex, but he wouldn't take long to come once Tate got his hands on him. Not with how many times he'd relived the hand job in the club.

Realization sparked in Tate's eyes. His expression went from pleasant to hungry in the blink of an eye. Liam nearly fanned himself. The man could set the place on fire with one look.

"I'm sure it will be tight." Tate winked. "I'm counting on it, actually."

Liam's jaw dropped, and he blinked at the alien sitting across from him. Then shot his most playful look Tate's way. "Why, Tate I-Don't-Know-Your-Last-Name, did you just flirt with little old me?"

He arched an eyebrow. "It's Sutton, and you know damn well I'm flirting with you."

"Well, then, in that case..." Liam stood. Excitement zinged through him. Too bad they had an hour's drive before he could get some relief. Jetting into the coffee shop's bathroom for a quickie probably wouldn't work out as well as it had in the club. "I'll meet you back at my studio." He gathered his trash and walked to Tate's side of the table. "Don't forget your measuring tape. There's something I measured by seeing how far down my throat it could reach, but I wanted a more precise measurement," he whispered in Tate's ear. "I'm guessing it was around eleven inches."

Tate's bark of laughter as he stood and strode to the exit had Liam chuckling under his breath.

It'd be a miracle if he wasn't pulled over for speeding on the way back.

## Chapter Six

*Eleven inches.*

That little fucking shit.

Tate mashed the gas pedal against the floor the entire drive from Tulsa to Swan. His cock was hard and trapped the entire ride. He'd tried pressing the heel of his hand to his crotch to find some relief, but all it did was make him growl with need.

He also hadn't been able to wipe the smile off his face.

Eleven inches.

Tate chuckled. He had a damn good cock, if he said so himself, but eleven inches was a bit generous.

As the miles passed and he grew closer to Swan, his enthusiasm morphed into nerves. This truck, with the company's logo, would be sitting in Liam's parking lot while he was inside fucking the man.

Someone would see. Swan was small enough that whoever spotted him could be a friend, a coworker, or a family member. He'd be asked about it. By now, almost everyone in town knew that a dance studio would be opening in the next few weeks. They also knew the owner to be a gay man.

Randy would hear.

*Yo, T, what the fuck were you doing back at the studio in the middle of the afternoon? Heard the truck was there for more than thirty minutes. What gives?*

By the time he pulled into the parking lot outside the studio, his palms were sweaty, and his pulse jumped in his neck.

He should leave.

His stomach churned.

His chest tightened.

A figure appeared in the large front window of the studio.

Liam.

He stood in the studio's front room, watching, waiting. Talking with him today had been fun. More than fun. He'd made Tate smile and laugh, which he did not do much of. He'd also made him hard. No, he hadn't had a queer friend before. Aside from sneaky hookups in the club bathroom or back alley, he hadn't had any interaction with queer people. If any lived in Swan, they kept their mouths shut like Tate. And he hadn't tried to make friends with anyone he'd met at the club. What the fuck would he tell Randy when his brother asked why he was going for drinks with a queer guy?

No, it wasn't worth the risk to his identity.

But this? Another chance to touch Liam?

That just might be worth it.

He sat there clenching the steering wheel for much too long, considering the clock ticked down to his next job. He wanted to walk in with his head high, grab the sexy man watching him, and kiss the hell out of him. What a normal thing to do—see someone he was attracted to and wanted him and act on it. How many times had he seen Randy kiss Whitney over the years? How many times had Randy swatted her ass or made a raunchy joke in front of their friends? How often did she hop on his back and tease him about taking her for a ride?

Countless.

They didn't think twice.

All Tate did was think about keeping his attraction to

someone from showing. It consumed him. And now there was a man he wanted to fuck enough he was considering taking the risk of being caught.

*Go in or leave?*

If he puked at Liam's feet, the decision would be made for him.

"Fuck."

Unsmiling, Liam pushed away from the windows and stalked across the wooden floor. The way he moved, even when walking, revealed his years of dance training. He flowed, muscles in perfect harmony like a sleek jungle cat.

Christ, the man was turning Tate poetic.

When he disappeared into the locker room they would soon be renovating, Tate's heart sank.

He'd blown it.

"Fuck." He slammed the heel of his palm against the steering wheel. "What the fuck do you expect?" he whispered. "Sitting on your ass like a damn wuss."

Disappointment settled heavily on his shoulders as he reached for the key to restart the ignition. Jerking off alone would feel like a mockery, highlighting his inability to man up and take what he wanted.

What Liam freely offered.

The sight of Liam walking back out of the locker room froze his hand on the key.

"Holy shit." Tate nearly swallowed his tongue.

Liam had shed his shirt and swapped his stylish jeans for light gray dance tights. The way they cupped his muscular ass and molded to his firm thighs should be fucking illegal. The erection, which had waned with Tate's freak-out, surged back to life so fast it made him lightheaded.

Without so much as a glance at the parking lot, Liam grabbed the wooden bar along the wall of mirrors. Tate clutched the steering wheel and leaned forward. His heart lodged in his throat. He didn't dare blink as Liam lifted his leg to the bar and executed a series of stretches that made Tate sweat.

Fuck, the man could bend.

His imagination ran wild, thinking of all the ways they could put that flexibility to good use.

After loosening up each limb and his spine in ways that had Tate panting, Liam moved to the center of the room. This time, he looked straight at Tate.

"Fuck me," Tate whispered. He was so damn hard. Instead of soft denim encasing his dick, his jeans felt like a steel cage imprisoning his erection.

Liam winked.

Tate's cock jumped.

Then it was on. Liam rose onto his toes, lifted a leg, and began to dance. Tate stared, completely mesmerized by the complicated twists, leaps, and tricks. He understood nothing about dance technique, yet somehow, he knew every move and pose, and every pose was perfect. Liam would accept nothing less.

He was stunning. As the minutes passed, Tate was transported back ten years to the time he first realized he was attracted to the same sex. It'd been a dancer back then too. He hadn't accepted it that day. Hadn't understood it was inevitable. He'd had no control over who his body wanted back then, just as he had no control over this intense attraction to Liam.

He understood himself now, ten years later. His desires made sense, and he'd embraced them. Owned them.

*Have you?*

Spying on Liam from his car like a Peeping Tom instead of going inside didn't scream self-acceptance. Neither did hiding his sexuality from the entire world.

Liam arched into an impressive back bend with one leg in

the air and one on the ground before spinning into a complicated twirl that tested his balance. He didn't bobble once. Then he kicked his leg so high his knee reached his ear before bending forward, giving Tate a prime view of his mouth-watering ass in those fucking tights.

Tate clenched the steering wheel until his knuckles ached. He itched to barge in there, tear the ass-hugging material off Liam, bend him over, and—

"Fuck it."

He opened the car door and surged into the early afternoon warmth. He powered toward the building after slamming the truck door so hard the whole vehicle rocked. Liam must have noticed him because he was already on his way to the hideous seventies locker room by the time Tate made it inside.

It felt as though he was walking with a damn brick in his pants. As soon as they were surrounded by old, beige tiles, Liam closed the locker room door and turned the deadbolt. He made eye contact, ensuring Tate understood they had complete privacy and security.

Sexy and considerate.

"I only have fifteen minutes," Tate said. If he hadn't been a coward, he could have had another twenty to do with Liam as he pleased. But then, he wouldn't have had the pleasure of the private dance.

Liam pouted. "Guess we better get to work then, huh? Too bad we don't have longer. The drive here gave me plenty of time to think about what I wanted you to do to me."

"Next time," Tate said as he crowded Liam against the wall.

One perfect eyebrow rose on Liam's gorgeous face.

Yeah, he got it. He'd just committed to another hookup. It wasn't something he wanted to talk about right then, but he wouldn't deny it either.

Instead of talking, he cupped the bulge, trying to burst through Liam's tights. It was hot, hard, and so fucking tempting. "You put these on to fuck with me, didn't you."

Liam's head hit the wall. "Ah, I, no... I always wear them when I da... oh shit."

Tate squeezed him. "You knew exactly what they would do to me." He rubbed up and down the outside of the tights, alternating the pressure.

Liam's pupils blew wide. "I... oh fuck, you're a sadist. I thought you needed some motivation to come inside. Worked, didn't it?"

"Much as I'd love to *come inside*, we don't have time for that today. Get these fucking tights off. I want to see your pretty cock."

A smug grin curled Liam's lips. "You think my cock is pretty?"

"I think all of you is pretty." He'd never been one for compliments and didn't care what the guys he fucked thought of him, but seeing the mix of happiness and desire all over Liam's face as he praised the man's cock might have him rethinking that policy.

"God," Liam whispered. His hands shook as they went to the waistband of his tights. He wiggled, shimmying them over his slender hips and round ass. The damn things were so pasted to his skin that his dick sling-shotted out once free.

Tate tore at the button on his jeans. He shoved them over his ass, hissing when his dick popped out. Liam reached for him, but he batted the other man's hand away.

"Mine," he said with a growl as he thrust his shaft against Liam's and wrapped his hand around both of them. Even dry as the desert, the slide of Liam's cock against his caused a full-body jolt of pleasure.

"Fuck, I love your hands," Liam said, panting as his own hands latched onto Tate's waist.

He snorted. "They're beat to shit. Covered in scars and calluses." He stroked them with a light fist.

Liam moaned. "Yes, exactly. Feels out of this world on my soft dick."

"Ain't nothing soft about this dick," Tate said, increasing the pressure.

Liam's chuckle turned into a gasp. "Y-you know what I mean."

Tate released them, snickering when Liam whined. He held his hand up to Liam's mouth. "Spit."

The dancer's eyes flared. "Why is that so fucking hot?"

Tate waited until Liam complied and then he brought his hand to his mouth and added his own spit to the homemade lube.

"You're filthy," Liam whispered.

He winked, then grabbed their cocks again. This time, the slide of their combined spit eased the way. He tightened his fist and stroked them together. Liam leaked like a fucking sieve. Within seconds, their precum joined the spit, providing the perfect, slick tunnel.

"Yes," Liam said. His gaze left Tate's face and focused on where Tate jacked their dicks. "Harder, Tate. I love it harder."

*Fuck yes.*

He slapped his free hand against the wall beside Tate's head as he sped up and tightened his fist. The hot glide of Liam's cock against his amped the pleasure tenfold. His eyes grew heavy, and his breathing notched up. The way they looked side by side in his grip, both hard, flushed, and dripping, added to the pleasure.

It was sexy as fuck.

"God, Tate, I'm close already."

They both stared down, mesmerized by the sight of themselves.

"Me too," he ground out as he shuttled his fist along their

shafts. "Look at me."

Liam lifted his gaze until it met Tate's. His eyes were hooded and dark with lust. Pink flushed his cheeks. His unkissed lips were begging for his attention.

So Tate gave it.

He crushed their mouths together with the same intensity he used to stroke their cocks.

Liam moaned into his mouth, thrusting his tongue deep. He bucked his hips, fucking into Tate's fist.

"That's it, Luxe," Tate muttered against Liam's lips. "Give it to me."

"Now. Oh, shit." Liam shuddered as warmth flooded Tate's fist.

As soon as he felt the rush of Liam's cum, he lost the last of his control. His dick jerked and spurted as his balls emptied into his hand, and ecstasy washed over him. As his brain fuzzed, he stopped stroking and held their dicks against each other in a light grip.

"Mmm," Liam said with a satisfied smile. He slumped against the wall, limp with his eyes closed. "Now that was damn good."

"It was." Now that it was over, Tate prepared for the familiar impulse to get the fuck out of there.

But it didn't come. Instead, he felt a foreign desire to stay with Liam. To wrap his arms around the man and keep him as close as possible. To kiss him, touch him, and simply watch the man breathe.

"We're messy," Liam said without opening his eyes.

"I can take care of that." An alien force must have invaded his body because Tate had never, not once, given a shit what a guy did after he came. He could stick around, go, stay covered in spunk, or clean up. Tate didn't give two shits. So, the man shuffling to the sink with his jeans at his ankles, grabbing some paper towels, and waiting for the water to warm with the goal of cleaning Liam up couldn't be Tate.

His brain cells must have shot out his dick with his jizz.

Once the paper towels were damp, he turned to find Liam watching him with a curious expression.

"You don't need to do that," he said in a low voice. "I know you have to head out."

"I know." He didn't add that he wanted to or anything sappy like that. He just used the warm towels to clean the evidence of their hookup, then tossed them in the trash across the room.

"Thank you," Liam whispered as he tucked himself back in the tights.

Tate put his dick away as he nodded. His throat felt thick and uncomfortable. Liam's continued stare made him want to back away, but he forced himself to look the man in the eye.

"So," Liam finally said with a smirk. "Next time?"

Tate found himself grinning back wondering what the hell had happened to him.

## Chapter Seven

Liam hung up the phone with a smile. He couldn't stop himself from shimmying in his seat. Three, *three* classes at max capacity before he'd opened his doors. That had to be a good sign, right?

At the very least, his name was circulating in the community, and people wanted their kids to learn dance. At this rate, he'd need to hire a second teacher earlier than expected. That was a very desirable problem to have.

The loud clank of shattering tiles had him glancing toward the locker rooms with a flinch. This might be a good time to stop returning phone messages for the morning. The construction sounds didn't make the best background music.

Still, excitement surged through him. This was happening. *Really* happening.

He owned a studio, had classes booked up, and the renovations were underway. Tate and his brother arrived about an hour ago to begin the demolition of the old tiles. He'd been instructed to keep his eyes peeled for a third team member who should arrive at any time.

Since making calls was off the table, he dove into his mountain of unread emails instead. After swiping two more tasks off his to-do list, the door opened, and a man dressed in ratty jeans and a wife beater strode into the building. He had a buzzed blond haircut, a cigarette behind his ear, and a forearm tattoo of a large-breasted woman.

Liam learned long ago not to judge a book by its cover, but he had a hard time imagining this guy not being a homophobe. Still, he prided himself on giving people a chance, so he walked out from behind the front counter with his hand extended.

"Hey there, I'm Liam. You're here to work with Tate and Randy?"

He had a mildly attractive face with a blond goatee and dark brown eyes, but any appeal vanished when he sneered. "This a fucking joke?"

Liam blinked. "Excuse me?"

"Fucking Randy." He laughed. "Always busting my balls. He make you wear that shirt?"

What? Glancing down, Liam frowned. Ahh, the T-shirt. He'd dressed casually today after Tate warned there was no way to keep the dust contained to the locker room, and he hadn't thought twice about wearing a shirt from last year's Pride event in New York City. A rainbow Statue of Liberty with glitter shooting out of the torch adorned his chest.

*Here we go.*

Sighing, he steeled his spine and prepared for a barrage of prejudiced garbage. "Uh, no, got this baby in New York last June. I was the headline performer at a club during Pride." He struck a sassy pose as though that would help him win over this Neanderthal.

"So this ain't a joke?"

"Nope."

"I can't believe we took this fucking job," he muttered.

"Excuse me?" Liam narrowed his eyes.

Daryl stalked toward him, getting right in his personal space. "Listen, fairy, you can prance around in a rainbow tutu all fucking day behind closed doors, but keep it the fuck away from me." He jabbed a finger in Liam's face.

Time froze, and Liam's chest seized. Fear washed over him, making his stomach sour and his hands shake. It'd been a long time since someone came at him with such aggression, but the memories were the kind that lived in every cell of his body. He wanted to smack that hand away, twisting the thumb until Daryl sank to his knees, begging for relief. But instead, he stood there, eyes wide and legs like spaghetti noodles.

Where the fuck were all the self-defense classes he'd taken over the years? The ones where he'd learned how to put bullies like this one out of commission. There was no fight in his body right then, just flight.

"Daryl," Tate's furious voice cracked into the room like a whip. He marched out of the locker room and grabbed his coworker by his ear, yanking him away from Liam, who scrambled back behind his desk. The two-foot barrier helped settle his nerves.

"Ow, T, what the hell?" Daryl cupped a hand over his ear once Tate released him.

"The fuck is wrong with you, talking to a client that way?"

"What's wrong with me? What's wrong with you? The boss know we doin' this job? He know we're working for a fucking fa—"

"*Don't!*" The lethal warning in Tate's voice made Liam tremble. "Don't fucking finish that sentence. Get in there and do your job with your mouth shut."

Daryl shook his head with a disgusted snort. "You talk about wanting to start your own business. You don't have the balls to run a business. This," he pointed to Liam. "Working with people like this is how you run your business into the ground."

Well, that was just stupid.

"You've always been too fucking soft." With that, Daryl

stormed into the locker room, ramming Tate with his shoulder as he stomped by. A loud crash sounded, making Liam flinch. It was followed by a shout and a curse from Randy.

Liam swallowed. These were the men Tate associated with day in and day out. He'd mentioned this Daryl asshole was his brother's best friend. He lived thirty seconds from Tate and Randy, and they'd grown up together and now worked together. No wonder Tate didn't feel safe coming out. No wonder not a single person in his life knew he was gay.

With friends like that, Tate didn't need a single enemy.

Liam's heart splintered. No one should have to grow up afraid to be themselves, yet so many people did. The lucky ones were surprised to receive the support they deserved when they finally revealed themselves, but then there were the Tates of the world—the kids who grew into closeted adults and knew nothing but anonymous hookups and loneliness.

His pulse fluttered as he met Tate's sorrowful gaze.

"On behalf of our company, please accept my apology, Mr. Brady," Tate said, though his eyes said so much more. They revealed how Daryl's words pierced him as much, probably more than they did Liam. "I promise this won't happen again. Daryl won't come near you while he's working here." He paused, then said, "But if he makes you uncomfortable, I can remove him from the job."

It took Liam a few seconds to find his voice. "No," he said after clearing his throat. "If it gets the job done faster, he can stay. Just…"

Tate nodded. "You have my word."

Daryl wouldn't be allowed to harass him again.

"Okay." He tried for a smile, but it felt flat. "Then get back to work, mister," he said with false authority in his tone. "Those tiles aren't gonna lay themselves." Their eyes locked.

There were so many things Liam wanted to say, but who was he to Tate?

No one.

Just a guy he'd hooked up with a few times and could be—*fingers crossed*—planning another.

The problem was, aside from loving the orgasms Tate provided, Liam liked the man.

Genuinely liked him. They didn't have much in common, but something drew him to Tate and seemed to attract Tate to him as well. And he had dreams of starting his own company? The guy had layers. Liam could see there were many, and they went deep. How amazing would it be to peel them back individually and discover the man at the center?

"Sure. Sorry for all the noise. We'll break around noon for lunch."

"It's not a problem."

Tate nodded, then turned for the locker room.

"Tate?"

He spun around.

"He's wrong. Daryl, that is. You handled that well... like a boss. For what it's worth, I think you'd be the perfect person to break out on your own. If that's what you wanted."

FOR WHAT IT was worth?

Liam had no idea, not a single clue, just how much his words were worth. A couple of months ago, after a few too many beers while they'd been chilling after work, Tate let it slip to Randy that he'd considered starting his own tile company. He loved big, complex jobs where he could use his creativity and innovative techniques. Their boss was stuck in the dark ages. He didn't care about design trends, and it showed in the jobs he accepted. Tate was good with the clients too. Worlds better than Randy or even their boss.

His brother had laughed so hard that beer foamed out of

his nose. Then he'd slapped Tate on the shoulder and said, "Keep dreaming, asshole. But thanks for the laugh." Then he'd stumbled off and fucked Whitney in the damn bushes behind his trailer.

What a lucky lady.

Liam hadn't laughed.

When was the last time someone had believed in him?

His parents sure as hell never did. Hell, he hadn't seen his father in three years. Or was it four? The last time he'd blown through town, he'd stolen a hundred bucks from Tate's wallet, grabbed Whitney's tit and tried to sleep with her, and smacked his ex-wife across the face. His Father of the Year award must have gotten lost in the mail.

His mother barely recognized up from down and sure as hell had no idea what Tate got up to these days. He could be the CEO of a Fortune 500 company, and she'd never know it. He couldn't forget Randy and their group of hick friends. People who didn't know the real Tate would shun him if they did and certainly didn't care about his goals and dreams.

Then there was this compassionate, sexy, accepting man who'd given Tate more in a few encounters than the people who'd been in his life for two and a half decades.

He couldn't think of something worthwhile to say, so he merely said, "Thank you," and turned his back on Liam before the man saw more than he wanted to reveal.

When he entered the locker room, he found Daryl taking his anger out on the tiles. He smashed them like a gas-powered machine, muttering and curing as he worked.

"Well," Randy said as he strode over with a shit-eating grin. A fine layer of powder covered his face and lightened his hair. His dust mask rested on his forehead over his safety glasses. "At this rate, we'll be done with the demo by the end of the day. You pissed him off good."

Tate grunted.

"What the fuck happened out there?"

"He ran his stupid, disrespectful mouth to the client. Practically had him fucking cornered."

"Hmm."

"What?" Tate rounded on his brother, who held his hands up in surrender.

"Nothing." Randy took a step back, shaking his head.

"No, you got something to say, so fucking say it." He curled his hands in a give-it-to-me motion. He couldn't hit Daryl in front of Liam, but back here, without those pretty eyes watching, he'd be happy to clock Randy in his stupid mouth.

"It ain't right, T, you coming at Daryl so strong like that."

"Excuse me?" His ears burned. "That shit makes us, meaning the company we work for, look unprofessional and backward. He got off easy. I should have kicked his ass for how he talked to our client."

"See, there you go again."

Tate threw his hands in the air. His blood boiled. He was walking a fine line, and if he wasn't careful, he'd show his hand.

"Look," Randy said, lowering his arms. "I get it. Daryl's a stupid fucker. He shouldn't antagonize the clients, but you gotta understand how this one is different."

"And how exactly is that?" he asked, narrowing his eyes.

"It's fucking uncomfortable, man. Working here knowing how he is and what he likes." He gestured toward the locker room exit, where Liam sat at his desk in the lobby.

Tate prayed he couldn't hear a word of their conversation.

He wanted to throw up. All he could think of was Randy screaming at him someday, "Knowing how *you* are and what *you* like."

"He fucking looks at me when I walk in the door," Randy said, kicking a loose tile.

"What do you want him to do, stare at the floor?" Tate was proud of himself for his voice's leveled control.

"Yes!" Randy shouted. "That's exactly what I want him to do."

He'd known his brother was a small-minded bigot. It'd be impossible not to, and there'd been plenty of times over the years when he'd wanted to smack the shit out of Randy for the stupid shit he said, but he'd never hated him. Part of him had always held hope that Randy would eventually come around if he learned of Tate's sexual orientation.

This conversation was quickly killing that faith.

And in that moment, he hated Randy.

"Times are changing, Randy," he said as he grabbed his chisel. "You can't say shit like that and expect people to agree with you."

"Times are changing." Randy snorted. "Maybe, but that don't make it right." He stared Tate in the eye. "There's gonna come a time when you gotta make a choice, man. Stand by your people or his. I hope you make the right choice." He pulled his mask down, lowered his safety glasses, and gave Tate his back as he went to work.

Were the words a threat, or was it just Randy running his mouth? Either way, they cut deep and emphasized the problem. Tate couldn't have it both ways. He couldn't be himself and remain part of his family.

Whatever morsel of hope he'd clung to died a painful death right there in Liam's studio.

Twice now, he'd connected with Liam in a way he'd never connected with another man. It'd been fun, freeing, and addictive. They'd talked about a next time, and Tate didn't want to let that pass him by. Being with Liam felt life-changing in a way his soul craved.

Randy would kick him in the nuts if he could hear his thoughts.

The inevitable barreled down on him with the speed of a runaway train.

*There's gonna come a time when you gotta make a choice, man.*

Randy was right.

Tate hoped he was strong enough to make the right choice when the time came.

The choice that would change his life forever.

## Chapter Eight

The next week followed much of the same pattern. Liam woke at six thirty, chugged a cup of coffee and a protein bar, then made his way downstairs to the studio. After a solid half hour of stretching and warm-up, he worked on choreographing routines. Once he had the studio up and running, he hoped to start a competition team. To do that, he'd need to attract skilled dancers, and the best way to reel them in was with stellar choreography. Just because he lived in a small rural town didn't mean there wasn't incredible talent to be discovered.

Tate and Randy showed up around eight each morning. The last three days, Tate had brought him an iced caramel macchiato. It'd been a welcome surprise, and he'd had a hard time not gushing in excitement. Randy gave him dirty looks but didn't ask how Tate knew Liam's coffee order. At least he didn't ask in Liam's earshot.

Thankfully, there hadn't been any more issues with Daryl. He tended to show up late and with a scowl, but he'd kept his mouth shut and worked. As soon as Liam saw him pull into the parking lot, he made himself scarce until Daryl disappeared into the locker room. The situation wasn't ideal, but he'd take it if it kept the peace and made things easier for Tate.

What he hated was the professional way Tate spoke to him and how they hadn't had so much as spent thirty seconds alone together. After the epic frotting session in the locker room, Liam had hoped for more. That night, he'd gone to bed imagining stolen moments, sneaking kisses, and maybe a scandalous lunch break in his apartment.

But, no. It'd been crickets from Tate, and while Liam practically had to tie himself to his desk chair, he didn't make a move either. If it were up to Liam, they'd get each other off daily, but the ball was in Tate's court. He was the one with something to lose. So, Liam had behaved himself and had spent more time jerking off over the past few days than he had in high school.

It was becoming a problem.

This morning, the tilers weren't scheduled to begin until eleven, which worked in his favor. Liam had a date with eight very sassy ladies, and he'd have hated to cancel on them.

"All right, my lovelies," he said, clapping his hands. "Should we run it again?"

"Let's do it," Dot, the spunkiest of the crowd, rushed to the front of the studio.

After an hour of class with her, Liam learned she loved to be front and center and soaked up attention like a dry sponge.

A few of the others rolled their eyes. "He's gay, dear," Barbara said with a tut. "He wouldn't have wanted you even thirty years ago."

"Oh, stuff it, Barb. You know this isn't about me." Dot shifted her gaze to Liam. "I do, however, have a very lovely nephew who recently broke up with his boyfriend. Just saying." She batted her seventy-eight-year-old eyelashes. "The only problem is he lives in Chicago, but what's a little distance between soulmates?"

Liam's face heated. "That's very sweet," he said, patting

Dot's slender shoulder. "But I'm just going to focus on my business for a while."

And maybe, God willing, a very attractive country boy who brought his favorite coffee each day. Not that Tate gave him any indication they'd be doing more than casting sidelong glances at each other for the foreseeable future.

Liam was still clinging to the *next time* they'd promised each other.

It would happen.

*Desperation, thy name is Liam.*

"Good idea, sweetie," Mary, the youngest of the group at sixty-six, said. "Men are nothing but trouble. Trust me, I know."

"Yeah, you did marry five of them, after all," Dot said with a snort.

"Five?" Liam mouthed to Mary, who shrugged. "What can I say? I liked dick, and I wasn't one to give the milk away for free."

Unfortunately, he took a sip of his water at the exact moment those words came flying out of Mary's mouth. The liquid slipped right down his trachea. He choked, spewing water all over the floor as his lungs fought to keep from drowning.

"Careful, dear." Dot whacked him on the back. "Take a breath."

"Thank you," he rasped when he could breathe again.

Who knew sweet Mary, with her snowy white hair and orthopedic shoes, had it in her?

Five of them, apparently.

"Okay…" He needed to get this train back on track before he completely lost control. People thought teaching kids was tough, it was nothing compared to a group of mischievous seniors. "Let's work through the dance a few more times before we run out of time. The senior center's talent show is in a few weeks, and I'd hate myself if I sent you ladies out there unprepared."

"It's so nice of you to do this for us before you officially open, dear."

"It's my pleasure, Mrs. Snow. Okay, everyone in their place?" The group of senior ladies all nodded. "And five... six... seven... eight..." He hit the music, and the studio filled with the song they'd requested—*Jailhouse Rock*. As Elvis belted out the lyrics, the ladies began to dance. It was a bit of a disaster, but they had fun, laughed, and teased each other, so he offered a few corrections. After running it several times, they had it down, and Liam felt comfortable calling it a day.

Dot had other ideas. She'd begged him to play the rest of Elvis's album. Once the other ladies joined in the pleading, he had no choice but to give them what they wanted. Who could resist a bunch of sweet grandmas itching for a dance party?

By the end of the second song, he was dancing with them, spinning, dipping ladies left and right, and laughing his head off. His friends in New York wouldn't recognize him. Who would believe that in the span of a few weeks, he'd gone from being a lead performer in the New York City Ballet to choreographing a dance for the local senior center's talent show?

But this type of dance fed his soul—fun, no pressure, and pure joy. It was the kind of dance professionals often forgot about in their pursuit of perfection. So, he embraced it, crooning along with Elvis and getting his fifties groove on.

He was mid *Rock Around the Clock* with The King when he spun, thrust his hips, and came to a dead stop. Tate stood propped against the door with his arms folded and a smirk on his handsome face.

Liam rushed to his phone on the floor near the mirror and killed the music.

"Hey!" Mary called out when the room fell silent. "Oh,

who do we have here?"

"Leave him alone, Mar. He doesn't want to be your number six," Dot said with a snicker.

"Oh, Tate, hello dear," Mrs. Snow said with a wave for the bad boy lurking at the door.

"Hey, Miz Snow." He waved before folding his arms again. "So, what are you crazy kids getting up to in here?"

Liam's face was hot enough to melt off his body. "Uh, we're just having a quick lesson."

"This sweet boy is helping us by choreographing a dance for the senior center's talent show." Dot looped her thin arm through Liam's and tugged him closer to Tate. She had a mischievous gleam in her eye that he needed to squash immediately.

"Sorry, we ran late. I meant to be finished before you got here to work."

"I'm a few minutes early."

"Tate, why don't you come dance with me?" Mrs. Snow shuffled over. Her hot pink spandex pants were stretched to capacity by her hefty frame, and her top could only be described as a mumu. It was bright, bold, and told the world she didn't give a crap what people thought of her style.

Color leached from Tate's face, which made Liam chuckle. He had no problem with the spotlight leaving him and shifting to Tate.

"Uh, no disrespect intended, Miz Snow, but I'm gonna have to pass. I'm not much of a dancer."

Liam's eyes met Tate's, whose expression remained pained. Liam winked. The man had been a great dance partner the night they met in the club, but then he hadn't had to do more than grind his hips and rock back and forth.

"Hmm." Mrs. Snow tilted her head and studied Tate.

What did she see? Could she tell he had secrets?

"How's your mama, boy?"

Tate stiffened. " 'Bout the same as usual, Miz Snow. You know how it is."

With a shake of her head, she said, "I know she's trouble. Marissa was trouble in school, and she's trouble now. You two boys practically raised yourselves, with you taking the brunt of it, if I'm not mistaken."

Discomfort rolled off Tate in waves so thick Liam could practically see them. He squirmed, then shrugged. "Not all of us are lucky to have had you as a mama."

"Don't you try to sugar me up with sweet words, boy. I once made you scrub the whole bathroom after you dropped that cherry bomb in the toilet. I have no problem taking you to task again. You hear me?"

All that was missing was her shriveled finger wagging in his face. As it was, Liam could barely contain his laughter.

The smirk returned, and Tate seemed to shake off whatever cloud had momentarily rolled in. "Yes, ma'am." He faced Liam. "Miz Snow was my mama's fifth-grade teacher. By the time I came through school, she was the principal. Meanest one I've ever had."

Liam's eyes bugged, and he whipped his head toward Mrs. Snow to find her laughing instead of being offended.

A wide grin stretched her soft face. "Don't you forget it, boy. Same time next week, Liam?"

What on earth was happening here? "Yes, ma'am. Same time, same place."

"I can't wait." She shuffled on by, patting his arm as she passed. "You're a good boy, Liam." She narrowed her eyes at Tate. "You'd do well to try to be more like this one," she said, shaking a crooked finger in his face.

There it was.

"Yes, ma'am. Can I help you to your ride?" He held out an arm, and Mrs. Snow took it with a harumph, but she still smiled.

All bark and no bite.

Liam grinned. The whiplash of emotions and information overload from the past few minutes had left his head spinning and his heart aching, which was becoming a common theme the more he learned about Tate's life.

As Tate escorted Mrs. Snow to the shuttle that would take them back to the senior center across town, a beat-up car holding Randy and Daryl pulled into the parking lot. They hopped out of the vehicle and strode to Tate and Mrs. Snow, greeting her with smirks and probably a lot of sass.

Without warning, Mrs. Snow walloped Daryl on the side of his head with her tan leather purse.

Daryl yelped and hopped away from the woman. She didn't miss a beat, treating Randy to the same smack.

Liam covered his mouth, which did nothing to hide his laughter. Tate, on the other hand, didn't bother to disguise his. Instead, he held a fist out to Mrs. Snow, who bumped her knuckles against his, making Liam snicker even more.

The spunky old lady just became his favorite person.

He tried to keep from feeling warm and gooey inside as he watched Tate, who had a solid foot and a half on Mrs. Snow, help her onto the shuttle bus, but the effort failed. After Mrs. Snow climbed the step into the shuttle, Tate remained and helped each lady in turn as they filed out of the studio.

Randy and Daryl unloaded supplies from Tate's truck.

Liam stared from the window the entire time.

"He really is a good boy."

He glanced down to find Dot at his side. "Seems like it," he said with a smile.

"Always thought he was so much better than where he came from. And I don't mean because of where he grew up or the fact that his family doesn't have two pennies to rub together. Those details don't make up a person's quality."

He couldn't tear his eyes off Tate even as he listened to

Dot. Watching him this way, with such focused, hungry attention, came too close to crossing the line. If he wasn't careful, Dot, or worse, Randy and Daryl would notice the desire in his gaze.

But he couldn't stop.

"It's the hatred," Dot said, and those might have been the only words capable of pulling his focus from Tate.

Liam glanced down to find her also watching the man they spoke about. She had a soft fondness in her gaze.

"They hate everyone," she said. "Always have. My Henry and I lived in the same trailer park they did when those boys were kids. There is so much hate, especially of those different from them." She sighed. "Guess it's hard to raise children who can love when you don't love yourself." She patted his arm. "You have yourself a good week, Liam. Thank you for today. I've had the most fun since my date with Roger a few months ago."

He nodded but couldn't speak. His attention was already back on Tate, who extended a hand to Dot as she walked toward the shuttle.

Instead of answering his hundreds of questions about Tate, his family, and life, she'd only added to the mountain.

What had his childhood been like?

What was Mrs. Snow referring to when talking about his mother?

How did he pull himself from a pit of darkness and hatred to become the man he was today?

And would he ever chance revealing his authentic self to the world?

## Chapter Nine

With only one day left on the studio's tiling project, Tate could feel his chances to be with Liam slipping through his fingers. How many times over the past week had there been an opportunity to sneak into a corner and take a hit of Liam's sweetness? How many evenings did he think about texting the man whose number he'd stolen off the work order? How many nights had he laid in his bed alone with his hard dick in his hand and Liam's name on his lips?

All. Of. Them.

Countless times, he'd thought about driving back to the studio after dinner. His cock had been hard more often than not ever since he'd stumbled upon Liam dancing with a bunch of batty old ladies.

He needed his head examined because there'd been nothing sexy about that day, yet every time he pictured the joy on Liam's face, he got horny as hell. The man in his element was the most beautiful thing Tate had ever seen.

He craved more of Liam's kisses, fantasized about the way their dicks felt sliding against each other, and dreamed of what it would feel like to glide into his flawless ass.

There wasn't anything he wanted more than skin on skin with Liam.

And what did he do about it?

Nothing.

Not a damn thing.

Tate did hookups. Quick and dirty hookups where he could bust a nut and get the hell out before any risk of discovery. Liam might have started that way, but he no longer looked at the dancer the same. If he touched Liam again, they'd be starting something. What? He had no fucking clue, but something more than a hookup.

The idea of being with Liam appealed to him on a level he'd never allowed himself to tap into. But it also terrified him to his very soul. Liam thought he understood the risk if Tate were outed, but he'd led a charmed life. He'd grown up in New York, where he'd never had to fear for his physical safety from the people who claimed to love him if they found out he preferred fucking men.

But by the end of the week, when he'd had to see Liam's beautiful face every single day, Tate broke. If he didn't get his hand on the man before night's end, he'd fucking implode. He wanted Liam, but he didn't want it to be the same quick orgasms against a bathroom wall. They should be able to take their time. He didn't know how Liam's nipples felt against his tongue or what his balls tasted like. He had no idea how tight Liam would squeeze him as he finger-fucked his ass—though he had a feeling it'd be damn fucking tight. Maybe they should hang out, too, before devouring each other or even after.

He could do that, right? Maybe share a meal or watch a movie?

It might be nice to hang out with someone besides his idiot friends. Someone like him. Someone who could show him how to just be.

Before he could talk himself out of it, he jogged out of his trailer and over to Randy's. "Yo, Rand, you here?" he asked as he pounded on the door.

"What do you want, fucker?" came the reply.

Chuckling, he let himself in to find his brother sitting on the couch in a pair of cutoff jean shorts and nothing else. He had a beer in one hand and the remote in the other.

"Dude, you can't even fucking button your jorts? You look like a goddamn slob. How does your wife not leave you?"

"They ain't fucking jorts," Randy said, flipping him off around the remote. "Soccer moms wear jorts."

"Are they jean material?"

"Yes," Randy grumbled.

"Are they shorts?"

"Fuck off."

He laughed and plopped on the couch beside his brother, who had an old NASCAR race on the television screen. The couch had seen better days. Hell, their whole trailer had seen better days. Sun-bleached curtains covered the small window above the television. The couch was a freebie they found on a corner in front of someone's house in the burbs. It had been nice when they found it a few years ago, but it now had a deep indent from Randy's ass, always sitting in the same spot. The faint smell of cigarette smoke had been there for so long Tate barely noticed it anymore.

"Want a beer?" Randy asked without taking his eyes off the race.

"Nah. Got a question for you, though."

"Shoot."

The cars zoomed around the track with a loud whir that reverberated through the room.

"What do you do if you wanna do something nice for Whit?"

"What do you mean?"

"What do you mean, what do I mean? Like, I don't know… if you want to make her feel good. Do something romantic or some shit."

What the hell were these words coming out of his mouth? Thankfully, Randy seemed too caught up in the race to put his one brain cell toward noticing Tate had lost his mind.

"I don't know. Sometimes, if I feel up to it, I'll pick her up a lotto ticket on the weekend."

He blinked. "Seriously?"

"What? She likes 'em."

"A lotto ticket. That's what you do when you wanna impress your wife? You buy her a fucking dollar lotto ticket? Can you please turn the fucking volume down? I can't hear myself think."

"Hey, fuck you, Mega Millions costs two bucks," Randy yelled, but he hit the mute button.

"You're useless," Tate said as Whitney walked out of their bedroom.

"Hey, T, what's up?"

"What's this bullshit about anyway?" Randy asked.

"Hey, hon," Tate called to his sister-in-law. Still, as pretty as she'd been in high school, Whitney wore a flowy skirt and crop top showing off her flat midriff. Her looks mattered above all to her, and most of her paychecks from the salon where she worked went toward her appearance.

"What are you guys talking about?" She went into the kitchen and pulled a pan from the sink. After a quick inspection, she placed it on the stove. "Anyone want a grilled cheese?"

"I do, babe," Randy said as Tate declined. "Listen to this shit, Whit. Tate came over to ask what I do when I wanna do some nice shit for you."

Her laughter sounded more like a cackle. "This oughta be good. What'd you tell him?"

"Told him I give you my dick. Ain't nothing nicer, right, baby?"

Whitney snorted. "And you wonder why I call you a

dumbass."

"You know what, forget it." It'd been a stupid idea anyway.

"No, wait." Whitney stood at the counter, buttering a slice of white bread. "You talking about a date or something?"

Forget a stupid idea, this was a *terrible* idea. What had he been thinking? He should scrap this whole thing. But he knew Whitney. That woman was like a dog with a bone. Now that she'd gotten involved, she wouldn't let up until she had all the details.

"Yeah, maybe. Something like that." He shrugged.

"Wait, this about your piece in Tulsa?" Randy asked after taking a swig from his beer. "Shit, I thought you were just getting your dick wet. You wanna take this bitch out on a date?"

"Randy, could you maybe try not calling all women bitches? It's offensive," Whitney said, shaking her head. She dropped two buttered slices into the pan and began to layer the cheese on top. "I think it's sweet, T."

"It's not... I don't know. You know what, never mind. It's stupid."

"It is stupid. Why the fuck would you go to all that trouble when you already got her willing to fuck you?"

Whitney glared at her stupid husband. "How about a picnic?" she said, shifting her gaze to Tate.

"A picnic?"

"Oh God." Randy rolled his eyes. "You and your fucking picnics."

Shrugging, Whitney topped off her sandwiches with a final piece of bread. "It's nice. You get to eat but have more privacy than a restaurant. You can take your time, be outside, and it shows effort." She shot a glare Randy's way. "Women like effort."

"Yeah, well, men like pussy, babe."

Tate had been lying about his sexuality for so long that

he'd gotten used to hearing them talk about him with women. Obviously, he'd never corrected them, but it hadn't ever bothered him. It was just another layer of protection for himself.

But hearing them assume Liam was a woman soured his stomach. Liam didn't deserve to be lied about as his dirty little secret, and that's exactly what he'd be, what he already was by getting involved with Tate.

And yet he found himself saying, "A picnic, huh?"

"Yep." Whitney stood with her hip propped against the counter and a spatula in her hand.

He could arrange a picnic. What did he need, a blanket, some snacks, and a good spot?

Easy. He already knew the perfect place and had a feeling Liam would love it.

Excitement bubbled in his veins, but he tempered his expression. The last thing he wanted was more questions. "Thanks, Whit," he said as he hopped up and walked into the kitchen, kissing his sister-in-law on the cheek.

"Hey," Randy called out. "What about me? I helped. Where's the love, man?"

Tate flipped him off.

"Oh yeah, what'd you suggest, Rand?" Whitney asked, rolling her eyes. "You tell him to buy a lotto ticket?"

Tate snorted a laugh as Randy's face screwed up, and he muttered something unintelligible under his breath.

"Hey," Whitney called out as Tate reached the door. "You're a good man, Tate. She's a lucky lady."

He nodded, then jogged back to his place as her sweet words ate a hole in his heart. A good man wouldn't lie about the very foundation of who he was. A good man wouldn't hide Liam in the shadows and pretend he was someone he wasn't. No, he wasn't a good man, but maybe he could make up for some of his shortcomings by doing something nice for

Liam.

Liam, now, there was a good man.

About an hour before sunset, he drove out of Swan Trailer Park and started the short trip to Liam's place. With each passing second, the brick in his stomach grew heavier.

What the hell was he doing? Liam would probably laugh in his face. He'd never so much as taken someone to a movie, and now he was planning picnics?

Fuck, this was a terrible idea.

He turned right onto Main Street, where Liam leased his studio and apartment.

How had he gotten here so fast? When had he ever driven through town without hitting a red light?

Tonight, of course.

The building grew closer and closer as his heart beat faster and faster.

"I can't do this," he muttered, flicking on his blinker. He could swing a U-turn and be back on his way home in seconds.

He glanced in his rear-view mirror and prepared to shift lanes as movement fifty feet up on his right caught his eye.

Liam.

He'd know that smooth, cat-like walk anywhere.

Instead of turning around, his car seemed to move of its own volition, slowing next to his obsession as he strolled down the road. Liam jumped, and then his eyes widened when he saw who sat behind the wheel of the car, lowering the passenger window.

"Tate," he said, his voice ripe with surprise. He glanced around as though worried someone might catch them. It drove a spear of guilt straight through Tate's stomach. "What are you doing here?"

As usual, Liam looked effortlessly stylish in pale yellow shorts and a short-sleeved white polo. He was fresh, happy, and mouthwatering. On the other hand, Tate wore his usual ratty jeans and plain shirt. "I was coming to see you, actually."

"Oh." Liam leaned his forearms on the open window. "Are you sure this is wise? You stopping me like this?" Concern marred his voice.

"Probably not. Maybe you should get in the car before someone spots us. I'll drive us somewhere else."

Surprise lit his face. "Really? You and me?"

Tate nodded. Beautiful as the man was, he was never more stunning than when he smiled.

"Where are we going?"

Nerves fluttered in his stomach as he realized he was about to ask a man on a date for the first time. Christ, his insides shook like a teenage boy asking his crush to prom. "I was thinking a picnic. There's someplace I wanna show you."

Liam probably wouldn't have looked so shocked if Tate had run him over with his car instead of stopping to talk to him. But the surprise didn't last long. The most radiant smile lit up his entire face. "Really?" he squealed. "A picnic?"

The excitement must have been contagious because Tate found himself grinning back. "Yep."

"Oh my God, yay. Yes, I love picnics." He glanced down at himself. I was just on my way to grab some dinner. Am I okay like this, or should I change?"

"You're perfect." *So fucking perfect.*

"Sweet talker." Liam opened the door and climbed into Tate's car. If the old fast-food wrappers crunching under his feet bothered him, he didn't mention it. Instead, he clapped his hands. "I am so excited. I haven't been on a picnic in years."

*Thank you, Whit.* He'd be sure to send some flowers to his sister-in-law. Better than a damn lottery ticket.

"So where exactly are we going? Wait, no, don't tell me. I

want to be surprised."

"It's nowhere fancy," Tate said with a grunt. Shit, now he'd be second-guessing his location choice the whole ride. Why the hell did people do this dating shit? It was way too stressful.

"I don't want fancy," Liam said with a shrug. "I just want you."

Well, shit. Tate swallowed a lump of emotion he'd never tell anyone about. Why did that simple statement make him feel as though someone flipped him inside out?

## Chapter Ten

Anticipation zinged through Liam as he settled into the passenger seat of Tate's beat-up old car. If someone offered him a million dollars, he couldn't name the type of car, but he had a feeling it wasn't made in the last decade, maybe a decade and a half.

Not that he cared. Hell, Liam hadn't even owned a car until a month ago when he purchased a used Ford Explorer. Cars didn't impress him. Living in New York City, he barely knew anyone who owned a motor vehicle. What did impress him was a man showing up for a surprise date, so obviously out of his comfort zone, just to be with him.

*Swoon.*

His heart wouldn't stand a chance if Tate did things like this often.

Had he admitted too much a moment ago when he said he wanted Tate? Hopefully not. Tate had to want him, too, right? Why go through all this trouble otherwise? And knowing what he knew about Tate, it had been trouble. The kind of mental trouble that involved overthinking and second-guessing himself.

"So," Liam said as he turned to face the sexy man he'd jerked off to that morning. And the night before. Possibly twice. Tate looked good behind his car's steering wheel, comfortable in his command and control of the vehicle. His jeans were a familiar pair he wore often, but the short-sleeved blue Henley he hadn't seen. The fabric hugged Tate's muscles in a way that had Liam fighting an erection the moment he climbed in the car. "Tell me something about yourself."

Tate cast him a quick side-eye before focusing back on the road. "Like what?"

Cornfields stretched on as far as the eye could see. They were heading south and west in a direction Liam had yet to explore. Still, it was funny how quickly he'd acclimated to seeing the flat farmlands out his window as he traveled.

"Like… what's your favorite movie?" They could start with something light and easy to keep Tate from getting spooked.

"My favorite movie, huh?" He sat with one arm outstretched, gripping the top of the steering wheel and the other propped against the closed window. The car's air conditioning chugged along, doing a fair to poor job of cooling the inside, but if they opened the windows, it'd be hard to talk, and Liam wanted to hear everything Tate had to say. The man fascinated him. He was a mess of contradictions, thanks to being surrounded by narrow-minded assholes.

Liam had a feeling there was so much more to Tate than met the eye. Even in the short time they'd known each other, Tate changed around him. He let his guard down a smidge, but Liam was selfish enough to want the whole package. He wanted Tate to trust him enough to be himself if the poor guy even knew who that was.

"*Fight Club.*"

Liam smiled. "Oh, interesting. You like a movie with a little bit of a mind fuck, huh?"

That drew a laugh out of Tate. "I do. Always have. *Momento, Requiem for a Dream,* those kinds of movies have always done it for me. Psychological thrillers and dark comedies are my two favorite genres."

*Interesting.* Liam soaked up the information. "You know, I can see it."

"I love Chuck Palahniuk. I read *Fight Club* after watching it, then read everything else he wrote." Tate shrugged and glanced at Liam, who could barely contain himself in his seat. "What?"

"You're a reader?"

The switch flipped, and Tate went from open to closed-off in the blink of an eye. "What? No, I mean—"

"Okay, let's get one thing straight... or not straight since it's us." Liam chuckled as Tate rolled his eyes. He turned in the seat, tucking his legs under him so he could fully face his driver. "This is serious, so listen. I'm not going to judge you."

Tate's eyes narrowed.

"I'll say it again. I am not going to judge *you*. When we're together, like this, just the two of us, you're free." He waffled his hand back and forth between them. "Understand, Tate?"

He watched as Tate's grip on the faded steering wheel tightened. Maybe it was stupid to push the man as tense as he'd become, but this was vital to their relationship.

And to Tate's self-acceptance.

Liam continued, "No matter what you tell me about who you are and what you like, I will not judge you. And if you've been hiding so long you don't know who you are yet, I am a safe place for you to explore that. So, tell me you like to read, tell me you like to make fucking aroma therapy soaps in your trailer, and I will do nothing but ask you to tell me more because I really like every single thing I learn about you."

Tate's throat bobbed as he swallowed. For a moment, it seemed he wouldn't respond, but then he spoke. "I... this is new to me."

"I know."

"You've met some of the people in my life. They're assholes on a good day." He glanced at Liam with a fierce expression. "I'm used to keeping my shit on lockdown."

"I know that too. I'm not asking you to spill your guts to me. I get it might take you a while to feel like you can trust me, but I just want to make sure you know you can. I'll keep your confidence and never judge you. I am and always will be a safe place for you, no matter what happens or doesn't happen between us."

Tate cleared his throat. Was he struggling to accept what Liam said? Or could he be feeling the same intense connection and desire to be closer to Liam, not only sexually but in all ways? After a few tense seconds, he rasped, "Thank you."

"Trust me when I tell you it is my pleasure." Liam extended his hand, palm up, resting it on the center console.

He counted the seconds as Tate's gaze bounced between his hand and the road ahead. Liam would give it until twenty, then pull back. When he got to twelve, Tate shifted, taking the steering wheel with his left hand and placing his right on top of Liam's.

Triumph surged through him, but he fought to keep calm and not bounce in his seat. Instead of cheering like he wanted, he closed his fingers around Tate's and said, "He's gay. Did you know that?"

"Huh? Who?"

"Chuck Palahniuk."

"Oh, yeah. I did know that."

The conversation lightened after that, flowing without any effort on Liam's part. They continued talking about books and movies and discovered they had similar tastes in many things, except food. Tate had never eaten sushi, a horrifying fact Liam planned to remedy as soon as possible.

After thirty minutes of driving through farmland, Tate

turned onto an unmarked road Liam never saw coming. It was more of a dirt path than a road and ended at a creek after about a hundred yards.

"Whoa." Liam craned his neck to get a better look at their surroundings. "Where are we?"

"This is the back end of a huge commercial farm."

His eyes widened. "Are we allowed to be here?"

Tate's chuckle made his cheeks burn. "Not sure, to be honest, but I've been here hundreds of times and haven't been caught yet, so…" He shrugged.

"How do you know about this place?"

"My old man worked here when I was a kid. For about a decade after he split, he would randomly show up at the trailer park every six months or so. Mom loved it. She'd make him take Randy and me to work with him until he disappeared again. There wasn't anyone to supervise us while he worked, so we did a lot of exploring and found this place. Around the time I turned twelve, my old man didn't come around for two straight years. But I managed to get myself here sometimes and still come when I need… space."

Their gazes locked. Liam saw the vulnerability staring back at him. Tate let him see the vulnerability. The weight of the responsibility of protecting this man's sacred emotions pressed down on him, but he was up to the challenge. "And you brought me here."

A single nod was all he received in reply. It was enough.

Liam squeezed Tate's hand and then released him as he turned toward the door. "Well then, let's get to picnicking."

"This time, I wanted space… with you," Tate spoke to his back, but the position didn't dim the impact of the admission.

Afraid his emotions would show all over his face, Liam kept his back to Tate. "That sounds perfect to me."

After they climbed out of the car, Tate went to the trunk while Liam absorbed their surroundings. The creek ran so clear the water looked drinkable. They were in a smallish clearing surrounded by cornfields on either side of the creek. The tall plants provided privacy and made him feel as though they were the only two souls for miles.

Maybe they were.

"This is beautiful." He inhaled, drawing in the sweet scent permeating the air from the growing corn. It was one of the first things he learned to love about driving through farm country. "So, what's the plan?" He spun around, and his jaw nearly hit the dirt. "Tate…" he whispered.

The man had pulled a duffle out of the trunk and now kneeled, setting up an idyllic picnic. He'd spread a red blanket over the ground and unloaded food containers. Liam happened to turn as he was pulling a bottle of white wine from the duffle.

Wine? Somehow, he didn't peg Tate as a wine drinker, which meant it was for him.

His heart swelled to near bursting.

This man was proving to be very dangerous to Liam's heart. If Liam wasn't careful, he'd fall down the slippery slope of romantic feelings and end up hurt. He was almost certain Tate had never dated another man. The first was always memorable but rarely lasted.

It was the starter relationship, the training boyfriend, not that they were even boyfriends. Ugh, if he didn't get out of his own head, he'd miss this incredible experience and spend the next month kicking himself, so he swallowed down the surge of emotion.

"Tate, this is incredible. I can't believe you did all this."

He'd never have thought it possible, but the man turned an adorable shade of pink. He rubbed the back of his neck, staring down at two chipped wine glasses in his hands. "I didn't know what you liked so…" He shook his head.

"I'm easy. Whatever you have is perfect." He walked over

to the blanket. Tate's gaze shifted up as he approached. The other man watched as Liam sat with his legs curled to his side like a mermaid.

Chucking, Tate said, "You even sit gracefully."

Grinning, Liam shrugged. "Two decades of dance training will do that."

"Two decades?" Tate unscrewed the wine and poured some into the glasses.

"Yep. Started when I was five, which is after many of my co-performers." He accepted the glass from Tate and then held it up between them. "To safe havens, whether they be a beautiful place or an unexpected person."

With a nod, Tate tapped his glass against Liam's. "To safe-havens," he whispered.

As he took his first sip, he kept his gaze on Tate over the glass's rim. A crisp, fruity flavor filled his mouth, and he smiled. Sauvignon Blanc, his favorite.

Tate's nose wrinkled before he swallowed. He pulled the glass away from his mouth and stared at it for a second before shrugging and going in for a second taste.

"Like it?"

"Not bad. Though I can think of something much more delicious to taste."

There wasn't anything better than Tate letting his guard down. The few times he'd allowed himself to flirt, the effort sent butterflies through Liam's stomach.

"There you go, flirting with me again," Liam said with a wink.

"That a problem?" An eyebrow arched into Tate's forehead.

"Um, hell no. Quite the opposite. I love it. Flirt away."

They grinned at each other.

"So, what did you bring me to eat?"

The man had enough food to feed an army. He'd brought cheese, crackers, grapes, an assortment of finger sandwiches, a fresh pasta salad, and one large cupcake for dessert. Liam couldn't wait to share it.

"Seriously, Tate, this is amazing. Thank you so much for doing all this."

"It's nothing," he said as he ripped open a bag of crackers.

"It's not nothing." Liam scooted until his knees bumped Tate's thighs. "This is really wonderful. No one has ever put this much thought into planning a date for me. You made me feel really special tonight. Thank you."

A world of emotions burned in Tate's gaze—fear, lust, pride, and hopefully the same magnetic draw Liam was experiencing. He cupped the back of Tate's neck and drew him close, pressing their lips together.

Tate gasped at the contact, and Liam took the opportunity to slip his tongue into the man's sexy mouth. He tasted of wine, and the flavor went straight to Liam's head. Unlike their other kisses, this one had no end goal or time limit. They weren't in a club racing to get off or in his studio hiding from prying eyes for a frantic few minutes before Tate had to leave.

Liam took his sweet time exploring every corner of Tate's mouth with licks and strokes of his tongue. He kept his hand on Tate's neck, playing with the unruly strands of hair at the nape. How on earth did he get it so silky?

When Tate moaned and grabbed Liam's thighs, pulling him until he straddled Tate's lap, his cock hardened to near aching. The man beneath him was just as rigid but seemed to realize the same thing Liam did—they didn't need to do anything about it right then. They could enjoy kissing and touching for the sake of being close and connecting.

But later, he wanted Tate in his bed and in his body.

"Come home with me tonight," he whispered as he rocked his erection into Tate's, drawing a harsh curse from the man. "After this, come to my apartment. Sleep in my bed. Fuck me."

"Jesus Christ." Tate nibbled along his jaw, squeezing his ass with those very strong hands. "We gotta stop, or I'm gonna lose it."

It took Herculean effort, but Liam managed to wrench himself away. "What do you say?" he asked as he crawled back onto his own spot on the blanket.

"Yeah," Tate said as he ran a hand through his hair and pressed the other one to his crotch. "Fuck, yes. I'll stay with you tonight, Luxe. There's nowhere I'd rather be."

His heart threatened to beat out of his chest. "Then let's eat because you, my friend, will need your stamina. It's been a while for me, and I have a lot of pent-up desire."

Tate lifted his glass in salute before downing the entire glass of wine in three gulps. The tremor in his hand had Liam grinning. Yeah, Tate wanted him so badly he was shaking with it.

Who wouldn't love that?

For the rest of the evening, they alternated between eating, drinking, and kissing. As the sun dipped below the tall stalks of corn, Tate produced a battery-operated lantern to illuminate their private area. He'd thought of everything.

"So, tell me about wanting to start your own business," Liam said as they lay side by side, looking up at the stars. He had his head resting on Tate's outstretched arm and felt a sense of peace he'd never had in bustling New York City. The air had chilled, and if it weren't for the warmth of the man he cuddled up to, Liam might be cold.

"Oh, it's just a silly thought. Doubt I'll ever make anything of it."

He frowned. Tate was a master at dismissing his own worth. Not on Liam's watch. That garbage would stop now. With a huff, he pushed up onto his elbow, glancing down. Scruff dusted Tate's jaw as though he hadn't shaved in a few days. He couldn't resist stroking a hand through the soft bristles that had tickled his cheeks and chin moments before.

"Tell me."

Time ticked by as Tate stared at him. One thing Liam quickly learned about the man was his need to take a few minutes to process his words before he spoke of anything deep. Instead of turning away, assuming his command would be ignored, Liam waited.

Eventually, Tate spoke. "You might think it's dumb, but I actually like what I do."

"Why would I think that was dumb?"

"Because you make art with your fucking amazing body. I put ceramic on the floor."

"Tate!" Liam socked him lightly on the shoulder. "That is the stupidest thing I've ever heard. I'm instituting a rule. Every time you say something disparaging about yourself, I withhold sex."

A loud burst of laughter rumbled the body beneath him. "So, you're saying I'm not getting any tonight?"

Well, shit, he hadn't thought that one through. "Just shut up and tell me your dream. We'll start tomorrow."

Still laughing, Tate wrapped his arms around Liam and fully pulled him onto him. They now lay chest to chest, nose to nose. "No one ever gives a shit what I want."

Ugh, stab me in the heart.

"Well," he said, trying to keep the sadness of that statement out of his tone. "That changed when you met me."

"My boss is close to retirement. He doesn't really give a shit anymore. We accept easy local jobs because he isn't motivated to go for anything bigger or learn more modern techniques. With social media and stuff, we could expand our market and reach new customers. But, as I said, he doesn't give a shit anymore."

"And you have ideas to expand?"

Nodding, Tate ran a hand up and down Liam's back. He

swore he purred like a happy cat under the touch.

"A crapload of acreage was sold recently to a developer. They're planning multiple communities and looking for subcontractors right now. I do good work and enjoy the design side of things. I also keep up with modern trends and what people are looking for. The shit they're planning to build is ritzy as fuck, and I bet they're going to have some really unique, intricate work. I'd love in on that."

The passion lacing his voice captured Liam's attention. This was more than a flash-in-the-pan idea—he'd given it serious thought.

"So do it," Liam said. "Break away. Take your brother and Daryl." He couldn't keep his nose from wrinkling as he said that jerk's name, but thankfully, Tate didn't seem to expect him to like his friends. "Break away and approach the developer."

"Just like that, huh?" The man below him smirked.

"Yes. Just like that. It doesn't need to be more complicated. I recently went through a lot of the process with my studio, so I can help you."

"Luxe…"

"Nuh-uh." He placed his fingers over those tasty lips. "Don't say no yet. Think about it first. It's a really great idea. You'd make a fantastic boss. Just think about it. Okay?"

Nodding, Tate said, "Okay," but the word was muffled by the fingers squishing his lips.

"Good." Liam beamed.

It was the best date of Liam's life, hands down. It probably ranked in the top five evenings of his life, period. With each passing second, keeping his hands off his date grew harder as did his cock.

When Tate snuck his tongue out and licked along the seam of Liam's fingers, he sucked in a harsh breath.

"Kiss me," Tate ordered in an impossible-to-resist growl.

They spent the next long while kissing and groping beneath the vast, starry sky. The longer they went at it, the more desperate Liam became, and before he knew it, he was rutting against Tate for all he was worth.

"Wait!" He tore his mouth away and rested his forehead against Tate's. "Holy shit, we have to stop or I'm going to come."

"And that's a problem?"

"Right now, it is. I don't want to come again until you're inside me." He lifted his head, and the white-hot stare gazing up at him had sweat rolling down his back.

Fire blazed in Tate's eyes as he squeezed Liam's ass. "Then let's get the fuck outta here."

## Chapter Eleven

"This is nice." Tate shoved his hands in his pockets to keep from attacking Liam the second they entered his apartment. After spending the past few hours touching, kissing, and learning about the pretty dancer, his cock was harder than the porcelain tiles he worked with.

But a hard cock wasn't anything new. Maybe he didn't usually want inside someone as much as he did Liam, but he understood sexual arousal. What he didn't understand was the fluttery feeling in his chest or the way his blood zinged with jitters as though he'd downed a pot of coffee on an empty stomach.

He didn't want to fuck this up because he wanted it to happen again, and it hadn't even happened yet.

That's what he didn't understand.

Who anticipated the next time they'd be with someone when they were already in their presence?

Saps, that's who.

*And me, apparently.*

"If by nice you mean tiny, then yes, this place is very nice." Liam dropped his keys in a silver dish on a small table by the door.

With a snort, Tate followed him into the small apartment. "Do you have to turn sideways to fit down the hallway?"

He'd been side-stepping to his bedroom since he hit puberty.

"What? No. Why?"

"Then it's not tiny."

"Well, it's not big by any stretch of the imagination. The hallway is only about two feet long. It leads to an itty-bitty bedroom." He spread his slender arms with the same grace he did when dancing. Then, this is the rest—a baby kitchen and a little den.

Tate took a good look at the space. Sure, it wasn't big, but Liam was one guy. How much space could he need? In the short time he'd lived there, Liam managed to create a homier environment than Tate's place, and he'd lived there his whole damn life. "What I meant was you made it look nice. It's cozy and classy." He shrugged. "Like you."

"Oh." He beamed. "Thank you." Art prints and photos of ballet dancers hung from the walls. The beige loveseat had a plush, olive-green blanket draped over one arm, with two matching pillows on each end. Then, there was the small end table with a candle and a framed photo of who he assumed was Liam and his parents.

A thick silence fell between them. Tate didn't fit in this stylish place with this sweet, caring man with his fragrant candle. He belonged ten minutes away in the trailer park with an ashtray full of cigarette butts on the kitchen table, a mountain of empty beer cans in the trash, and mismatched dishes.

As much as he didn't fit here, Liam wouldn't work in Tate's world even more. He tried to imagine the dancer in his trailer, meeting his mother, and befriending Whitney, but the vision wouldn't come. Liam was too good for his world.

"You're thinking awfully hard over there," Liam said.

He stood at the mouth of the small hallway leading to his bedroom, looking like a tasty treat in those trendy yellow shorts and the white polo that clung to his fit frame. Peeling him out of the outfit would be like opening a Christmas present he'd wanted his entire life.

But it would change things. Tate couldn't figure out how he knew that, but he did. Sex never changed shit for him in the past, but it would this time. He could feel it in his gut.

"Anything you wanna share?"

His instinct was to keep his mouth shut and his thoughts to himself. Hell, he'd been perfecting that skill for most of his life. But Liam's words from earlier came back to him.

*I am and always will be a safe place for you.*

So, instead of sealing his mouth shut, he swallowed his nerves and said, "I was thinking about how different our worlds are."

Liam tilted his head. "Ahh, and probably talking yourself out of this *thing* we have going on in the process."

"Maybe." Why did the man have to be so damn attractive? Tate's dick felt crushed in its denim prison.

Liam propped his hands on his trim hips. "Well, I want to come."

Tate sucked in a breath. Jesus, he wanted that too. Fuck, he had no choice but to press the heel of his hand over his cock. The way Liam's eyes darkened in approval as he licked his lips had Tate groaning. Damn tease.

"I want you to be the one to make me come. Preferably, with that thick cock pounding my prostate. So maybe you could save your freakout until after that."

Tate chuckled. "Fuck, you're mean."

Liam shrugged, and a smirk curved those pouty lips. "I'm gonna head on in there," he said, thumbing over his shoulder toward the only bedroom. "I'd say take your time thinking about what you want to do, but I'm gonna get started. So don't take too long." He winked, spun on a toe like the perfect ballet dancer he was, then started down the hall. His pert ass mocked Tate with every swish of his hips. Before he disappeared into his room, he glanced over his shoulder. "There's one very important way our worlds align, and I'm dying to prove it to you, so choose wisely."

Tate's head dropped back, and he groaned at the white ceiling.

No way was he strong enough to resist an offer like that. Liam won. He knew he'd won, the little minx.

So much could go wrong.

What if someone saw his car? He'd parked behind the building as Liam instructed with promises that no one else parked back there, but shit happened.

What if Randy saw through the lies when he asked about the woman he took on a picnic and then spent the night with?

What if Liam decided he was a lost cause and dropped him?

It would hurt.

Shit. It would hurt if Liam ended this. How on earth had that happened? It didn't matter how. It was too late—he'd crossed an invisible line—and there was no going back. He might as well reap the rewards before it all went to shit.

He forced himself to stroll instead of charging into the bedroom like a raging bull. The fifteen seconds it took to get there felt like eons. Walking wasn't easy with a lead pipe between his legs and a heart beating so fast and hard he could feel it in his neck.

Breathing ragged, he stepped into the room and nearly swallowed his tongue.

"Jesus Christ."

Liam lay in the center of his queen-size bed completely naked, with his sculpted legs spread and his stiff cock in his fist. All Tate could see was the red, angry tip peeking out of that tight grip. The grin on Liam's face was pure sex.

"I see you made the right choice." His voice dropped two octaves, coming out husky and full of need.

"I think so," Tate responded through a closed throat.

"Oh, I know so. You have no idea what my ass can do, Tate, but you're about to find out."

"Fuck, Luxe." That confidence was a damn aphrodisiac. "You're beautiful." And he was. Incredibly so. All rolling hills and valleys of muscle wrapped in creamy smooth skin. Liam had minimal body hair and no tattoos or piercings. A small scar marred his right shoulder as though he'd had surgery in the past, but it was the only blemish on an otherwise perfect specimen. His own body was riddled with scars from a rough, unsupervised youth and the few tattoos he'd gotten over the years. If he still had any functioning brain cells after this, he'd ask about the shoulder, but most likely, he'd be too drunk on Liam to remember.

"Get naked," the gorgeous object of his inspection said.

Tate didn't have to be told twice. As his hands went to his fly, realization slammed into him with the force of a Mack truck, and his knees wobbled. This was the first time he'd been with a fully naked man. It was the first time he'd be fucking in a bed. It was the first time he didn't have to rush. He could take his time exploring every inch of Liam. He could draw it out until the man begged for release, begged for Tate's cock. He could shout and demand Liam put a voice to every delicious sensation Tate wrung from him.

His uncertainty fled. He didn't have enough blood to fuel his brain and cock at the same time, and right now, all of it was charging down south. He toed off his sneakers, stepping onto the soft carpet. As he unzipped his jeans, he moved to the edge of the bed for a better view of the sexy man pleasuring himself.

Liam's hand stilled. He propped himself up on one elbow. "Keep going," he whispered, staring as though enraptured by the strip show.

Tate hooked his thumbs in the side of his jeans and briefs

together, pushing them down. A harsh sound hissed from his lungs when the material scraped over his dick.

As his clothes hit the floor, his cock flopped forward, heavy and leaking without being touched.

"Damn," Liam said on an exhale. "That is going to feel so good inside me."

"About as good as your ass will feel strangling it, I bet."

"Yes. Take your shirt off. You look hot as fuck with it on, but I'm over it."

Chuckling, Tate crossed his arms at his waist and hauled the Henley over his head. "Demanding, aren't you?"

"Desperate," Liam responded.

"Christ." Tate gripped his cock and pumped his fist twice, using his precum to lube the way.

"Your body is incredible." They watched each other for a moment, stroking their cocks and drinking in the sight of each other, aroused and flushed with need.

"Please come here. I've got supplies." A few condoms and a tube of lube lay next to Liam on the simple navy comforter. "Don't make me wait."

Tate smirked. Oh, he was going to wait, all right.

"Oh, shit, that's a wicked grin."

Tate placed a knee on the edge of the bed, still playing with himself. "Let go of your cock. Hands up and under the pillow."

Liam's eyes flared. "Oh God."

"Do it, Luxe." As he spoke, he crawled up the bed over Liam's body. His cock, which pointed straight out, trailed a line of precum up Liam's flat stomach.

They both cursed.

"You're gonna be bossy as hell, aren't you?" Liam whispered, gazing up at him.

Tate licked a stripe up the side of his neck, stopping at Liam's ear. He tasted like heaven on earth. "Fuck yes, I am.

Now put your fucking hands under the pillow, and don't you dare move them."

"You're going to torture me, aren't you?"

"That's the plan." Little did he know, Tate would be torturing himself just as much. "Just think of how hard you'll come by the time I'm done with you."

Liam groaned but did as Tate commanded, shoving his hands under the pillow beneath his head. This position put him on full display for whatever Tate could dream up—and he'd been dreaming of this for years. Those dreams had intensified since he'd met Liam.

His hands shook as he placed them on Liam's torso, but thankfully, the other man didn't call him out on it. "Your skin is so soft," he said as he stroked up and down Liam's ribs.

"Thank you. I do try."

That had him chuckling. As his fingers explored, he let his lips have their way with Liam's neck. Liam turned his head, allowing Tate full access. He licked and sucked small kisses all over the warm skin. Within seconds, Liam's breathing increased, and he shifted beneath the touch.

Tate slid his hands up, brushing his thumbs over Liam's puckered nipples. The man beneath him jerked at the contact and spat out a curse. He lifted his head and did it again with similar results. "You like that. Your nipples are sensitive?"

"Yes. I love to be touched. Anywhere. Everywhere. Do it again."

This time, when he pinched Liam's nipples, he was rewarded with a harsh cry. He kissed down Liam's sternum, pausing to lick the nipples he'd played with. The moans and whimpers he drew from his partner satisfied him in a novel and consuming way. Never had he cared what his hookups thought or felt as long as they got off. And they always did, so mission accomplished.

Tonight's assignment was much more involved than giving

one orgasm. He only hoped he could hold out long enough to make this the most epic fuck of Liam's life.

"Your hands feel incredible."

Tate smiled against Liam's skin. "You mentioned that last time."

"I meant it then, and I mean it now."

He trailed down Liam's flat stomach, pausing to rim his belly button. It made Liam squeak and then giggle. The muscles in his stomach twitched under Tate's tongue. He tasted so damn good. Warm, a little salty, alive. He'd lick every inch of the man if he could and still want more.

When he reached Liam's jutting hip bones, he nipped the taut skin. His hands continued to play as he explored with his lips and tongue. Occasionally, the briny taste of his own precum hit his senses as he lapped at Liam's torso.

"Tate..." Liam panted and squirmed but kept his hands in place. "I'm gonna rip this fucking pillow in half. I want to touch you too. Please let me touch you."

He lifted his head, meeting Liam's desperate gaze. The man's pupils had blown wide. His bottom lip had indents from his teeth, and his deep pink nipples jutted out.

"Not yet," he whispered. "Let me have my fun. I've never..."

Understanding dawned in Liam's wide eyes, and he nodded. "Just don't blame me if I blow before you get inside me. You're driving me out of my mind. I love this, Tate. Being with you like this. It's more than I thought it would be."

For him too. And that was the problem. But instead of sharing those fears, he just whispered, "Me too," which wasn't a lie.

He bypassed Liam's cock, chuckling at the growled protest, and made his way down one sleek leg. He sucked a hickey onto Liam's inner thigh, licked the back of his knee until he threatened violence, and nibbled his way down the man's calf. Liam's head thrashed back and forth as he babbled nonsense and every few seconds, his hips jutted off the bed, searching for relief.

*Not yet.*

Done exploring one long, sexy dancer's leg, he went after the other with the same treatment. This time, he ran the flat of his tongue up Liam's inner thigh so close to his erection, it brushed across Tate's cheek.

"Oh God, please fucking suck me. I'm dying." His body was flushed and dewy with sweat. He couldn't stay still, writhing on the bed as though hooked to live wires. His biceps bulged with the force of trying to tear the pillow to shreds.

*So fucking hot.*

"Please, Tate." Liam's body arched. "Please suck me or fuck me. Do something. I can't take it anymore." He'd been reduced to whining and begging.

*Gorgeous.*

Tate's balls hung so heavy and full they ached like hell. He had no right to complain, considering the way he'd been tormenting Liam, but he'd been fucking with his own control as well.

And it wouldn't last much longer.

"Roll over," he growled. "Up on all fours. Let me see your pretty hole."

"Oh, yes, finally," Liam whispered as he scrambled onto his hands and knees faster than should have been possible.

Tate's focus immediately reached for the firm backside jutting out at him. He wanted to spend hours doing everything he could dream up to that incredible ass. But damn, if his own cock wouldn't hold out that long, and he'd rather die than come without being surrounded by Liam's blistering heat.

He gripped the round cheeks and pushed his hands apart,

spreading Liam's ass wide for his viewing pleasure. In the center was the pink, tight hole he'd fantasized about for days.

"Goddamn, that's a pretty sight," he whispered.

"Admire it later," Liam said, breathless. "Hell, I'll send you a framed picture you can stare at all fucking day. Right now, you need to lube up and get something inside me before I take matters into my own hands."

His cock twitched as though trying to obey Liam's command.

Who knew a pretty, elegant ballet dancer could have such a filthy mouth?

## Chapter Twelve

If he had enough brain power to think, Liam might have been embarrassed by Tate's up close and personal inspection of his most intimate area. As it was, the only thought running through his head was how badly he wanted Tate to put something inside him. A finger, his tongue, his cock, something to end the ache.

"So impatient," Tate spoke so close to his ass Liam could feel the breath wafting over his cheeks. He felt like a rubber band stretched to capacity. With one flick, he'd shoot across the room with punishing force.

"Tate, please..." He gripped the sheets so hard his knuckles cracked.

His cock hung down heavy and angry red from neglect. If they didn't hurry, he'd blow all over his sheets from the anticipation alone. Already, his arms trembled, but it was more from desire than the effort to hold himself up.

"I need to feel it," Tate muttered.

The sound of lube being squeezed onto Tate's finger preceded the click of the closing tube.

*Hold on for a few more seconds.*

Nothing happened, and Liam imagined Tate behind him, warming the lube with his fingers. Then, there was a light touch to his rim without the cold shock that often accompanied a hurried or careless partner.

"Yes," he said, panting. "Touch me." He peered over his shoulder to find Tate with a look of wonder and awe as he focused on his finger circling Liam's asshole.

"Ready?" His voice was ragged, close to the edge.

*Join the club.*

"Beyond ready."

A thick finger breached his hole, pushing in with maddening slowness. "Fuck, that's good." He loved this part. The initial burn and sting as his body stretched to accommodate the intrusion.

"Fuck, Luxe, it's so goddamn tight. You're just sucking me in." Tate played around, testing the depth and moving his finger in and out.

"More," Liam said as he moaned. "Another."

"Shit, yes." He added another finger, ramping up the burn all over again, but within seconds it turned to a warm pleasure radiating out from Liam's ass through his entire body.

Tate scissored his fingers, stretching Liam and giving him a thorough finger-fucking.

His head swam with happy chemicals, making it hard to do anything but feel. He thrust back on those curious fingers.

"More," he said again.

"God, I love this. You're a fucking mess, just begging for my cock, aren't you?" As he spoke, Tate probed deeper, hitting Liam's prostate.

A powerful shock of electricity had him crying out and arching his back. Precum dribbled onto the sheets below him. His balls were full and heavy, threatening to unload if he had to endure much more of this.

"Now, Tate. I'm ready. Now. Fuck me now."

"You sure?"

He heard the thread of uncertainty in the question.

"I don't want to hur—"

"You won't. Just fucking fuck me already."

The sound of the condom wrapper made his insides clench with anticipation. Next time, he'd be the one to smooth the latex over Tate's erection. A few seconds later, the head of Tate's cock notched against his hole two seconds before powerful pressure swamped him. Tate pushed inside his body, slowly, so fucking slowly. The grip on Liam's hips tightened with each inch. He shut his eyes, breathing through the intensity of the burn as he bore down to accept the intrusion.

"Christ, it's fucking obscene the way your ass is stretching for my cock. Take it, Luxe, take every damn inch."

"Yes." He groaned. Tate's obvious appreciation made the experience ten times hotter. It was exactly what Liam wanted. He wanted his ass to take Tate to a place he'd never been before. To lock him in and make it impossible for him to walk away. "Give it to me."

When Tate bottomed out, he cursed and rested his head between Liam's shoulder blades. "Fuck, you're so goddamn tight. I've never felt anything better."

*Victory.*

"That's because you're big as hell." And he was. Liam felt stuffed to capacity in the best way possible.

"Give me a minute. I'm too close to the damn edge." His fingers dug into Liam's hips, and he held them glued together while they both adjusted.

It wasn't long before Liam's body relaxed around the thick cock lodged inside him, and the need for more took over. Teeth grazed the back of his neck, ripping a near-violent shudder through him.

"Oh God. Shit, Tate, you feel incredible."

"You like it?" He nipped Liam's ear. "You like your ass full of my cock?"

"Yes. Yes, I love it. But you gotta move. You're killing me."

"Mmm, I think I can do that." The heavy weight of a man left his back as Tate straightened. He pulled his hips back with the same agonizing pace he'd entered Liam. But when he drove forward, he did it with a fierce, powerful thrust that had Liam crying out.

"Fuck yes. More. Wreck me with your cock, Tate."

The words seemed to snap something inside the man. He growled and began fucking Liam in a fast, pounding rhythm like he was trying to split him in two. Liam slammed his hips back, meeting Tate thrust for thrust. When the pleasure of his prostate being hit jolted through him, he shouted, "Yes! Oh, fuck yes, there. Right there."

Like a man possessed, Tate hammered his prostate over and over. Liam's arms gave out, and he crashed onto the mattress, but Tate didn't miss a beat. He used his hold on Liam's hips to jerk them together again and again.

Sweat dripped from Tate onto his skin. If he were on his back, he'd capture some for a taste, but then they'd be face-to-face and he'd be exposed. As it was, he used the mattress to hide whatever strong emotions had to be plain as day in his expression. Liam wasn't exactly known for his ability to hide what he was feeling like Tate could.

His stomach coiled, and his balls drew up tight, ready to blow. "Tate," he said with a moan. "I need to come." He started to reach for his dick only to have his hand slapped away.

"Mine," Tate growled, then his big, rough hand closed around Liam's cock.

"Fuck!" he shouted as that hand pumped his dick with quick, sure strokes. Four tugs in, he lost control of his body. Stars burst behind his eyelids, and pleasure so intense he roared exploded from deep within. Cum shot from his dick, coating Tate's hand and spraying the sheets below him.

"Fuck, oh fuck, you're choking my cock," Tate said, then thrust twice more before shouting a savage curse and slamming as deep as he could get as he erupted into the condom.

Not once had Liam fucked without a condom—he'd never even wanted to—but now cum was all he could think about as he lay twitching beneath Tate and how badly he wanted to feel the man's load dripping from his ass.

If he said that out loud, Tate would probably run from the apartment naked and covered in cum, so he kept his mouth shut. After a moment, the heavy weight of a satisfied man collapsed on top of him. The softening cock slipped out, making Liam grunt. He'd have loved to stay connected a little longer.

Tate breathed hard, and his muscles jumped every few seconds.

Liam smiled. Was there anything better than feeling the mass of a cum-drunk man on top of him?

He didn't think so.

A soft kiss on the back of his neck had him sighing in bliss. Another followed, then a third. "Are you okay? I didn't hurt you, did I?" There went another of those kisses.

Who knew Tate would be so sweet post-fuck?

"No, you didn't hurt me. Not even a little bit. But no, I'm not okay."

The big body on top of him tensed.

"I don't think I'll be okay until we've done that at least a few dozen times. Just to make sure we have our technique down pat."

Tate snorted, then rolled off Liam's back. They both shifted until they were facing each other. At some point, they needed to get up and deal with the condom and wet sheets as well as their messy bodies, but neither seemed willing to break the intimate spell.

"A few dozen, huh?" Tate asked. The damp hair around his forehead was plastered to his skin, and Liam couldn't resist smoothing it back.

"That work for you?"

He stayed quiet, letting Tate work through his answer. This was the moment of truth. Tate would either put up his walls and flee or stick around. The choice was his. After all, he was the one with something to lose. Liam had never been closeted. The first time he felt attraction to a man, he'd gone to his mother and asked her about it. She hadn't so much as blinked as she told him boys liked girls and some liked boys. No big deal.

He'd been ten. He came out to the rest of the world at twelve.

"Yeah," Tate said after a long pause. "I'm down for that."

Inside, Liam did a happy dance and a backflip, but on the outside, he kept his excitement muted. "Great. Um…" he said, not feeling an ounce of the calm he portrayed. "Do you want to stay? A while or… all night?" He held his breath as he waited for Tate to process that question.

A range of emotions played out on Tate's face, but Liam didn't know him well enough to decipher them or read his mind. Eventually, he shook his head. "I want to," he said, eyes sincere. "I hope you believe that. This was…" He smoothed his hand over Liam's hip, coming to rest on his ass. "This was one of the best nights of my life, no bullshit. And I mean it when I say I want more, but…"

Time to put the poor guy out of his misery. "But you're not ready for a pajama party. I get it, Tate. No worries. And no pressure. I get this is uncharted territory for you. I told you I was your safe space, and that includes not pushing you into things you aren't ready for. Just know the offer stands. Seriously, after that performance, you're welcome in this bed any time you like."

Thankfully, his quip had the desired effect, and Tate chuckled. "Good to know. Let me deal with this condom and clean up a bit, then I'll get out of your hair."

"Bathroom's that way." He pointed toward the door leading to the only bathroom in the apartment.

Liam watched as Tate climbed out of the bed.

Look at all those yummy muscles.

Tate stumbled when he took his first step. "Shit, I think I need to lie upside down to get some blood back in my head," he said as he laughed. Once steady, he slipped into the bathroom and was back a few seconds later, clean and without the condom.

"I'll walk you down," Liam said as Tate located his clothes.

The sexy man shook his head. "Not necessary. Stay and relax."

"Okay." He tucked his hands behind his head and settled. "No argument here. I'm enjoying this show too much to get up anyway."

"You like watching me put on my clothes?"

"I like watching you do anything."

Tate paused, shirt in hand, and gave him a soft smile.

"Thank you for my date. This whole night has been unreal in the best way." It also messed with his head, and now he'd have to work to keep from fantasizing about things he could never have.

"It has." Tate's low, sincere tone did nothing to prevent Liam from having stupid dreams.

"Now that you have my number, feel free to text anytime. I'll try to resist sending you a dick pic, but it's gonna be hard now that I know what a good fuck you are." He winked— time to get this conversation on a lighter note.

Tate laughed. "No one knows my passcode or uses my phone. Send away."

His spent dick tried to rally, but even though he could go a few more times tonight, he'd need at least a couple of minutes to recover.

As soon as Tate's jeans were up and covering that beautiful cock, Liam pouted. "Well, now I have nothing fun to look at."

There went the shirt, hiding his sexy chest. Most of his favorite spots were now covered up, though Tate's face was eye candy enough.

"Well then, maybe I'll be the one sending you a dick pic." He winked, and Liam's jaw dropped.

"Swear to God I'm more shocked when you flirt with me than I'd be if you sprouted wings."

"Good. Gotta keep you on your toes, Luxe. Don't want my big-city dancer getting bored with this small-town boy." He shoved his feet in his shoes and then strode over. "We'll talk soon."

Then he did the most shocking thing of all. He gave Liam a goodbye kiss, and not a quick peck, but the kind of kiss that ensured Liam would be hard again and thinking about him all night long.

Hell, when he walked out the door, Liam's cock was already waking back up.

Teasing bastard.

*My big city dancer.*

*Swoon.*

## Chapter Thirteen

Liam piled his cart high with the same nutritious foods he'd eaten as a professional ballet dancer. Though no longer performing daily, old habits died hard, and he had yet to stray from the stringent diet his career had required—except for one vice.

Cereal. He'd always loved a good cereal, and a mega box of Cinnamon Toast Crunch was typically hidden among his kale, ground turkey, and brown rice. But he'd polished off the last of it that morning and needed to replenish the stock before his next craving hit.

The closest grocery store wasn't much larger than a mini-mart, so he headed out of town about fifteen minutes to the next town over, where they boasted a full-size grocery chain. Still, it wasn't what he'd call huge, and he'd had to order a few specialty health food items online since he couldn't find them anywhere close enough he'd be willing to drive for a product or two.

This town, Culpepper, seemed about twice the size of Swan, which made it only slightly bigger than tiny. Most of Liam's clients had found out about his new studio through the extensive social media push he'd been working on, but it never hurt to try and garner local traffic through more traditional means. He'd made sure to bring a stack of flyers and a few business cards in case an opportunity to post them arose.

Done shopping, he wheeled the full cart to the only open checkout lane. The clerk appeared somewhere around Liam's age. He had pale skin with rosy cheeks and a nose that might have seen too much sun. He'd styled his curly auburn hair in an artful yet trendy way. What really caught Liam's attention was his name tag, which read *Jonah* but had a rainbow flag sticker in the top right corner.

"Good morning, welcome to Food Haven. Would you like paper or plastic bags?"

"Paper would be great, thanks."

The clerk eyed him with curiosity as he began scanning the items. "Haven't seen you in here before. You visiting someone?"

"Nope, I'm just new to town, and this is my first time here. Hey, is there a bulletin board where I can post a flyer?" he asked, showing Jonah a flyer. "I'm about to open a dance studio in Swan and would love to hang a flyer somewhere."

Two auburn eyebrows shot high into Jonah's forehead as he continued to scan Liam's groceries without missing a beat. "A dance studio," he said. "In Swan. You?"

"Yep. Swan, Oklahoma, gay population of one." He struck a pose and smiled his cheesiest grin.

Jonah snorted. "Holy shit, you're either the bravest guy I've ever met or the stupidest."

Thoughts he had himself at least ten times a day. "Probably somewhere in the middle, to be honest."

Jonah chuckled. "Uh, yeah, we got a bulletin board by the exit," he said, waving a hand in the direction of the door. "Feel free to pimp your business all you want."

"Thanks. I appreciate it."

"Dance, huh?" Jonah's assessing gaze took a slow trip up and down Liam's body. "You any good?"

The blunt question was all it took for Liam to decide Jonah would make an awesome friend. He had a friend back home with the same no-nonsense personality, and they got along like tutus and dance tights.

Liam shrugged and, without an ounce of humility, said, "I'm very good. I danced professionally in the New York City ballet for years before moving here."

Jonah's jaw dropped. "Well, dayum. Okay, now I'm going to be nosy as hell and ask why on earth you'd leave a fancy life in New York City to come to Swan. You fall on your head or something?"

Snorting, Liam shook his head. "Long story."

"It always is."

Jonah was cute. Not Liam's type, but attractive nonetheless. Hell, even if he'd been Liam's type, it wouldn't matter. He'd thought of little but Tate in the week since they'd fucked that first time. No other man blipped on his radar. If he hadn't slept with Tate three more times since then, he'd worry his libido had broken, but it worked just fine around the closeted small-town man. Too well, actually. Just thinking about Tate like this was getting him interested down south.

Not good.

"Let me guess." Jonah tapped his lips as though deep in thought. "You have a big, burly boyfriend who's a corn farmer, and you followed him here for true love?" He sighed with a dramatic flourish, placing his hand over his heart. "I can see it now. He gives it to you three times a day and would rip my nuts off for even talking to you, you lucky bitch."

Barking out a loud laugh, Liam shook his head. "Not even close." Though he could hope the three times a day would become a reality soon. "I did not move here for a man, though I did meet one here. But what I have is more of a... complication than a relationship."

"Oooh, a situationship… intriguing."

He snorted. "I don't even know if I'd call it that. I'm sticking with complication. Anyway, this is not the time to talk about that. Since I did just move here and have exactly zero friends if you're ever looking for another person to hang with, I'm down."

"No friends in Swan?" Jonah made the phoniest shocked face Liam had ever seen. "The town that thinks gay people are a wicked urban legend? What a surprise."

"Hey!" He tried not to laugh but failed miserably. "It's too early in our friendship for you to call out my poor life choices."

"Well, Mr. Complication, I am always open to making a new friend. How about this… I'm meeting some of my boys at a funky little coffee shop right down the street on Friday at ten in the morning. What do you say to joining us and making a bunch of friends at once?"

"Call me Liam. Mr. Complication is too long. And thanks for the offer. What's your number." He pulled out his phone and entered the ten digits Jonah rattled off. "Great, I just texted you mine. Just send me the name of the coffee house before then."

"Will do."

They chatted as Jonah finished checking him out. Liam couldn't help but feel a genuine buzz of excitement at the prospect of forming a friend group. Back in New York, he'd had a thriving social life, and while he expected it to be very different here, he'd love to have something to put on his calendar once in a while.

Maybe he could eventually introduce Tate to these guys if coffee went well. Then, if Tate came out, he'd have an instant support group. It was so important to—

*No. Oh no, you don't,* Mr. Complication.

He'd promised himself no less than ten times this week

that he would not plan any part of his life around Tate. Nor would he take on Tate's problems. If he started doing that, he knew exactly how this story would end. Liam would catch feelings. Tate would eventually realize he didn't want to come out of the closet and didn't want to risk being with a man so close to home. He'd break it off, and Liam would be left a weepy, heartbroken mess eating Cinnamon Toast Crunch three times a day alone on his couch.

This coffee outing was for him and him alone.

It had to be.

"YO, T, LOOK alive."

Tate glanced toward Randy, but he wasn't quick enough to catch the package of hot dog buns lobbed his way. It smacked him in the face, then dropped in his lap.

"Dude, don't smoosh them. I hate it when it's hard to open the bun for the wiener." Daryl scowled at Randy.

*And, queue homophobic jokes.*

"Bet that dancer… what was his name… bet he could teach you all about getting the wiener in the bun," Randy said as he cackled and slapped a hand on his knee.

Daryl's face screwed up. "Fuck you. I ain't going near that guy again."

As Tate sighed and tried to ignore the twist in his gut, Whitney came out of their trailer with a tray of hotdogs and a few bags of chips. She looked cute and summery in her denim shorts and cropped tank, her long hair in a high ponytail. "You still didn't get the fire going?" she asked as she set the food on the upside-down trash can serving as their table.

"Doing it now." Randy hopped up from his sagging lawn chair, grabbing the bottle of lighter fluid at his feet. They didn't have a fire pit in their trailer park, but an old trashcan lid did the job just fine. Randy had piled wood on it a few minutes ago. Now, he stood shirtless and in his favorite grungy cutoff jorts, squirting the logs with lighter fluid. When he'd soaked them enough to start a damn wildfire, he lit a match and tossed it at his creation.

*Whoosh!*

The stack of wood ignited in a rush of heat and sparks.

"For God's sake, Randy, why you gotta make it so big? One day, you're gonna burn down this whole trailer park," Whitney complained, whacking her husband on the back of his head.

"Wouldn't be the worst thing in the world," Tate muttered.

"What was that?" Randy sat back down. His chair cracked as a few of the stretched fibers snapped.

Tate couldn't wait until the day the chair finally quit and his brother's ass landed on the ground. Not that his own lawn chair fared much better. He'd picked it up at Goodwill almost six years ago, and it was almost as crappy as Randy's camping chair.

"Nothing."

"What the hell's up with you, man?" Randy asked as he hooked an arm around his wife's waist and dragged her onto his lap. She yelped, but it quickly became a giggle as she settled in.

"What do you mean? Nothing's up."

"Yeah, you've been weird as shit this past week," Daryl added.

Nodding, Randy said, "We've hardly seen your ass around here. You've been all quiet, sneaking in and out."

"Guys," Whitney said, shooting him a sympathetic smile. "Leave him alone."

"You got a side piece or something?" Daryl asked. He popped the tab on his beer, chugged half the can, then belched.

"I don't have a fucking main piece. How can I have a side

piece." Tate's skin tightened, feeling stretched over his bones. He fought the urge to squirm under the three nosy gazes directed his way.

"No?" Daryl's eyes glittered with evil excitement. "What about that one in Tulsa you been going to see? She got you all pussy-whipped? That why you're never here?"

"Yeah, you ditching us for city pussy?" Randy asked as he reached around Whitney for a hotdog. He shoved a stick down the center, then held it over the fire.

Fire-roasted hotdogs with a strong flavor of lighter fluid are the trailer park specialty.

"Nah, that's done." He motioned for Randy to hand him a hotdog. It didn't get stupider than giving up his cover story. All he had to do was confirm he'd started seeing this mystery woman in Tulsa more. They'd tease him for a few minutes, then get bored and move on to dumber topics.

But the lie lodged in his throat. It wasn't lying in particular he had a problem with—he'd been doing that since his teen years—but denying Liam in that way, pretending he was someone he wasn't, Tate couldn't make his mouth say the words. The dick he'd swallowed last night sure as hell didn't belong to some woman in Tulsa. It belonged to the gorgeous, compassionate, accepting, and sexy-as-fuck man Tate couldn't stop thinking about.

Liam was on his mind twenty-four hours a day. The first thing he thought of when his eyes popped open and the last thing he thought of before they closed again—alone in his bed. They hadn't gone on another date, Tate's fault, and they hadn't spent an entire night together. Again, Tate's fault. But they did have pizza one night in Liam's apartment and coffee the next morning in the same place. Tate had just gone home to sleep in his own shitty bed in between.

"I'm sorry to hear that," Whitney said. "Are you okay?"

"Done? So, what, this shit is you pouting or something?"

Randy asked, waving a hand in Tate's direction.

Whitney smacked the side of her husband's thigh. "Randy, you're so insensitive. He's hurting."

"Nah, I'm good. Just been a busy week." He avoided meeting anyone's gaze. Thank God he had the hotdog to focus on, or he'd be staring at his feet like a liar would.

Narrowing his eyes, Randy shook his head. "I ain't buying it. Something's up."

"I bet I know." Daryl pulled a charred dog from the fire with a smirk.

Tate's stomach turned over, and his skin prickled like icy needles were jabbing him all over. Was this it? Had Daryl seen his car parked behind the studio where Liam promised no one would discover it? Had Tate let something slip that should have stayed locked up in his mind?

He gripped the end of his skewer so hard it pierced his palm, but he barely felt the discomfort. Every ounce of his focus zeroed in on Daryl.

"What?" Randy asked. "Spit it the fuck out."

"He's working on starting his own tiling company. Am I right?"

*Oh, thank fuck.* Relief pummeled him, leaving him feeling weak and wobbly. "That's it," he croaked. His hand shook so hard that the hot dog looked like it was vibrating on the end of his stick. Christ, he needed to get his shit together.

"This again?" Randy rolled his eyes. "You got a good job. Why can't you just be satisfied with it? Nothing's ever good enough for you."

"It's called ambition, Rand, and it's usually considered a good thing."

Randy grunted as Whitney chuckled. "He's not wrong, babe," she said.

"Oh, come on, what the fuck does he know about owning a business? Jack and shit, that's what."

"I'm not an idiot." Tate pulled his dog from the fire and shoved it in the bun. "I can fucking learn," he said before taking a giant bite.

"Why now? Why you gotta change everything now? Shit's good." Randy tore into his hot dog with all the manners of a boar.

*Shit's good.* Yeah, for the married straight man who'd never had to hide his whole damn identity.

"Leave it, Randy," Whitney said. "Why you all over him tonight?"

"It's that guy," Daryl cut in with his mouth full of chips.

"What guy?"

"This one." Daryl lifted his hand and let his wrist droop forward. "He's about our age and owns a business. Tate got ideas in his head from working on his studio."

"The fag?" Randy gaped at him. "He's the one that's got your head all fucked up?"

*You have no idea.*

His nerves were already scratched raw from the fear of Daryl outing him. Having to listen to the man he was obsessed with described in a derogatory way was the last fucking straw. "Why do you two assholes gotta fucking describe him that way? You could call him the studio owner, our client... hell, you could call him *that guy*. What the hell does who he likes to fuck have to do with anything? It's twenty-fucking-twenty-four. Why can't you two cavemen just let people be who the hell they are? Live and let live."

Whitney stared at him with wide eyes and pursed lips. Randy looked confused as hell, gaping at him like he'd grown a third arm from the center of his chest. He'd even stopped chowing down on his hotdog, which proved how shocking Tate's tirade had been.

"What the fuck?" Daryl said around a mouthful of half-chewed hotdog. "That's what I am doing. I'm letting him live.

Hell, I ain't even tried to run him out of town, and I heard a cocksucker was opening a dance studio before any of you. That's fucking growth."

Tate pinched the bridge of his nose. "Can you not call him that? No one calls you a pussy eater."

Daryl grinned. "But they could, and I wouldn't give a shit."

Randy snorted. "He'd think it was a compliment."

"Damn straight." Daryl laughed, then focused back on Tate. "Why you always sticking up for him over us? You better be careful, or people will think you're one of 'em."

"Maybe he's just a more evolved person than you," Whitney said, arching an eyebrow at Daryl. She'd never been his biggest fan. Even as teens, they were like oil and water, even though Tate was pretty sure they'd hooked up a few times before she and Randy became permanent.

"Ain't about being evolved. 'Sabout right and wrong. But, like I said, I'm letting him live his life. I haven't bothered him none."

"Hmm." Whitney cocked her head. "What if it was Randy?"

"The fuck?" Randy shouted.

"Whatcha mean?" Daryl asked.

"What if you found out tomorrow Randy was banging a dude? Shut up, Randy, and let him answer."

Randy grumbled but kept it muted.

"Well, that's easy. I'd beat the fucking gay out of him."

Tate stopped breathing.

"For real? Be serious," Whitney said.

"I am fucking serious. That's what you gotta do. Make a negative association."

"Oh." Randy laughed. "Look who's all smart now."

"Fuck off. It's fucking science. You beat 'em bloody, then when he thinks about dick, he remembers the pain and don't want it no more."

*Christ.*

Tate shot to his feet, drawing shocked gazes from the other three. "I can't listen to this bullshit." He tossed the rest of his hotdog into the fire and stormed off without another word.

He reached his trailer as his mother was leaving with a man on her arm. Jim Bob from the fucking gas station. He had half a dozen kids with as many women and at least three arrests on his record, most for knocking his women around.

"Hi, baby," his mom said, already slurring her words. It would be a late night for her if she even came home.

Tate ignored them and stormed up the three steps into the trailer. He didn't bother turning sideways to fit down the hallway to his room, instead letting the faux wood panels scrape the side of his arms. The pain did little to distract from his fury. When he reached his room, he slammed the door, crawled onto his bed, and shoved his pillow in his mouth.

He screamed until his throat ached, then punched his mattress until his knuckles burned.

Fuck his life.

Fuck his family.

Fuck it all.

# Chapter Fourteen

The text message Tate woke to had him grinning like a satisfied fool before he even took a sip of coffee. And that's because he spent his first fifteen minutes awake, jerking his cock until he came all over his stomach while staring at the picture from Liam.

**I resisted as long as I could.**

The message came after Tate had exhausted himself, beating his mattress half to death, then passed out, but the photo accompanying those words was what had him hard and sweating within seconds of waking up.

A full-body shot of the dancer standing in a complicated pose with one leg straight up by his ear and an arm stretched up, holding his foot—fully naked. The flexibility boggled Tate's mind as he couldn't touch his damn toes. But what sent the picture over the top was the erect cock reaching for him and the heavy sac hanging down, begging for his mouth.

Instant erection.

*The fucking tease.*

Tate wasted no time getting to work on his dick, and after his cum splashed up his torso, he did something he'd never imagined he'd do in his lifetime. He snapped a photo and sent it back to Liam.

Three seconds later, he'd gotten a reply.

**Come over tonight. My ass misses you.**

Hot damn.

Who knew flirting could be so damn fun. He'd done it with girls in the past to keep up the façade of being straight, but it had always been a chore, and the banter nearly impossible to drum up. With Liam, it came naturally. He wanted the man needy and as obsessed as he was. It was easy to tease and play with such sexy inspiration.

**Come early, and I'll order dinner.**

Then there was that. He should absolutely decline and keep this to fucking only, but he enjoyed spending time with Liam as much as he loved his dick in the guy's ass. Or mouth. Or even his hand. Liam was funny and chill, and he didn't judge anything Tate told him, which was so opposite to everyone else he knew. It was refreshing, and being in his presence felt so damn good he couldn't stay away. After the shit he had to hear Randy and Daryl spouting last night, he could use a dose of Liam's positivity.

Before he could talk himself out of it, he texted Liam back.

**I'll be there.**

The kissy face emoji he received in return had a strange warmth expanding through his chest.

Tate dressed quickly and then went to the kitchen for some coffee and whatever the hell he could find for breakfast, which turned out to be a package of s'mores pop tarts. Randy loved them, and the asshole didn't own a toaster, so he kept a stock in Tate's kitchen.

His mom's door, on the opposite end of the trailer, stood wide open, which meant she'd either stayed out all night or had come home bombed and passed out face-first on her bed without so much as removing her heels. A quick peek revealed it was the first option.

Great. Another missed shift at the diner. He'd never know why the hell they kept her on the a.m. shift. For years, he'd been expecting her to come home in tears, claiming she'd been fired, but Bertha kept her on staff for whatever reason.

Probably pity.

The door opened, and Randy popped his head in. "You ready to roll?"

He shook his head as he poured his coffee into one of the travel mugs he'd stocked up on a few days ago. "I got an estimate over on Columbus Ave in Culpepper first thing this morning. It shouldn't take more than an hour, but then I gotta swing by the office. I'll have to meet you and Daryl at the job on Hemlock here in town."

"The fuck, dude? You couldn'ta told me last night?"

No, last night he'd been too busy trying not to lose his shit. "Sorry, just catch a ride with Daryl." Or maybe stop getting in so many fucking accidents so you can keep your damn license for more than a month.

"Oh, come on," he whined. "That means I gotta wake his lazy ass up. Remember what happened last time I woke that loser up?"

Tate laughed. He hadn't thought about that in a while. About six months ago, Randy was making himself a sandwich to bring to work for lunch. Since he couldn't do anything right, he dropped a butcher knife straight onto his foot. It made a giant mess of blood all over the kitchen floor. Randy freaked the fuck out, only making the chaos worse.

Tate had already been at work, so Randy hobbled across the way to Daryl's trailer and let himself in. He found Daryl passed out on the couch. When he tried to wake his best friend, he ended up with a major black eye to complement the six stitches he ended up needing in his foot.

Tate laughed his ass off.

"Just give him a warning before you touch him."

Randy scoffed.

"Or better yet, pay him back by socking him in the eye."

Maybe it'd knock some sense into the idiot.

That suggestion had Randy's eyes lighting up. "Shit, Tate, you're a goddamn genius. Thanks."

Were there two dumber men than Randy and Daryl?

Tate stuffed the pop tart in his mouth, grabbed the travel mug, keys, phone, and wallet, and then jogged to his car. As he slipped behind the wheel, shouting from Daryl's trailer had him laughing out loud.

The estimate went well, and within an hour, he had a fresh job booked for the following week. Once he'd finished with the new client, he ran by the office to finish some outstanding paperwork and send a few invoices. Their office was a town over in Culpepper, so he didn't make it in every day. This morning, he'd hoped to have another conversation with his boss about putting their name in the ring for the new housing development, but of course, Larkin wasn't there. His work ethic made Daryl look like a damn workhorse.

As he drove back toward Swan, Food Haven passed by on the right. The store beat the grocery store in Swan hands down. Should he pick up something to bring to Liam's for dinner? That's what dates did, right? Brought each other nice shit occasionally?

As he approached the next light, he pulled into the left lane and then swung a U-turn, imagining the surprised delight on Liam's face when he showed up with a treat of some sort. Tate knew fuck all about wine, but Liam had really liked the wine they'd had on their picnic.

It'd been white and called Sav-something. He could probably pull off finding one like that again.

Luck was on his side today. As soon as he walked into the store, he encountered a large display of some local brand of wine. They were featuring their Sauvignon Blanc. It sounded familiar enough, so Tate grabbed a bottle and got in line behind one man with a decent-size order. He seemed to know the cashier because they were chatting and laughing like old friends.

Tate resisted the urge to ask them to hurry the hell up and, with nothing better to do, tuned into their conversation.

"Is he hot?" the customer asked. He was of average height and a little on the skinny side, with pressed pants, suspenders, and a bright pink bowtie.

The cashier, a short redhead, nodded eagerly. "Smokin'. I'm telling you, I'd have dropped to my knees on the spot if we were anywhere else."

Tate's spine tensed. He glanced around the quiet store. No one else was around, but they had to know he was there, listening. Were they talking out in the open about this dude giving a guy a blowjob?

Laughing, the customer said, "You're such a slut."

"And proud of it." The cashier fired back without an ounce of shame as he waggled his eyebrows at his friend. The banter quickly turned into a groan. "Ugh, do you know how long I've been waiting for someone as sexy as him to move in around here? And to think he's a dancer. All those bendy muscles." He shivered dramatically. "Yum-my."

A dancer? Tate's stomach plummeted. Holy fuck, they were talking about Liam. Who the fuck did this asshole think he was? Talking about dropping to his knees for Liam.

"Listen, bitch, what makes you think you're gonna be the one to snag him?"

"Um, have you seen how pretty I am?" There he went, batting those stupid-fucking- eyelashes again. "And he's coming to coffee on Friday."

Something dark and ugly twisted inside Tate's gut. His chest tightened, and his hands curled into fists. He glared daggers at the oblivious cashier.

This guy had a date with Liam?

The earth dropped from beneath his feet.

*Over my dead body.*

There was only one man who got to suck Liam's incredible cock, and that was Tate.

His nostrils flared. He rolled his shoulders and cracked his neck. If these two didn't stop talking about Liam like they had a claim to him, they would regret it.

With each continued word out of their mouths, Tate grew increasingly tense. He felt like a wild animal backed into a corner—coiled and poised to attack.

"Fuck it." He slammed the bottle of wine onto the conveyor belt, then turned and stormed toward the exit.

"Hey! Mr.! Did you want that?" The cashier yelled after him, but Tate couldn't fucking turn back. If he did, he'd likely wrap his hands around the skinny fucker's throat and squeeze until his eyes popped out.

Without thought or a plan, he got into his car and just fucking drove without music, air-conditioning, or awareness of his surroundings.

Fifteen minutes later, he whipped his car into the lot in front of the dance studio and screeched to a stop between two parking spots. Sweat dripped down his face as he shoved out of the car and stomped into the building.

"Luxe!" he shouted.

For fuck's sake, he sounded like a madman. But he didn't give a single shit. There was only room for one thought alongside the anger in his head.

*Mine.*

*Mine.*

*Mine.*

"Lu—"

"Tate?" Liam appeared at the open back door. He wore an I-Heart-NY T-shirt and shorts with streaks of blue paint on the fabric and held a dripping blue paintbrush. "You scared the crap outta me. Oh my God, what's wrong?" His eyes were wide and wary. "You look... did something happen?"

Without answering, Tate thundered across the lobby and down the hall to the exit at the end. Liam backed up from his aggressive approach, stepping outside. When he reached the object of his obsession, Tate grabbed Liam's shoulders and turned him so his back hit the bricks next to the door.

The paintbrush clattered to the asphalt as Liam gasped and sputtered. "What the hell, Tate?"

Liam looked stunned and annoyed but not afraid as Tate lightly wrapped one hand around his throat, anchoring him in place. He pressed his hips forward in case Liam tried to kick to get away.

Oh, fuck, was Liam hard?

The firmness against his dick had him reacting in kind.

"You're going on a fucking date?" The words rumbled from deep in his gut.

Liam's eyes flared even wider. "What? A date? What the fuck? No." He shook his head so fast his hair whooshed back and forth on his forehead.

Tate tightened his hand, and the way Liam's pupils dilated made him fully fucking erect. "Don't fucking lie to me!"

"I'm not! Christ, Tate, you're all I can fucking think about. You're on my mind all freaking day. You feel this?" He thrust his hips forward, drawing a tortured groan from Tate as their cocks brushed against each other behind their pants. "You're losing your shit on me, and I still want you. Right fucking now!"

Tate breathed through his nose, struggling to quell his anger. He'd heard what he heard at the grocery store. There's no way they were talking about another sexy male *gay* dancer in Swan.

"The grocery clerk," he said with a growl.

"Jonah?" Liam barked out a harsh laugh. "That's what this is about?" He blew out a breath. "Tate, I'm not interested in

Jonah at all. He's not even my type. But even if he was exactly who I usually went for, *you* are the only one I want. I'm addicted to you," he said as he placed his hands on Tate's chest.

His heart went wild beneath Liam's palm. The words and touch brought his temper down a few notches but enflamed his desire. "He was talking to another guy about how hot you are and said you were going for coffee. You telling me he was making that shit up?"

Liam watched him for a moment before a sly smile curved up one side of his mouth. "Holy crap, you're jealous."

He thought about denying it. He really did, but what the fuck would be the point? Jealous didn't come close to describing the green monster clawing its way through his body. "Luxe…"

"He asked me out, and I declined but said I'd be interested in a friendship. Then he said he was meeting a group of his friends on Friday morning for coffee. Since I don't have anyone in town to hang out with, he invited me, and I accepted. As a friend. I don't know anyone here besides you, Tate, and…"

*And we can't even go out in public.*

He didn't need to say it.

"You don't want to fuck him?" As the anger leached out of him, need, just as violent and intense, took its place.

"No," Liam whispered, gripping his T-shirt and shaking him. "I want to fuck you. Just you."

Fuck yes. Tate released Liam's throat and coasted his hand down the man's chest, over his flat abs to the cock he couldn't get off his mind. "Now?" he asked as he gripped Liam through his pants.

Liam hissed. "Oh God, yes. Now. Let's go upstairs."

The fire heating his blood wouldn't wait that long. He ripped Liam's pants open and shoved his hand down into his skimpy briefs, wrapping it around his hard cock.

"Oh shit, Tate… fuck."

He loved the heat of Liam's dick in his hand. Acting on the attraction he had to men had always been about getting off. Until he met this remarkable man, he had no idea how much he'd enjoy touching for the sake of touching. Whitney and Randy were in a real relationship. Did they do this shit? Did they want to touch each other for no reason besides it made them feel good to have their lover's skin against their hand?

After three rough strokes, he yanked his hand from Liam's briefs to the music of the man's groan. "The apartment is too fucking far," he ground out as he turned Liam to face the wall. One second later, his hand was back around the dancer's dick, this time with Liam's shorts and briefs down below that perfect ass. "What the fuck are you doing to me?" he rumbled against Liam's ear before attacking his neck with biting kisses and grinding his own covered dick against Liam's bare ass. Liam leaked a stream of precum into Tate's fist, easing the way.

"Oh God, Tate. This… I…. I'm just letting you be yourself."

And, fuck, if that wasn't hotter than any fantasy he could dream up.

## Chapter Fifteen

Liam was burning alive with desire. The whiplash of the past few minutes from Tate's anger and jealousy to intense lust, had his brain playing catchup to his body, which was a hundred percent on board getting it on out back behind his studio.

It was private enough, even though technically, anyone could wander back there at any time. But he couldn't care less. The only thing he cared a lick about was getting fucked and getting fucked now.

"You're right. Upstairs is too damn far. Fuck me, now."

Tate ground his rock-hard erection against Liam's ass, making him moan.

"Jesus, Luxe, you sure? Right here?"

"Yes, do it now."

The pressure against his ass disappeared as Tate wrestled with his jeans.

Liam rested his forehead and palms against the warm brick of the building. "You have supplies?" he asked.

"Sure as hell do. Started carrying them around a few days ago. Never know when I'm gonna need you."

*I need you all the time.*

Thank God he had enough brain power to keep that clingy thought in his head. Instead, he said, "Good thinking, Boy

Scout."

He heard a snort and the crinkled rip of the condom packet before Tate said, "I'da been kicked out on day one."

Cool, slick fingers slid through his crease, making him jump. His breathing sped in anticipation of what was to come and how damn hot it would be.

"You good?" Tate asked.

"Yeah, do it. Just a quick prep. I can't wait."

Tate probed his hole, then slid two thick fingers straight in, immediately getting to work, loosening him up.

"Jesus," Liam whispered as the intense pressure made his knees wobble.

A raw chuckle sounded in his ear. "Like that?" Tate asked as he scissored his fingers.

"Yes." Liam slapped the brick wall. "Just like that." The fingers inside him twisted and stretched him, making him pant. "Enough! Good enough. Fuck me now."

"Damn, it's hot when you get all bossy. Sure you're ready?" His voice was strained as though someone held his throat.

"I was ready the moment you stormed out here like a jealous caveman."

Tate gave another of those dark chuckles as he lined his cock up with Liam's hole.

"Make me feel it for days." *Days.*

Tate's fingers flexed on his hips, and he swore a savage curse. "Why do I have a feeling you won't be so mouthy in a second?" he asked before he drove his cock inside Liam with a brutal thrust.

The pleasure was instant and overwhelming, riding right at the edge of pain. Tate nailed his prostate on the first thrust, and the combination of discomfort and pleasure had him shouting out Tate's name.

A palm slapped over his mouth. "Much as I love you

screaming my name, I don't want anyone to come investigate the noise. I'm the only one who gets to see you with my cock buried inside your tight ass."

Not because he was worried about being outed but because he had a possessive need to keep Liam to himself.

If he could have swooned, he would have, but the thick rod inside him made it impossible. Instead, he mumbled, "Fuck me!" against the palm smothering him.

Tate did just that.

Liam's entire world centered on the two of them in their bubble out behind his studio. He moaned and whimpered into Tate's hand as he endured the hottest, most primal fucking of his life. With the coarse brick digging into his palms, he pushed back, meeting Tate's every thrust with sharp punches of his hips. His prostate took the most delicious pounding. A constant buzz of electricity traveled out through his limbs.

"How is your ass this fucking tight?" Tate rumbled next to his ear before sucking on his earlobe. "Fucking heaven." His left hand trailed from Liam's hip to grip his cock.

Liam's eyes rolled back, and his knees tried to give out. The man was a righty but just as skilled at stroking cock with his left hand. Liam trembled, mind muddled, and body losing control. Every thrust brought him closer to what promised to be a world-changing climax.

This was it. The point of no return. There was no coming back from a fuck as good as this one because it wasn't just a fuck. Tate might not believe or understand it, and Liam was too chickenshit to admit it, but this time their sex was fueled by emotion as well as straight lust.

Teeth grazed his neck as the hand on his dick tightened.

"Oh God," he mumbled into Tate's damp palm. "I'm close. I'm so close."

The thrusts and hand stroking him sped to a furious pace

as Tate growled, "Me too." His mouth latched onto Liam's neck, sucking with the force of a damn Dyson and sending Liam over the edge.

He shouted into Tate's palm just as he felt the man jerk behind him with his own orgasm. Tate shouted through clenched teeth. Tate's grip on Liam's dick became punishing, as though he had no control over his strength.

A jangling bell registered through the fog of a powerful orgasm.

"Tate? Yo, T, you here?"

Randy's voice ripped through the sexual haze surrounding them.

"Shit." In a move so fast that Liam couldn't process it, Tate pulled out of him and sprang away like Liam was on fire.

Christ, he'd barely finished coming and couldn't process what was happening, but he could feel the deep freeze that took over Tate.

One glance over his shoulder revealed Tate standing statue-still with his pants at his knees, his condom-covered cock soft and dangling, and an expression of abject horror on his face.

They could handle this. They just needed to cover up and pretend Tate had come to help Liam paint. He reached back for Tate's hand.

"Don't fucking touch me." Tate jumped back so fast that Liam instantly yanked his hand away. The harsh whisper pierced his heart.

"Shit, shit," Tate muttered. He shoved his dick, condom and all into his underwear and did up his jeans in record time.

Liam tried to turn around so he could reassure Tate everything would be okay. He forgot about his shorts around his ankles and the second he took a step, he tripped. He bit his lip to keep from shouting as he crashed to the ground, landing on all fours with a painful crunch. The metallic taste of blood flooded his mouth.

"Tate? You out back or something?"

Liam stared up at Tate from his spot on the ground. There he was, eyes teary, bare, recently fucked, ass out for all the world to see, and palms and knees stinging like they'd been attacked by a swarm of bees.

Tate's eyes were wild and panicked as he glanced down. "I-I'm sorry," he said, shaking his head. Then he darted into the building and, in a voice that made it seem as though he'd been out for a Sunday stroll, said, "Hey, Randy. What're you doing here?"

"Uh, what the fuck are you doing here? I'm here cuz I saw your truck out front. There a problem with our work?"

"Oh, no, definitely not. I just stopped by to do a final check and make sure everything was in order for the guy's opening day. It's coming up soon."

"Uh-huh. Where's the little dance guy?"

Little dance guy? Guess he should be glad Randy hadn't used a slur.

"He was running out for some lunch when I showed up, so he just let me in to look around the locker room."

"Why is your hair messy? And you're all fucking flushed. Were you…" He started to laugh.

Liam's heart shot into overdrive. Shit. He couldn't do a damn thing to help. As humiliated as he was by what had just happened, no one deserved to be outed this way. It would destroy Tate.

"Were you jerking off back there?"

"What?" Tate laughed.

Could Randy hear the strain in it?

"No, you sick fuck, I wasn't jerking off in an alley behind a building on Main Street. The fuck is wrong with you?"

"Oh, my God, you totally have an I-just-came-face. You

whacked one off behind the dance studio. I'm proud of you, T. Always figured you were vanilla. Glad to know you got some freak in ya."

"Jesus, fuck, I wasn't jerking off."

Liam's hands and knees were in agony, but he didn't change positions, terrified he'd make a sound and draw Randy's attention.

"You were. But don't worry, your perverted little secret is safe with me. For now." Randy laughed, and then there was a slapping sound like he'd clapped Tate on the shoulder. "Wanna grab some lunch?"

"Fuck off."

"Aww, come on. Don't be like that."

"Fine," Tate said, sounding resigned. "But you're buying since you're an asshole."

As the sound of their footsteps faded, Liam realized he was still on all fours with his lubed ass uncovered out behind his building.

How had the hottest fuck of his life turned into the most humiliating and degrading experience he'd ever had?

Wincing, he shifted back on his heels to inspect the damage. Both palms had little flecks of gravel embedded in the skin, and his knees were bleeding. Guess he wouldn't be giving any blowjobs for a while.

He probably wouldn't be seeing Tate for a while, either, which, at the moment, he couldn't feel horrible about. His palms and knees hurt while the rest of him burned too hot with humiliation to feel his usual compassion. Then there was his fragile heart, which had stupidly started to get involved only to be ruthlessly stomped on two seconds later.

God, he was a pathetic mess. He sighed and gingerly climbed to his feet, flinching at the sting when his legs straightened. Once up and no longer cringing in discomfort, he carefully tucked his spent dick into his shorts. "This is what happens when you get involved," he muttered at his crotch like a crazy person. "Actually," he said, tapping a bloodied hand on the left side of his chest. "This is what happens when *you* get involved."

He sighed again and spun toward the door. Looked like he'd be taking a break from painting the shelf to go doctor his knees. As he turned, he caught sight of his cum dripping down the brick wall.

"Fabulous," he muttered.

After he patched up his knees, he could come back to clean up the evidence of his poor choices.

He'd fucked up.

God, he'd fucked up in the most spectacular way possible. This trumped the time he and Randy snuck onto Old Man Murphy's farm to set his animals free. The goats and pigs ate through an entire crop of corn in one afternoon. Man, had they gotten in some serious trouble. They'd spent the entire summer working their asses off on Old Man Murphy's farm without earning a single cent to make up for the damage they'd cost. Until a few hours ago, he'd have said it was his biggest fuck-up to date.

Well, he'd blown that out of the water.

"Oh, I forgot to tell you Daryl isn't gonna be workin' today," Randy said as they unloaded supplies from the truck.

"What? You're shittin' me. What the fuck's he doing?"

Randy shrugged, hefting a heavy bag of powdered grout onto his shoulder. "Ducky is getting out of prison, and Daryl's picking him up. He cleared it with Larkin."

"And nobody bothered to tell me?" Dammit, he'd planned to get Randy and Daryl set up and working the job, then slip out and rush back over to Liam's for some serious damage control. Now, he'd have to spend the entire afternoon doing Daryl's work.

"What's it matter?" Randy asked, shooting him a confused look. "This ain't even a big job. You and I'll get it knocked out in a few hours, no problem."

"It's just fucking irresponsible."

"It's Ducky's release day. You can't expect Daryl to miss that. Stop being a dick. You've been all over Daryl's case lately. It's starting to piss him off."

He grabbed a few boxes of tiles, and they started for the older home. They'd been hired to add a simple backsplash in the kitchen.

"So let him be pissed off."

Ducky was Daryl's older brother and a complete shithead. He made Daryl look like an angel in comparison. Fifteen months ago, he was arrested for vandalizing a black-owned shop in downtown Swan. Being the racist idiot he is, he'd spray-painted slurs on the building, bumping the charges up from simple vandalism to a hate crime. He'd won himself a solid two-year-long stint in prison. Due to overcrowding, he'd received an early parole.

*Joy.*

Tate hated Ducky more than just about anyone. He'd idolized him at one point, but that only lasted until he was old enough to realize what a waste of space Ducky was. He used to hide in the bushes and throw rocks at Tate as he walked to school, steal his lunch—when he'd had one—and generally treated him like garbage. Once Tate realized his attraction to guys, it'd been Ducky finding out that terrified him most, and for good reason. He was as violent as he was prejudiced.

"He's not working with us." Ducky never had any interest in working for the tiling company in the past. Well, he'd never been interested in working for anyone, but he'd need a job now as part of his parole.

"That ain't up to you."

Another reason to start his own company.

"But I don't think it'll matter," Randy added. "I heard he's going to get a job working on cars. Daryl said something about Duck getting mechanic training in the clink."

Perfect. Whatever kept him away from Tate.

"All right," he said with a heavy sigh as his chances to fix things with Liam evaporated. "Let's get this over with." Now he'd have hours to plan his apology speech and obsess over what a fucking idiot he was.

Would Liam even speak to him?

And how could Tate blame him if he wouldn't?

He'd gone over there snarling and snapping with jealousy. There wasn't another word for it. The thought of that Jonah guy touching Liam had him seeing red. But then Liam shut that down, and all he could think of was fucking the man.

And, boy, had he fucked him.

It had been like nothing he'd ever experienced, and he was pretty sure Liam felt the same. Hot, raw, and primal, they'd been like two animals focused on nothing but pleasuring each other.

And then he'd heard Randy call his fucking name and felt as though a bucket of ice had been poured on him.

*He got hurt.*

Liam fell because Tate was an enormous asshole who'd jerked away from him.

He felt sick.

MOSTLY BECAUSE HE couldn't promise it wouldn't happen again.

He didn't deserve Liam and never would. Not as long as he lived in the closet, and he couldn't envision a world where he didn't. And now, with Ducky coming home, it felt as though the universe was playing games with him and laughing at his expense.

"Dude, what the fuck?" Randy called from the front door.

"You just gonna stand in the driveway all damn day? Swear to God you've been weird as fuck lately."

"I'm fine. Let's do this."

He spent the next few hours working like a madman to distract himself from his mistakes. It didn't work. The look of shock, pain, and pity on Liam's face when he'd stared up from where he'd fallen taunted Tate the entire time he worked. If Randy noticed, he kept his mouth shut but shot Tate concerned glances.

When quitting time rolled around, they silently cleaned up and loaded the truck. "Hey, I'm meeting Daryl and Duck at The Nail for a few drinks later. You game?"

The Rusty Nail or The Nail as the locals called it, was the lone bar in Swan. Every night it was full of drunk rednecks and farmers blowing off steam after a long day. Tate had been there countless times, but even if he didn't have a problem to fix tonight, he wouldn't go with Ducky.

"Nah, man, I've got some shit to do."

Randy scoffed.

"What?" Tate asked, glancing at his brother in his periphery.

"I'd ask what the fuck it is you gotta do, but I doubt you'll tell me. You've been such a secretive motherfucker lately."

He turned onto the highway. "You sound paranoid. I just got some shit to do. No big deal. Am I dropping you at The Nail?"

"Yeah." They were both dusty and dirty, but The Nail wasn't the type of place anyone cared about that shit.

Tate pulled into the lot and braked at the door.

"Thanks. We'll be here a while if you change your mind," Randy said as he hopped out. "I heard Kathy Baker was in town." He winked. "In case you need a little pick-me-up," he said.

"Oh, yeah, thanks," he said, voice flat. "I'll keep her in

mind." God, the words tasted bitter. Every time he denied Liam, he felt worse, and after today, he might as well be flaying his chest wide open.

After dropping his brother at the bar, he drove to the mini-mart across the street. They usually had a display of somewhat hearty flowers, and it couldn't hurt to show up with a peace offering.

He knew less than nothing about flowers, but they were colorful, alive, and arranged in a way that made them look pretty. That's all that mattered, right?

Would Liam care about the type of flowers? Most of them had a sticker that said assorted wildflowers. A few were plain roses, even Tate recognized those. Should he get roses? They only had pink. Were roses good for an apology, or were they about love?

*What the hell is wrong with you?*

He stood there like an idiot for a solid fifteen minutes, staring at the case and driving himself insane, when an older woman in a grass-green store vest wandered over. "Celebration or screw up?" she asked with a twinkle in her blue-gray eyes.

"Oh, uh, screw up. Big one."

"Ah, I thought so. You have that deer-in-the-headlights look a man gets when he messes up for the first time in a new relationship. Am I right?"

He glanced down at her. She was at least a foot shorter with tightly permed gray hair and a kind smile. "Something like that."

"Then go with these." She stretched to reach the largest bunch of wildflowers. "They have a little something for everyone. And the colors complement most people's décor."

The flowers had to match Liam's house?

"Uh, thanks." He accepted the bouquet. "Appreciate the help."

She patted his arms. "Let's get you checked out so you can win your girl back."

His heart stuttered. "S-sounds good." Every time he hid the fact Liam was a man, his body responded in a visceral way. Right then, he felt a painful pressure in his chest as though someone had reached in and squeezed his heart.

The short drive to Liam's studio was spent rehearsing an apology speech and trying not to vomit. He could barely control the car with how hard his hands shook, and he peeked at the flowers no less than twenty times as though they could somehow leap out of the car and run away.

This time, he parked behind the studio, as he should have done that morning and would have if he'd been thinking clearly—if the green-eyed monster hadn't eaten his brain.

Flowers in hand and speech prepared, he jogged up the outdoor staircase to the small balcony outside Liam's back door. After blowing out an unsteady breath, he knocked.

The door opened, and the second he saw Liam, his tongue dried up, and he forgot every word he'd planned to say.

He could only stare at the two large bandages covering Liam's knees.

*That's your fault, asshole.*

When he dragged his gaze back up, he found the man staring back at him with one raised eyebrow.

"I fucked up."

So much for everything he'd planned to say.

## Chapter Sixteen

By the time evening rolled around, Liam had worked himself into a tizzy. Round and round, he'd gone through the spectrum of emotions from anger to embarrassment to sadness and even compassion.

Right now, he was back to anger. "I get that he's not ready to come out," he muttered as he yanked the cork out of a bottle of wine. Not the same brand Tate had purchased for him. That would be sad and pathetic.

Fine. It was the same.

"I really do get it. And I respect it." He poured a healthy glass of wine. "But for fuck's sake, did he have to act like I was a damn leper? I was the one who suggested we go upstairs to my bed where we could have had privacy." He gulped a large swallow of wine. "But he was all, 'It's too far away.' Damn him and his hotness."

Liam sighed and took another sip of wine.

"And now I'm talking to myself again." As he'd done way too much that afternoon.

Just as he was about to pull a box of cereal from his cabinet, a heavy knock came at the back door.

He stared at it, knowing full well who'd come to see him.

Was he ready for this? Was he willing to listen to Tate's apology?

If he didn't, he'd spend the entire night awake, staring at the ceiling as he wondered what thoughts were going through Tate's head. He'd also worry whether Tate was okay and if Randy suspected anything, which pissed him off. Why the hell should he be worried about someone who obviously didn't give a shit about him?

Good. This was the energy he needed to have when faced with Tate. He shook out his arms and legs, then marched toward the door leading to the itty-bitty balcony behind his apartment.

He yanked the door open, prepared to blast the man, only to freeze. Tate stood there holding a giant bouquet of beautiful wildflowers. Had a man ever brought him flowers? It didn't take more than one second to think back through the men he dated and come up with the answer. A big, fat no.

The gorgeous bouquet wasn't enough to distract from the man who looked like shit. Bits of grout and dust covered his white T-shirt and work jeans. He even had some in his disheveled hair, but it was the devastation and self-hatred on his face that had Liam's anger melting away.

*Dammit.*

"I fucked up," Tate blurted.

Liam didn't say anything.

"These are for you." Tate thrust the flowers into Liam's hands. "I didn't know what kind you like or if you even like flowers, but the lady at the store said this was a good idea because it had a bunch of different flowers. Something for everyone, I think she said. She also said it should match well with whatever your house looks like. If you hate them, I can, I don't know, give them to my mom or something."

Holy crap, a nervous, bumbling Tate was adorable. There he stood, filthy from work, tall, gruff, and completely out of his element. The flowers were charming, but the awkward speech was what had him saying, "Come on in."

He stepped back to allow Tate into the apartment. They stared at each other for a moment, tension thick until Tate's gaze fell to his knees again. "I'm so sorry. Is it bad?"

Shaking his head, Liam said, "Just some deep scrapes. It doesn't feel good, but it's nothing major. Though I won't be on my knees giving blow jobs for a bit." He chuckled at his dumb attempt to break the tension, but Tate didn't laugh.

"I panicked," he said.

"I know."

"Yeah." Tate ran a hand through his hair. "I'm really fucking sorry."

There wasn't a doubt in Liam's mind that he meant the words.

"I know that too." The urge to reach out and hug Tate was strong, but he sensed there was more the man wanted to say, so he stayed where he was and waited.

"I—" He shoved his hands in his pockets, probably to keep them out of his hair. "I don't know how to do this. I'm freaked out all the fucking time. Not just for myself, though. I'm worried about what will happen to you if Randy sees us together."

Liam knew exactly what could happen to someone who wasn't accepted in this town. "I can take care of myself."

"Yeah, well…" He shrugged. "I like you, Liam. A lot."

*Oh, this man.*

"Can I hug you?" Liam set the flowers on the table and stepped closer to Tate, who nodded.

"Yeah."

He wrapped his arms around the bigger man and held tight. Tate's rigidity lasted another two seconds before he melted into Liam's embrace, burying his face in his neck. A long, shuddered sigh left the tortured man.

They stayed that way for a while, holding each other by the door. When Tate finally loosened his clasp, Liam did the same and stepped back. "Maybe next time we try for a little exhibitionism," he said in another attempt at humor. " I'm the one who should fuck you against the wall. Less risk of bodily injury."

Tate froze.

*Shit, too soon?*

"I don't do that," he said, voice devoid of emotion.

Liam winced. He shouldn't have assumed anything. Just because he was vers didn't mean everyone enjoyed it both ways. "Sorry, I—"

"It's too—" Tate said at the same time.

*Wait one second.* Liam tilted his head. "Too what?"

With the expression of somebody caught in a trap, Tate shook his head. "Never mind."

Oh, hell no. He was not about to say what Liam thought he was about to say. "Too what, Tate?" he asked, jamming his sore hands on his hips. "Too gay? Is that what you were gonna say?"

"What? No, I—" He sputtered as his face paled.

Well, *now* Liam was pissed. It was one thing for Tate to keep his truth from the rest of the world, but to lie to himself and Liam after all they'd done together? That was unacceptable.

"Newsflash, buddy," he said, stepping into Tate's personal space. "You are gay."

The man's face went from pale to sickly gray. "No, I'm... I... no..."

"No?" Liam threw his hands up, stalked away, then came back. "You know what? My bad. I know better than to label someone's sexuality without their input. So gay isn't the right word. How about bi? Pan? Which one is it, Tate?"

Later he'd feel the hot sting of shame for pressing Tate to label himself when he might not even know for sure, but right then, Liam was too damn mad to think rationally.

"You know what? It doesn't even fucking matter. The word you want right now is queer. Because all the others fall under that umbrella. You are queer, Tate, and you have as much of a fucking problem with that as your dipshit brother and his stupid friends have." He was shouting now, waving his arms like a madman as Tate stood there and took it, looking like he might get sick on the floor.

"Here are some words for you, Tate. Internalized homophobia." The confusion on Tate's face told Liam what he already knew—it wasn't a concept with which the other man was familiar. "Now get the hell out of my apartment and go look it up." His chest heaved as he breathed as though he'd just run through a grueling rehearsal.

Instead of leaving, Tate said, "I'm not lucky like you, Luxe."

"Don't call me that."

He winced. "You've never had to live with this fear. You've never seen the viciousness of hateful people like I have. You have no idea how cruel life can be."

Laughing an ugly sound, Liam said, "You don't know a goddamn thing about what I've seen and lived with, Tate. You want to talk fear? You want to talk hate? How about this? When I was fifteen years old, I joined a traveling dance company for the summer. I spent those months performing at state fairs all over the country. Or I did until I came to Swan, Oklahoma. After our performance at the state fair not two miles up the damn road, I was jumped by some bigot who got his rocks off beating on the little fairy dancer kid."

Tate gasped and stumbled back until he bumped the door. "No," he whispered, face like he'd seen a ghost. "You're... him?"

"Him? You heard about that? Yeah, I'm him. They broke my shoulder and busted my ribs. I was covered in deep, painful bruises. I couldn't dance for months. You have no idea how hard it was to get back to where I was in time for college auditions. You have no idea how much therapy it took to make the nightmares go away. So don't you dare tell me I don't know fear, and I don't know hatred." He jabbed a finger into his own chest, practically hyperventilating as he finished screaming the words at Tate.

"Why?" Tate whispered.

Liam knew exactly what he was asking. "I'm here to prove to myself and the fucking world that I am stronger than the hatred. I am here to show these backward assholes that anyone who wants to dance deserves to, regardless of their gender, ethnicity, or sexuality. And fuck anyone who gets in my way."

Tate's big body was shaking as he turned. "I'm sorry," he muttered, scrambling to open the door. "I can't. It's too much. I'm sorry." He bolted outside. His footsteps pounding down the stairs faded as the door slammed closed behind him.

Liam stood there, shoulders slumped, breathing hard as regret washed over him. "Shit," he whispered, then ran to the door, but when he reached it, he couldn't get himself to open it. Instead, he rested his forearms against the wood and screamed at the top of his lungs.

Memories of the pain and fear bombarded him from all angles. The frustration of fighting an uphill battle to regain his dance skills. The shock and disappointment of his family and friends when he told them where he wanted to move.

He turned until his back met the wall, then slid down. When he hit the floor, he tugged his knees into his chest, wincing as the abraded skin stretched.

He'd handled that so poorly. Screamed at the man who was only trying to prevent himself from meeting the same fate Liam had. It was then he realized something that had him burying his face against his knees and sobbing.

He was the only person in the world who knew Tate's

secret. The only person Tate trusted to know him without judgment. And he'd just thrown everything Tate told him back in his face as though it didn't matter.

It mattered.

Tate mattered to him.

Maybe more than anyone else.

Why did that make the pain in his chest hurt so much more than the pain in his knees?

# Chapter Seventeen

I-N-T-E-R-N-A-L-I-Z-E-D  H-O-M-O-P-H-O-B-I-A

It took two days, but Tate finally worked up the courage to type into a computer at his office the twenty-two characters Liam had shouted at him. That was, of course, after ensuring he could erase the search history and checking that no one else was in the building.

Now, he just had to press enter and see what the internet gods had to teach him.

Instead of depressing that one little key, he sat there paralyzed, replaying the pitying expression on Liam's face as he'd hurled his anger Tate's way. His very justified anger.

He missed Liam. He'd never missed anyone before, and it wasn't a pleasant sensation. A heaviness had moved, making everything he'd done over the past few days take a monumental amount of effort. He felt weighted down from the inside out, and nothing provided relief. Not cigarettes, booze, or working out at the makeshift gym a few guys set up at the trailer park.

Nothing.

The number of times he'd thought of Liam, started to text him, and nearly driven to his place in the past forty-eight hours bordered on pathetic. He didn't deserve to be around Liam until he figured out some of his shit. Disgust with himself kept him from following through on his attempts to contact Liam.

That, and the fact that he now knew Liam was the kid he'd seen attacked at the fair all those years ago. The kid he'd tried to save.

The gorgeous dancer who'd mesmerized him.

The first guy he'd been attracted to. The one who started it all. Learning that had been too much information at once. Too overwhelming. Which was why he'd run like a little coward instead of telling Liam who he was. That he'd been there. That he'd seen it all and walked away with a few bruises of his own.

After all Liam had suffered that horrible day, he'd come back to live in Swan.

It was either the bravest or stupidest move Tate had ever heard.

One thing was for sure, he'd never be worthy of breathing the same air as Liam until he pulled his head out of his ass. And he wanted nothing more than to be worthy of Liam's attention, so he'd better stop lying to himself and make some changes.

He jammed the enter key down before he could talk himself out of it yet again. Two seconds later, he had a host of search results to choose from. He clicked the top one and leaned closer to read. After a few minutes, he sagged back in the chair, shaken to his core.

Liam hit the nail on the head.

Why did that fill him with so much shame?

He was guilty of exactly what the website described. He'd taken the homophobic bullshit he'd heard his entire life and turned it on himself. There he was, thinking himself so much more enlightened than Randy, Daryl, or the rest of the town because he didn't give a shit who someone wanted to fuck. But when it came to himself? He'd made his sexuality a shameful secret that festered for years until he couldn't even say "I'm gay" to the man he was fucking.

*Why?*

Did he believe, like Randy and Daryl, that something was wrong with him?

Maybe he had on some level, and he'd forever be ashamed of that. But meeting Liam, spending time with Liam, and being *with* Liam opened his eyes to who he was and how he wanted to live. He wanted to be comfortable in his own skin, to live as his authentic self, to be happy and free just like Liam. And the only way he could get there was to start with himself.

A sense of urgency stole over him. He gathered his stuff and shut down the computer—without deleting the search history, baby steps—then ran out to his car. Once behind the wheel, he pulled down the visor and stared into the old, distorted mirror.

"I'm gay," he whispered to the man staring back at him.

He held his breath as seconds ticked by.

The world didn't end.

Despite recognizing his attraction to men for the past ten years, despite fucking them in dark corners of the club, he had never dared to utter those words aloud.

"I'm gay," he said again, louder this time. Relief washed over him like a tidal wave, making a crazed laugh bubble out. "I'm gay!" he shouted at the top of his lungs and then slumped forward. Tears clogged his throat, and a few escaped his eyes.

If Randy or Daryl walked by, they'd call him a pussy for crying and laugh their asses off, but for the first time in his life, he didn't fucking care. He felt so damn good.

"I have to tell Liam," he whispered, then straightened. After starting the car, he glanced at the clock. Five in the evening. Today was Liam's grand opening from three to six.

He'd decided to run it like an open house without any formal class times. There'd be food and beverages as well as demos if—when—he had enough interested people checking out the studio.

Tate could stop by. He should stop by. Today had been a great first step, and while he wasn't ready to scream his sexuality from the rooftop of Swan's town hall building, he could, at the very least, show the town he and Liam were friends.

Baby steps.

When he arrived at the dance studio, a giant grin broke out across his face. The place was packed. Cars filled the lot and lined the shoulder up and down the street.

"Fuck yeah," he muttered, pulling around the back of the building. This time, it wasn't to hide his car but because he had no other options. Party music and children's laughter greeted him as soon as he stepped out of the vehicle. He hadn't even taken a step toward the studio and could already tell the event was a huge success.

Someone had propped the back door open, probably to let some air in the crowded building, so Tate headed inside. As he reached the door, memories of days before came rushing back. He'd fucked Liam right there in broad daylight, and it had been like nothing else. Hotter than the fucking sun, but also intimate. He'd never wanted it to end.

And then he'd fucked it all up.

Today, he hoped he could fix it.

He *would* fix it.

Sighing, he slipped through the open door and strolled down the hallway toward the noise. Liam had three practice rooms in total, but the party was in the main studio, the one visible from the parking lot. Mostly women, but a few men mingled, chatting as they snacked from a large, decorated table full of everything from one of those charcuterie things

Whitney was always talking about to a fancy cupcake tower.

The place was packed and hot as hell. Tate leaned against the wall in the mouth of the hallway. Kids danced around in pink, frilly ballet outfits and some in street clothes, giggling and having a blast.

And there, in the middle of it all, was Liam.

Tate's breath caught in his lungs. How had he managed forty-eight whole hours without seeing the beautiful man?

Liam looked radiant in a black, sleeveless, fitted top and navy dance tights. He was completely in his element, beaming as he demonstrated some choreography. He executed a dance move—Tate had no idea what the hell it was called—and all the children tried to copy him. Some were perfect and others were a hot mess. Smiling the entire time, Liam went around to each child, heaping praise and correcting form in a way that built the kids' confidence, even the ones who sucked. Not only was he a natural on the dance floor, but he also had a gift when it came to teaching. The children hung on his every word, practically floating off the floor when he complimented them.

A lump lodged in his throat. He tried to swallow it down, but it held firm. He did not deserve a man half as good as Liam in his life, but he was too damn selfish to walk away now. Liam would be his, and today started the journey to making that happen.

Who knew how long he stood there, propped against the wall with his arms folded, staring at Liam in his element? Interested dancers came and went, registering for classes on the iPad Liam set up at the front desk. If this crowd was any indication of how business would go, Liam would need to hire additional teachers before long.

Pride filled Tate's chest. Liam had come here with a lofty goal and made it happen. Now that he understood why Liam chose Swan, his admiration grew exponentially.

Liam approached a tiny little girl in a pink tutu who stood a bit away from the rest of the kids. She had a thumb in her mouth and watery eyes. "Hey," he said as he crouched down. "I'm Liam. What's your name?"

"Tammy," she said, mouth full of thumb.

"Hi, Tammy. You look so pretty in your leotard. Do you know how to twirl?"

The little girl's eyes widened, and she nodded, making her riot of blonde curls bounce all around.

"Can you show me?"

She shook her head, which made Liam chuckle.

"What if we do it at the same time?"

She tilted her little head and stared at him for a moment before finally nodding.

"Yay!" Liam clapped his hands as he stood. "Ready?"

Out popped the thumb. The little girl spun and spun until she stumbled and nearly fell. Liam, who only twirled once, laughed and clapped for her. After steadying her, he crouched again to tell her how wonderful she'd done.

She beamed, and Tate rubbed at his chest.

As if he finally sensed hungry eyes on him, Liam lifted his gaze and met Tate's stare. His eyes widened with surprise.

They stayed that way, focus locked on each other for long seconds until Liam finally smiled. He waved and pressed a hand to his heart. "Thank you for coming," he mouthed.

Tate felt like a balloon someone had forgotten to tie off. Immense tension he hadn't even realized he'd been holding rushed out of him with a nearly audible whoosh.

Liam didn't hate him. There was still so much work to be done to repair their fragile connection, but it didn't seem nearly as hopeless as it had earlier in the day.

"Wait upstairs?" Liam mouthed, pointing at the ceiling.

Tate nodded. No one paid him any mind, so he did something he never imagined himself doing in a million years. He kissed the tips of his fingers and inclined them subtly in Liam's direction.

The dancer's eyes nearly fell from his head. He blinked quickly as though fighting tears before nodding. The little twirling girl grabbed his hand and tugged, breaking the spell. When Liam turned to face her, Tate took the opportunity to head up the stairs and wait in Liam's apartment for him to finish up the successful open house.

HE SHOWED UP. Tate showed up.

The open house had put Liam in the best mood he'd been in for days, but the second he spotted Tate, he nearly exploded with glee.

He came.

What did that mean?

Concentrating on the final half hour of his event became impossible. All he could think about was the man upstairs, waiting in his apartment. It spoke to how deeply entangled he was with Tate if the man took up more of his brain than this night he'd been planning for years.

"Thank you, Liam. This was just wonderful." A woman who'd introduced herself as Cathy and showed up with three rowdy children in tow hugged him. "I have all three of them signed up."

"Excellent. Classes will begin next week. And if you know anyone who is a dance teacher looking for work, please send them my way. It looks like I'll need to hire another teacher right away."

Not a bad problem to have. Every class advertised had filled, and he even had a waitlist forming for his nonexistent second teacher.

"Absolutely. I have someone in mind, so I'll pass her your information."

"Thank you so much. I look forward to teaching your little

ones."

He had similar conversations with many lingering customers, and within fifty minutes, everyone cleared out, and the studio fell blessedly silent. Liam killed the music and then fell into the front desk chair, completely exhausted. The night was a success beyond what he'd ever imagined, and he felt like he was floating on cloud nine.

The studio was a mess and would require a few hours of dedicated cleaning, but Liam had something much more pressing to attend to. He forced his tired body up, turned off the lights, locked the exterior doors, and practically flew up the stairs to his apartment.

When he walked in, he found Tate reclined on his couch, snoozing. Liam smiled. The man had shed his shoes and socks, leaving those large feet bare as they rested on the couch. As usual, Tate wore a T-shirt and jeans. His shaggy hair was mussed, giving off a sexy, disheveled vibe. Liam's hands itched to mess him up even more.

He didn't bother to change out of his dance tights or fitted tee. Instead, he walked straight to the couch and climbed on the dozing man, straddling his lap.

"Luxe?" Tate asked in a sleepy voice before he opened his eyes. His hands were already full of Liam's ass by the time he completely woke.

"It's me." Nothing had been settled between them, but he couldn't resist reaching out and sifting his fingers through Tate's hair.

"Mmm." Tate leaned into his touch with a near purr. His eyes opened. Sorrow and pain reflected up at him from those deep blue orbs.

"I'm sorry," they said at the same time.

"What? No." Tate shook his head. "What the hell do you have to be sorry for? Jesus, Luxe, I was an ass. You were so right. We just met. I don't know your past or what you've gone through in your life. I never should have said that shit."

"And I shouldn't have tried to label you or force you to label yourself." He ran his hands through Tate's hair again to feel the softness on his fingers. "You never have to pick a label if you don't want to. It was wrong of me to throw that in your face. I was upset about what happened earlier in the day and overreacted."

"No." He shook his head. "You didn't. You were right to be upset and to call me out. I looked up that internalized homophobia stuff you mentioned."

Liam winced. "I shouldn't have thrown that at you." He'd forever hate how he'd let anger control him that day.

Tate swallowed. "I'm-I'm gay." He nodded once. "Gay. That's how I identify."

Liam felt the grin stretch his cheeks. "First time?"

"No," he said with a sheepish grin. "I said it to my car mirror earlier today. I never even realized how I had taken the garbage I had been told my whole life and turned it on myself. I thought I was so open-minded, accepting others for who they were, but I couldn't do it for myself."

"I'm so proud of you." He kept his hands in Tate's hair, massaging while he enjoyed the cool strands against his skin.

He snorted. "I might fuck up sometimes, but it will never be like it was the other day. I'm so fucking sorry for how I reacted when Randy almost found us. I'm so sorry you got hurt."

"That's in the past. And I'm fine. My hands are practically healed already, and my knees don't hurt anymore. Promise me you won't beat yourself up over that anymore."

"I'm still a work in progress, Luxe."

He wasn't the only one. "I get that. And I understand years of learning, even if it's wrong, doesn't go away in one afternoon. But you've taken a huge, scary step. I'm allowed to be proud of you."

Tate squeezed his ass. Liam rocked forward as he shivered in pleasure.

"Speaking of proud…" Tate said as he kneaded Liam's cheeks over his tights. "Damn, you did good down there tonight, Luxe. You're incredible with those kids. They worship you already."

Throwing Tate a sassy grin, Liam said, "I did do good, didn't I?"

Laughing, Tate nodded. "Hell, yeah, you did. And your modesty is admirable too."

He'd be lying if he said the approval didn't send him to the moon. "What can I say? I'm a performer. We all have a bit of a praise kink."

"Is that so?" One of Tate's eyebrows rose. "So, you'd like it if I told you how sexy you look when you're dancing? How you command the room and captivate everyone in your presence. How you're so beautiful, not a single person can look away."

"I mean, I wouldn't hate it." He blew on his fingernails, then buffed them on his shoulder, making Tate laugh again. "I like it when you laugh."

"You bring it out of me. We should celebrate your big night."

"Oh yeah?" He ground his hips into Tate's quickly growing erection. "What did you have in mind?"

"That, definitely that," Tate said as he rocked up, meeting Liam's thrust. His face went serious. "But there's something I need to tell you first."

Liam stopped moving. "Well, shit. Nothing good ever starts with that sentence."

## Chapter Eighteen

Tate grabbed Liam's hips as he started to climb off his lap. "Stay." It sounded more of a plea than a command.

Liam stilled, frowning down at the man beneath him. "Yeah?" Part of him needed the physical separation, something to keep his heart from becoming too entwined with Tate's and ending up battered if this news was negative.

Who was he kidding? It was far too late to keep his heart out of the picture. It became involved the moment he realized Tate hid a vulnerable soul beneath his tough exterior.

"Yeah. I mean, if you want to." The uncertainty in Tate's tone ate at Liam's heart. He wanted to soothe this man, to promise that no matter what Tate was about to say, everything between them would be okay.

*But will it?*

"I want to," Liam said as he settled back down astride Tate. "I like any excuse to be close to you, but I'm not gonna lie, you're making me a bit nervous." Or extremely nervous.

"I know." Tate chuckled, but it held no humor. There went that hand again, running through his hair. If this turmoil continued, he'd be bald before his twenty-sixth birthday, whenever that was. Something for Liam to discover.

After blowing out a long breath, Tate cleared his throat. "I have a story to tell you. It, uh, might be hard to hear, and it might change how you feel about this… us… me."

"Okay…" With each passing second, tension coiled tighter. Tate's solemn expression did nothing to ease Liam's nerves. Whatever story he was about to tell, it would suck. "Go ahead." Doubt was clear as day in his voice, but he didn't shy away from hearing Tate out. He'd promised to be a safe space for the other man, so he worked to keep from judging before he knew anything. He slipped his hands under Tate's shirt, splaying his fingers across those delicious abs. The warmth of Tate's skin grounded him.

"I like your hands on me."

"Good." He smiled as he stroked all over Tate's torso. "Then I'll keep touching as long as you start talking."

Tate grimaced. "Okay, um… where to start? I guess at the beginning." His mouth turned down. "Every summer since we were kids, Randy and I, along with our friends, uh, went to the county fair together."

The county fair. *Oh God.* Liam's hands stilled. He stared down at Tate with dread creeping down his spine.

*Stop talking.*

He couldn't speak.

Tate looked everywhere around the apartment but at Liam. "My dad was long gone by the time I could talk in full sentences, and my mom, well, you've heard a bit about her, so as far back as I can remember, Randy and I walked there ourselves. Sometimes with our friends, sometimes alone. The summer I turned fifteen,"—*Fifteen. I can't breathe.*—"Randy couldn't wait to get there because, uh, Whit, his now wife, had promised him a BJ if he got to her before another, Daryl of all people."

He peeled his thick tongue from the roof of his mouth. "Wow, sounds like true love." He'd never know how he managed a joke despite the enormous weight crushing his chest.

Tate grunted. "Something like that. Anyway, he ran ahead, and I took my sweet time walking there. When I finally made it, I wandered around for a bit, looking for my crew." He stroked his thumb back and forth over Liam's thigh in a move that seemed more to soothe himself than anything else. "I didn't find them, but I saw this stage with dancers who looked like they were in high school."

Liam gasped. Memories of that performance swarmed into the forefront of his thoughts.

Swan Lake.

At the time, they'd all grumbled about performing Swan Lake in Swan, Oklahoma. How cheesy they thought it had been to match the ballet to the town. He'd played Prince Siegfried. And he'd loved every second of it. Until everything imploded.

"Uh, most of the dancers on stage were girls," Tate continued. "But there was this one guy who caught my attention and completely captivated me. I stopped looking for my friends and watched him. He was so hypnotizing I couldn't even breathe."

Liam's jaw hung open. Speaking of not breathing. He didn't dare inhale for fear of missing even one word of Tate's story.

Finally, Tate lifted his gaze to meet Liam's. Liam fell headfirst into the powerful emotions capturing him. Regret, suffering, longing. So many dominant emotions this poor man had no idea how to handle. "He was so beautiful, Luxe," he whispered. "I stood there watching him for what felt like hours. I couldn't tear myself away. I didn't want to."

"Tate…" He gripped the man's hands to keep them from diving through his hair again. They trembled slightly, stilling only when he squeezed Liam back.

"It was the first time I felt attracted to a guy. It was confusing. I didn't get it at first. Everything was too overwhelming, but I was so spellbound I couldn't stop staring or even be worried about what my feelings meant. I have no idea what ballet it was, but it was incredible."

"Swan Lake," he whispered.

Tate's half smile held a world of pain and sadness. "Fitting."

"Yeah."

"Eventually, my friends caught up with me while I was standing there gawking. I played it off but still got all sorts of shit from them. Why the hell was I watching? Did I have a thing for girls in tutus? What was with the male dancer? A fairy, they called him over and over."

"Fairy," Liam said with a roll of his eyes and as much haughtiness in his tone as he could muster. "I was an elegant swan, not a flitting fairy." No point in pretending they were talking about anyone else.

"Yeah." Tate let go of his hands and reached up to cup Liam's face. "Prettiest swan there ever was."

*This man…*

He couldn't keep from nuzzling his cheek against that coarse palm.

"Uh, anyway, we hung out for a while and did the usual fair shit. I stopped to take a leak before we left, and when I came out of the bathroom, I couldn't find anyone. At first, I thought they ditched me, but then I heard what sounded like a fight."

*Oh God, here it comes.*

Liam couldn't keep his eyes from filling with tears as traumatic memories he'd worked so hard to leave in the past came flooding back. He sucked in a stunted breath and blinked as fast as he could.

"Want me to stop?" Tate ran his hands up and down Liam's thighs. The man had a lucrative career as a masseuse if he ever wanted a change.

179

"No," he whispered, shaking his head. "I want to hear it all." He had to hear it all. He tried to focus on the feel of those warm, strong hands instead of his turbulent emotions.

With their eyes locked, Tate continued, "I followed the sounds around the back of a trailer and found Randy and Daryl watching someone taking a serious beating. It only took me a second to recognize the victim was the dancer I'd watched earlier."

*Yes, he was.*

"I lost it. I didn't know who had attacked him, but I knew why, and I lost my shit."

He didn't need to close his eyes to conjure clear images of that night. "They wore ball caps and bandanas over their faces," he whispered. "I tried to grab one guy's bandana so I could see his face, but I was in too much pain. All I could do was curl in a ball and try to protect my vital organs. 'Fairies didn't belong in our town.' That's what they'd said before they knocked me down. I told them they were as stupid as they were ugly if they couldn't tell the difference between a fairy and a swan." Maybe someday he would chuckle at the memory of that smartass quip, but the memory of the punch that followed his bold statement ensured that day hadn't come yet.

"Jesus, Luxe, you've got balls."

Liam shrugged.

"You'd been so perfect on that stage," Tate said, seeming unaware he'd started talking about Liam directly instead of the anonymous dancer. "I couldn't... I couldn't stand to see someone hurting you."

Tears spilled out of Liam's eyes. "You yelled. Screamed for them to stop."

Nodding, Tate said, "They didn't listen, so I... I tried to stop them."

It was the most horrible night of his life, and Tate had been there. He'd been Liam's savior. Whatever perceived wrongdoing Tate punished himself for, it wasn't necessary. He had been the only person to stand up for a beaten gay kid, the only one to help.

"You saved my life, Tate." He inched his hands back under Tate's shirt and resumed touching as much skin as he could reach. "It was bad. The doctors told me if it had gone on much longer, I'd have suffered internal bleeding and possibly died."

Tate shook his head. "I didn't do shit. They were bigger, and there were two of 'em. I got my ass handed to me and then fled like a coward, like the rest of them, when the cops got close."

Was that how he viewed it? For years, Liam had wondered about his mystery protector. Little did he know the brave man had been right in front of him for weeks. "No, Tate," he said, withdrawing his hands so he could cup the man's face between his palms. "You took the attention away from me without thought for your own safety. I was able to breathe and hold on until the security guard showed up and called an ambulance." His voice caught. "I thought I was going to die that night. And then there you were, and I had hope."

"That was the night I realized exactly what would happen to me if I was gay." Tate's voice took on a faraway tone as though he'd gotten lost in the painful memories. "I ran away so fast and hard I eventually collapsed. I puked my guts up in a cornfield, just fucking *knowing* I could not be gay. I said it over and over. 'I am not gay. I am not gay.'"

The tiny fraction of Liam's heart not destroyed by this story splintered, joining the rest in a mess of broken pieces. "Tate, I'm so sorry."

"I'm gay, Luxe."

Liam smiled, a real one this time. "I know, baby. And I am so lucky that you are."

They kissed. It was slow, sweet, and delicious, like a velvety red wine. Neither rushed to get naked or raced to get off. They explored each other's mouths with lips, tongues, and teeth while their hands roamed for what felt like hours. Liam slid his hands back under Tate's shirt, needing to feel his warm skin. He ran his thumbs over the man's nipples as he licked into his mouth.

Tate moaned a slow, sensual sound that had Liam shivering in his lap.

"Love your hands on me," Tate whispered. "Love your mouth. I'm fucking obsessed." He nipped Liam's lower lip as his hips made a slow roll, rocking their erections together."

"God, same," Liam chased those lips until he got his tongue back in Tate's mouth. He loved the feel of them sliding against each other in an unhurried yet playful manner.

"I want to taste more of you, Luxe. I want your cock in my mouth. Can I suck you?"

Liam groaned. "Always." Then jutted his lip out in an overdramatic pout. "But I wanted to suck you."

"Me first." Tate grabbed his ass and squeezed until Liam was grinding on him.

"Or…" he whispered in Tate's ear, "… we could do it at the same time."

"Yes. That. Oh, fuck yes. Let's do that."

"Glad you like my idea." As Liam scrambled off his lap, Tate went to work, tearing his own clothes off. Within seconds, he was naked and sprawled on the couch with his hard cock pointing straight out as though trying to reach for Liam. "Damn, you are one sexy bastard. All those muscles. Mmm." He licked his lips as he imagined repeatedly running his tongue up and down over those abs until he got his fill. Another time.

"Why the fuck are you still dressed, Luxe?" Tate asked as

he played with the head of his cock.

"I got caught up in the show." Instead of getting naked as fast as possible as Tate did, he took his sweet time peeling himself out of his tight dance clothes.

"Are you trying to fucking kill me?"

"No," he said with a sly grin. But I am trying to make you sweat a bit."

"I'm drenched." He shifted until he was lying on his back on the couch. "Get those goddamn tights off and sit your pretty ass on my face before I'm covered in my own cum."

"Well, since you said my ass was pretty…" He finished undressing much quicker. His cock was so damn hard it bobbed as he closed the distance to the couch.

"Everything about you is pretty."

"Yeah?" Liam couldn't help himself and took his hands on a slow journey down the front of his body, loving the way Tate practically drooled as he watched.

"Hell yes. So damn smooth. I love your body. You're so muscular but not bulky like me. So sleek. Yeah, that's the word. Sleek and pretty."

Liam preened.

"You're such a praise slut," Tate said with a laugh.

"Hmm, I think you might be right. Hearing you call me pretty makes me want to do all sorts of nasty things to you." He swung a leg onto the couch behind Tate's head, then settled the other near the edge. His ass and balls hovered directly over Tate's face.

"Goddamn, that's a view."

"Tell me about it." The unobstructed landscape of Tate's magnificent body lay before him—rippling abs, a few tattoos, and miles of tanned skin culminating in a long, thick cock that was all his for the night.

Strong hands gripped his ass, parting his cheeks as a warm tongue licked over his ball sack. Liam hissed. "Yes."

He leaned forward, giving Tate closer access to his balls, then licked across the top of Tate's cock, gathering a dribble of precum. The salty burst of flavor had him moaning like he'd tasted his favorite treat.

Who was he kidding? Tate's cock was by far his favorite treat.

Tate continued to tease Liam with licks and sucks to his balls, leaving his cock untouched and aching. He got his revenge by sucking the head of Tate's dick into his mouth, playing with it while not allowing him any deeper.

"Jesus, Luxe, your cock is drooling all over my goddamn chest."

"That's cuz you won't suck it, you sadist," Liam snapped, making Tate howl with laughter.

"Oh yeah?" he said, still chuckling. "Well, what's with you just tonguing my tip like I'm a damn lollipop?"

"Revenge," Liam said with a dark snicker. "I... oh shit."

White hot suction enveloped his entire cock as Tate swallowed him to the root. Liam's entire body convulsed from extreme pleasure.

"Now we're talking," he muttered before mirroring Tate's action and inhaling his dick. Was it normal how much he loved having a mouth full of cock?

*Who cares?*

They didn't speak again, too focused on driving each other crazy. Every erotic sound and thrust of Tate's hips had him spiraling toward orgasm as much as the suction on his cock. And when Tate finally unloaded down his throat, Liam swallowed every drop like a parched man in the desert as his savior's orgasm triggered his own.

He had one final thought before his brain melted out through his dick.

*I will do anything I have to in order to keep this man.*

## Chapter Nineteen

Things changed after the night of Liam's grand opening. First off, Liam's schedule went from busy to insanity as his studio took off without needing training wheels. Every class he offered had a waitlist, and every mom in town was abuzz with how much they loved the new dance teacher. Tate heard some shit talk and slurs over the rainbow flag sticker on the entrance door as well, but in general, Liam was being accepted in town much better than Tate had feared.

Tate felt himself changing as well. Not overnight, but in small increments that moved him toward a life he never dared to hope for but wanted now. No, he wasn't ready to sit on a float in a gay pride parade, but he no longer hid his friendship with Liam. They weren't making out in public or even announcing their relationship, but they'd sat together at the coffee shop on a number of occasions when they *happened* to show up around the same time. They'd met for a drink one night, just two guys chilling after work. Tate had even taken him fishing in the creek once. That time, they'd been alone and probably scared a few fish for life with their inability to keep their hands off each other, but people in town knew they'd gone together since they rode to the bait shop in Tate's car.

So far, Randy hadn't given him any shit, but it was

coming. He could feel the curious stares and heavy tension at work and around the trailer park. He'd decided to get it the hell over with, so he'd accepted Randy's invitation to lunch at the diner between jobs today. Of course, he was the first to arrive.

The place had seen better days, for sure, with maroon vinyl seats that had cracks and exposed foam cushions. The floor always seemed just shy of sticky, and fewer than half the tableside jukeboxes worked. Most stole patrons' quarters while management claimed there was no possible way to open them up without the 'jukebox representative' who always happened to be scheduled the next day.

Such bullshit.

Still, Tate had practically lived at the diner as a kid, with his mom working there since she turned fourteen. The place held a nostalgia that nowhere else did.

Millie, a waitress he'd known since birth, sat him at his favorite booth. "You need a menu, kid?" She'd been calling him kid for the past twenty-three years.

"Nah." He knew it like the back of his hand. "Just waiting on Rand and Daryl."

"Okay, sugar. I'll get you some coffee while you wait."

"Thanks, Miss Millie." She turned to leave, but Tate stopped her with a, "Oh, hey, my momma come in for her shift this morning?"

"She sure did, sugar. Just left about twenty minutes ago."

Thank God. At least today had that going for it.

The bell above the door jangled, and Tate glanced up to see the second good omen of the day. The best part of any day. Liam strode in with a smile on his face. He had the same painted sleeveless tops he danced in but, thankfully, had slipped a pair of loose shorts over his dance tights. He spoke to the waitress at the hostess stand, indicating he had a to-go order to pick up from the counter. As he spoke, he noticed

Tate sitting there, and his entire face lit up like a damn holiday tree.

Instead of going to the counter, he walked straight to Tate's table and slid into the booth opposite him. Tate hated himself for the momentary flicker of nerves or the impulse to glance around and see who might be watching, but he resisted the urge and counted it a win.

"Well, hey there, handsome," Liam said in a low voice. "Fancy meeting you here."

"Damn, Luxe, why you gotta go around town wearing those tight-as-fuck shirts. They might give the wrong kinda man some nasty ideas."

He batted his eyelashes. "What? This old thang?" he drawled in an exaggerated Southern accent before bursting into giggles. "I'm between classes and just ran to grab some lunch. Dancing all day works up an appetite."

"Eat up, Luxe. You're gonna need some energy for tonight." He winked.

"I sure do enjoy flirty Tate," Liam said with a sly grin. "Glad he's coming out to play more and more."

The bell jangled again, and in strutted Randy, followed by Daryl. Tate couldn't help how his spine snapped straight and his breath caught. Fight or flight tried to kick in, but he focused on Liam's face instead of his internal freakout.

"I'll go," Liam said as he started to scoot out of the bench.

"No. Don't. It's okay." He wanted to reach across the table and take Liam's hand but hadn't reached that level of bravery yet.

"You sure?" Liam cast a sideways glance at Dumb and Dumber making their way over.

He nodded as Randy approached with a raised eyebrow and sneer like he'd smelled something rotten. "So, what? You're like buddies now?"

"Yeah, butt buddies," Daryl said, snickering.

Tate narrowed his eyes, but Liam was quick as hell with the comebacks. He rolled his eyes and snorted. "Wow, Daryl, that was super original. You think of that insult all on your own, or did a second grader teach it to you?"

"Shut the fuck up, you little—"

"Enough, Daryl," Tate barked. "And yes, Randy, we're friends. Deal with it."

The way Liam beamed made him feel ten feet tall.

"Shit, T, you don't gotta take in every stray you meet. Sometimes they're the kinda creature that'll hump your leg if you're not careful."

"Randy, shut your fucking mouth."

Liam sighed. "Look, Randy," he said with all the arrogance of someone who knew how much they had to offer. "What if I promise to never ever, not even once, not even in jest… that means as a joke, in case you didn't know…"

Tate snorted. God, this man made him horny as hell. The way he put Randy in his place made Tate want to dive across the table and kiss the hell out of him.

"What if I promise to never come close to hitting on you? Would that help you feel more comfortable around me?"

He shifted as though considering it.

"No," Daryl mumbled. "Answer's still no."

"Here's the thing, boys, I have a specific type of man I like to fuck."

They both turned a little green.

"And I promise you what I want in my bed is not a small-minded, pot-bellied redneck. So, trust me when I tell you, you two are very safe from all my evil advances." He wiggled his fingers as though casting a spell on them.

Randy and Daryl stood there, jaws on the floor like two gaping fly traps. It took everything in Tate not to reach out and take that kiss Liam was clearly begging for.

"Now, if you gentlemen will excuse me, I think I'll wait for my food at the counter and leave you to belch and talk about tits or whatever it is you uber-masculine men do." He winked at Tate, then climbed out of the booth with the grace of a prince and practically sashayed toward the counter.

Tate swiped a thumb across his lower lip to make sure he wasn't drooling.

Eventually, Randy and Daryl scooped their jaws off the floor. Randy slid into the booth next to Tate while Daryl took the seat Liam vacated. "This shit is getting out of control," Daryl grumbled.

"For fucking real," Randy added with a disgusted grunt. "This guy's got half the town eating out of his fucking hand. If we're not careful, there'll be more like 'im movin' here."

"So what the fuck do we do about it?" Daryl asked.

Tate rolled his eyes. "Hmm, considering it's twenty-twenty-four and you two idiots don't want to be arrested for a hate crime, not to mention you're stupid as fuck, I say you learn to live with it." He folded his arms across his chest and stared Daryl down with his most severe glare. The guy might flap his mouth like a runaway bull, but he didn't have the stones to do shit, thank God.

Ducky, on the other hand. As though his thinking conjured the scumbag from thin air, the bell jangled, and in walked Swan's most recent parolee. What the hell he had to swagger about, given he'd been in prison only a week before, Tate would never know, but he sauntered in like he owned the damn diner.

Unfortunately, it was the same moment Liam collected his to-go container and started for the exit.

Panic clawed at Tate's chest. "Shit," he muttered. "Rand, let me out," he said, tapping his brother's arm with the back of his hand.

"What? Why? You gotta piss or something?" He followed Tate's gaze, and a gleeful smirk crossed his face. "Hell no. I ain't movin'. That little fucker's got a mouth on him. Let him try it out on Duck."

Daryl whipped around. "Woo-hoo, this is gonna be fucking good."

He shoved his brother hard. "I said get the fuck out of my way, Randy."

Randy managed to grab the table before he hit the grimy floor. "Why the fuck do you give a shit about that fa—"

Tate's expression must have been fierce enough to keep Randy from uttering the slur. Either that or his brother remembered he was in public, and the entire world didn't think as he did, but that was too advanced for a Neanderthal like him, so it was probably the first thing.

Tate clenched his fists and spoke through clenched teeth while keeping one eye on Liam. "Swear to Christ, Randy, if you don't get the fuck outta this booth and let me pass, I'll stomp the hell all over your ass to get out."

"Fine, but don't expect me to jump in and help your stupid ass," he muttered. Randy scooted out of the booth and stood to allow Tate to pass. Tate followed so close behind his brother that he barreled into him as he rushed to get to Liam.

"Fuck's sake, T," Randy grumbled.

"What a stupid shit," Daryl said to his back.

He reached Liam just as Ducky stepped back to block the exit. He folded his beefy arms covered in new and shitty prison tats across his chest and glared down at Liam as though the man was shit on his shoe.

"Well, who do we have here? You must be that new dance teacher I keep hearing about. The one who just moved to town and wants to teach the kids all about being a gay."

"Excuse me," Liam said with an edge to his voice. "Just need to get to the exit."

Ducky glanced over Liam's shoulder. "Ah, Tate, defender of all the queers. You here to make sure I don't make this one cry?"

"Just let 'im pass, Duck. No need to cause a scene in the diner. You know Millie will whip your ass if you do." She'd whip Tate's, too, if he threw the first punch, though she seemed to like Liam, so maybe she'd forgive him for taking out a few of Ducky's teeth in her diner.

Liam propped a hand on his hip. "Oh, you're Ducky," he said with a tone of understanding.

Shit, here it comes. He put a hand on Liam's lower back, trying to convey with touch how quickly this could turn dangerous.

"Look, I get it," Liam said with a shrug. "You were in prison for a while, and it's weird being out. You miss being someone's bitch." He pressed a hand to his chest with a dramatic flair. "I'm honored you thought of me, really, I am, but like I told your brother over there, you're just not my type."

Ducky lunged forward. "You fucking—"

Tate managed to grab Liam and shove him behind his back as Millie shouted, "Donald Hayes, don't you dare." She shuffled over, shaking her finger at him like he was a naughty six-year-old instead of a full-grown man about to attack another. "I will not have any of that hatred in my diner, you hear me?"

His eyes narrowed, and he shot daggers at Tate, but even he wasn't stupid enough to cross Millie. "Yes, ma'am," he muttered.

"Now you got two choices. You can sit down and enjoy a nice meal with your people, or you can get the hell out and let my customers eat in peace."

"I'm hungry as hell, Miss Millie, I'll sit," he grumbled.

Ducky made sure to bump both Tate and Liam with his shoulder as he passed by, muttering something to Liam that Tate couldn't make out.

Liam opened his mouth, no doubt to further slice Ducky to ribbons with his razor-sharp tongue, but Tate pulled him back. He held his upper arm gently, stroking the skin with his thumb hidden up Liam's sleeve. "He's a violent prick," he muttered too low for anyone but Liam to hear. "Millie's warning will only go so far. Walk out the door, Luxe."

The use of his nickname seemed to grab Liam's attention. He nodded once and sent Tate a look that said they'd be talking about this later before slipping out the door.

Every instinct Tate had screamed at him to follow Liam. To make sure he wasn't too shaken and to drag him somewhere private so he could get his hands and mouth on the man to convince himself Liam wasn't too rattled. But it would lead to questions he wasn't ready to answer and possibly cause more trouble for Liam.

So, he turned back to the table he'd rather break his thumbs than return to.

"Better watch your fucking step, T," Ducky said as he reached the table. "You think you're a big shit, trying to be an ally or whatever the fuck, but all you're doing is helping poison our town."

"Actually, Duck, I'm just grabbing my stuff and going. Some of us gotta work today." He reached across Randy and grabbed his cell and keys from the table. Without a goodbye, he turned his back on the people he'd known his whole life and strode toward the exit, head high, trying to ignore the curious stares from onlookers.

"Watch your step, T," Ducky called out again before he shoved the door open.

Fuck him and fuck the others too.

Tate stepped outside, inhaling the fresh summer air. Liam had taken off already, and Tate only had twenty minutes before he had to return to the job site. There wasn't enough time to swing by the studio. He'd have to settle for reminding himself Liam was a grown-ass man who could take care of himself.

And he'd be seeing him later that night, where he could spend hours checking over every delicious inch of the man. Maybe with his tongue to be extra certain he was okay.

His phone chirped, and he glanced at it to find a text from the man who'd invaded his brain.

**Stop worrying about me. I'm good.**

A smile curled his lips as another text chirped.

**So fucking proud of you, Tate.**

*Well, damn.*

## Chapter Twenty

Liam locked the studio door behind him, then started the quick quarter-mile walk to the bakery down the street. Tate had mentioned last week that apple pie with a giant scoop of vanilla ice cream was his favorite dessert. Tonight, Liam planned to surprise him with exactly that. He picked up ice cream earlier in the day, and since he didn't have the skills or space to bake a pie, he ordered one from the local bakery.

His calves twinged as he walked, sore from the six classes he'd taught that day. Thank God he had three interviews set up next week for additional teachers. He was sore from head to toe, not just his legs. Over the last week, he'd ramped up his workouts to make sure he was in the best shape to teach his students, and now he was paying for the few months he'd taken off to move and set up his studio.

Then there was the ache in his ass. The one that had him grinning like a fool as he remembered the furious way Tate had taken him last night. They'd both been so busy they hadn't seen each other for a few days, and, apparently, that was too long for Tate. He'd been like a man possessed from the moment he walked into Liam's apartment.

He shivered at the memory of Tate tearing off his clothes and fucking him right there on the floor by the door.

God, it had been good.

Liam glanced around. If he wasn't careful, he'd be walking down Main Street with a tent in his shorts like some kind of pervert. Just what he needed when a third of the town already saw him as a deviant.

About halfway to the bakery, he spotted a woman walking —stumbling—on the sidewalk toward him.

He frowned but continued moving forward. After a few seconds, she dropped to her knees and vomited in the grass on the side of the road.

"Oh crap." Liam rushed toward her. "Ma'am? Do you need some help?" He stood over her as she heaved and unloaded her stomach onto the ground.

*Gross.*

When she finished, she stared up at him with dilated pupils and bloodshot whites of her eyes.

The sour stench was hard to ignore, but he tried his best. "Here," he said, reaching for the small backpack containing his phone, wallet, and water bottle. Grabbing the water, he crouched and held it out to her after uncapping it. "I haven't had any yet. Please take it."

"Twenty bucks," she slurred as she took the bottle from him. Her unsteady hands caused some to slosh over the rim of the plastic bottle.

"Excuse me?"

"You want me to suck your dick? It'll cost you twenty bucks."

"Oh, no. No, that's not… I just wanted to make sure you're okay. I don't want… anything else." Was she insane? She'd just thrown up all over the side of the road, and now she was propositioning him?

"Huh. You that new dance teacher?" Her stringy blonde hair needed to be washed at least a day ago. Despite being mid-summer, her skin was sickly pale, and her eyes had heavy purple rings beneath them.

"I am. My name is Liam."

She guzzled half the bottle of water, swaying as she tipped her head back. Liam reached out and caught her shoulder so she wouldn't fall over.

"I got a boy 'bout your age."

It looked like they were having a full-blown conversation now. "Oh yeah?" he said as he sat on the sidewalk next to her, careful to avoid where she'd gotten sick.

"Yep. Name's Tate. You know 'im?"

Oh shit. His heart sank. This mess of a woman was Tate's mother? There was no way in hell he could leave her here wasted on the side of the road, soliciting random men for twenty freaking dollars.

"I do know him. He's a... friend."

"Mmm, I bet he is."

*What?* He'd be ignoring that comment.

"Hey..." He climbed to his feet. "How about I take you home? My car is just down the road, and I know Tate would feel better if you were home so you could get some rest."

"You got any booze?"

He had wine at home, but there was no way he'd be giving her any. She reeked of alcohol, and he wasn't convinced it was the only substance in her system. "Sorry, fresh out. Here, let me help you up." He held out a hand, which she took. Hauling her to her feet was no harder than if she'd been a child. This woman needed to gain some serious weight.

"Whoa." She lilted to the right with a cackle.

"Easy there." Liam slipped a hand around her slender waist. "Lean on me if you need to."

The short distance back to the studio took twice as long as it should have since Tate's mother could barely stand. Two cars honked as they whizzed by, and one person leaned a head out the window to shout something about junkies.

Lovely people.

"Okay, here we go." He propped her against the car as he opened the passenger door. She practically fell in ass first. Liam had to lift her legs to turn her into the car.

"Remind me to give you a blowie as a thank you."

His stomach turned. Poor Tate.

"I'm gay, ma'am. Sorry, but the offer's wasted on me." Even if he was the straightest man in the world, he'd never take her up on it.

"Oh. I could peg ya. You want that?"

"Uh, no, thank you. I'm good," he said, nearly choking on the words. "Let's just get you home so you can get some rest." After making sure her limbs were out of the way, he shut the door and jogged to the driver's side. "I'm going to need you to direct me where to go, okay?" he said as he started the car.

Her head lolled his way. "Uh-huh. How do you know Tate?"

*Tate.* Shit, he should probably text him and let him know what was happening. He grabbed his phone and shot off a quick text, letting Tate know he'd be taking his inebriated mother to their trailer. "Uh, he did some tile work at my dance studio."

"He's a good boy."

"The best," he said as a lump lodged in his throat. "So where are we going?" he asked after swallowing.

Thankfully, she managed to navigate them to the trailer park without issue. Liam soaked in his surroundings as they drove through the park. Some trailers seemed nice enough, well-maintained, and cared for. Others had been neglected and sat dilapidated on their lots. Tate's seemed somewhere in the middle, though a bit closer to the cared-for side.

"Park anywhere," she said, waving a hand. Before he'd managed to kill the engine, she was out of the car and stumbling toward the few steps leading up to the door.

"You good, Marissa?" A woman's voice sounded from across the dirt road.

"Get off my ass, Whit. This nice boy's just taking me home."

Whitney. Wasn't that Randy's wife? God, hopefully, she wouldn't think this was something it wasn't.

He followed her up the steps and into the trailer. Before disappearing inside with her, he cast a glance over his shoulder and saw Whitney frowning at them with a wrinkled brow.

This was the first time he'd been in Tate's space, and he'd be lying if he said he wasn't curious as hell. He wanted to explore every inch of the place and see what else he could learn about the man he'd become smitten with, but he had a very intoxicated woman to contend with.

"I need a drink," she mumbled as she staggered toward the refrigerator.

"Um." Liam gently cupped her shoulders and steered her away. "How about you take a nap first? Which way is your room?"

Huffing like a disappointed child who'd just been told no, she turned toward a small hallway. "It's down here." She bounced off the wall twice but managed to make it into her room without incident. A queen-size mattress and box spring were shoved in one corner without a bedframe or headboard. There wasn't room for much else besides the dark wood dresser. Piles of clothes were strewn around, and a crooked flower painting hung on the wall with a long cobweb dangling from one corner.

Marissa walked straight to her bed and fell face-first onto the mattress without taking off her shoes or setting down her cross-body purse.

Liam considered trying to help her remove them, but it seemed unnecessary. Better to leave well enough alone.

"Marissa, is there a small trash can I could leave by the bed in case you get sick again?"

The only response he received was the soft sound of breathing. He took a moment to locate a tiny bathroom and retrieved the trash can, leaving it near her head. Hopefully, she wouldn't need it, but better safe than sorry.

He glanced around with a sigh and an ache in his chest before making his way out of the room. Just as he was leaving, he heard a mumbled, "Tell Tate I'm sorry. He worries."

"I will," he whispered in response, though she seemed to fall right back to sleep.

With a heavy heart, he strode back down the hall toward the kitchen. The other hallway opposite Marissa's room must lead to Tate's room. His curiosity was at an all-time high, but he'd never invade Tate's privacy by snooping without permission. Instead, he reached for his pocket to text the man and let him know Marissa was safe and sound only to come up empty.

"Right," he muttered. "It's still in the car."

The door to the trailer flew open, and Liam jumped back about a foot. "Holy shit!" he yelped as his hand went to his racing heart.

Tate stood in the doorway wild-eyed and frantic. "Luxe?"

"Yeah, it's me. Your mom's okay," he said as he rushed over to his man. "I got her settled. She's sleeping it off."

As soon as he reached Tate, the man pulled him into a bone-crushing embrace. "Fuck, I was freakin' out." He buried his face in Liam's neck. "Are you okay? Did she... did she try anything?"

God, he hated to upset Tate with the things his mother propositioned, so he said, "Nothing I couldn't handle. I saw her walking, and she got sick on the side of the road. When she mentioned her son named Tate, I knew I had to help."

"I don't deserve someone as good as you," Tate mumbled into his neck.

"Hey." Liam grabbed a handful of hair at the back of Tate's neck and tugged. When Tate lifted his head, Liam said, "I do not want to hear that horseshit, okay?"

Tate nodded. "Thank you."

"My pleasure. Actually, if you think about it, I kinda lucked out. I get to see you earlier than I thought today."

Tate didn't take the bait and fire back with a sassy quip as he'd hoped. Instead, he stared deep into Liam's eyes, wildfire in his gaze. "Fuck, Luxe, I want you. I want you all the damn time."

"You have me, Tate." Always. Anytime.

They kissed. It started out soft and gentle, a comfort to battle the stress of the afternoon, but it quickly turned heated. Tate's hands went to his ass, squeezing and lifting. Liam got the message. He jumped up and wrapped his legs around Tate's waist, locking his ankles behind Tate's back. All that strength was sexy as hell. Tate stalked across the small kitchen until he could press Liam against the refrigerator.

"I need to fuck you," Tate growled in his ear.

"I'd kick your ass if you didn't." They both laughed, then went back to devouring each other. Once his head was spinning and his dick hard as stone, Liam ripped his mouth away. "Take me to your—"

"Tate?" The door flew open so hard it banged against the wall. "Whit said Mom's got some dude ov... oh fuck no!"

They froze.

Their gazes locked, and Liam saw resignation in Tate's. There'd be no getting out of this one. No zipping up and pretending nothing happened. Liam swallowed hard and tried to prepare himself for the fallout—for Tate to wall himself off and go cold.

But instead, he leaned in and pressed the softest kiss to

Liam's lips. "I'm sorry," he whispered.

"I knew it," Randy shouted as Liam unwound himself from Tate's body. "I fucking knew it."

His feet hit the floor, and Tate made sure he was steady before turning to face his brother.

Tate's Adam's apple bobbed as he swallowed. "Randy, take a fucking breath," he said, holding up his hands.

"Goddammit, I fucking knew some shady shit was going on between you two." Randy spun around and stomped out of the trailer, shouting and cursing the whole way.

"Randy, calm the fuck down." Tate marched after his brother with Liam hot on his heels.

Once outside, Randy paced a dusty strip across the dirt road, jamming a hand through his hair the same way Tate did when frustrated. He looked up and speared Liam with a glare that had his blood running cold. This was what Tate had warned him about.

What he'd feared all along.

"What the fuck have you done to him?" Randy's ice-cold tone would have penetrated six layers of snow gear.

"Randy, he didn't do a goddamn thing," Tate said, extending an arm in front of Liam like people do when they hit the brakes too hard and send their passenger careening forward.

"What the fuck have you done to my brother," Randy screamed at the top of his lungs as he charged toward Liam.

Liam didn't have time to react. No time to feel fear or decide whether he should run or fight. Tate dove between them, stopping Randy before he could touch Liam. "Don't you fucking touch him." He managed to coral Randy back a dozen or so steps.

"He's trying to turn you gay. You're trying to turn my brother fucking gay," he shouted over Tate's shoulder. They were nearly the same height, and Randy had a clear view of

Liam over his brother's shoulder.

Liam had no idea what to do or say. His normal cutting tongue and snarky comebacks wouldn't work here. His heart was so heavy for Tate, and his head spun from the whiplash of what had happened over the last half hour.

Randy continued to scream and rant as he tried to get around Tate.

"For fuck's sake, Randy," Tate eventually yelled back in his brother's face. "He can't fucking *turn me*. I've known I was gay since I was fifteen-fucking-years old."

Randy went eerily still. "What?" he whispered, stepping away from his brother.

Liam watched, helpless and heartsick. A few trailer doors opened, and heads popped out, but conflict must be common around here because he caught a few eye rolls, and then the observers disappeared back into their homes.

"Liam didn't turn me gay," he said in a more level tone. "I've been fucking guys since long before I met Liam."

"What the fuck?" Randy's fist came from nowhere, ramming into Tate's face with so much force that Tate stumbled back.

"Stop!" Liam rushed forward.

"Stay back, Luxe."

"Luxe?" Randy spat. "You have a fucking pet name for this queer?"

"Randy, I'm queer." Tate's voice held so much resignation and exhaustion that it seemed as though fighting this war for so many years had finally caught up to him.

"No, you're fucking not. This is a goddamn prank." He threw another punch, catching Tate's chin.

Liam winced. Memories of when he'd been on the receiving end of granite fists tried to worm their way past his defenses, but he shoved them aside to focus on Tate. Tonight would bring a nightmare for sure, but he'd deal with that shit when it happened.

"Fight me like a man, you pussy!"

Shaking his head, Tate held his arms out to his sides. "Hit me all you want, Randy. I won't fight you."

"Goddamn right, I'll hit you." The next punch landed on Tate's nose. Blood sprayed onto the dirt.

"That's enough," Liam shouted. "Fucking stop it, Randy. He's your brother."

Another car pulled up, and Daryl hopped out with a woman Liam had never seen. "What the fuck is going on?"

"Just caught Tate here messing around with the gay. They were practically fucking in the goddamn kitchen."

If the situation weren't so volatile, Liam would have snorted and rolled his eyes. Maybe Randy didn't know how to fuck because all their clothes had been on and their cocks hidden.

"You ain't fucking serious." Spit flew from Daryl's mouth as he yelled.

Randy swung again, connecting with Tate's chin. This punch knocked him to the ground.

Enough was enough.

Liam ran to his car, where he kept pepper spray and a taser. After retrieving them from the glove box, he sprinted back to the fight and jumped between Randy and Tate.

"Luxe, get the fuck in the car," Tate yelled, but it sounded nasal and all wrong.

He activated the taser. "Don't fucking touch him again," he growled in a sinister voice he didn't know he was capable of making.

Randy lurched forward.

"Come at me, asshole. Tate might be too good of a man to hit you, but I have no problem making you jerk on the ground in a puddle of your own piss." Daryl started forward. "Don't do it." Liam swung the taser in Daryl's direction.

"Get the fuck outta here," Randy said. "And take that pussy with you." He spat toward his brother but, thankfully, was too far away from Tate to reach. Liam might have tasered his ass for the fun of it otherwise.

By now, Tate had climbed to his feet. Blood dripped down his chin and onto his shirt. One of his eyes was already swelling shut. Hopefully, his nose wasn't broken. "I'm okay, Luxe," he said before Liam could even ask.

Blinking away tears, Liam nodded. The entire afternoon was catching up to him, and he needed to get them the hell out of there so he could take care of Tate before he broke down. "Let's go."

They walked backward toward his car, unwilling to turn their backs on Randy or Daryl. As soon as they were seated inside, Liam locked the doors. Finally, he took a breath.

Tate stared at his brother through the windshield. Randy was having an animated conversation with Daryl, shouting, pacing, and flailing his arms. Tate's face remained expressionless.

"Tate?"

Finally, he turned to Liam. "Get us the fuck outta here."

*Gladly.*

# Chapter Twenty-One

They didn't speak as Liam exited the trailer park in a cloud of dust and gravel spray. Tate stared out the window, unseeing as familiar sights whizzed by. His face hurt, and the blood drying on his neck itched, but the rest of him felt numb.

Tonight, the thing he'd spent his entire life terrified of happened, and he didn't know what the hell to do next. Or how to process it. Randy reacted as expected, with violence and hatred. Shouldn't he feel *something*? Instead, his insides were empty.

Beside him, Liam practically vibrated with rage. He didn't need to look at the man who'd become the center of his world to know how angry Liam was on Tate's behalf. The whole car trembled with it.

He listened as Liam inhaled and exhaled with slow, measured breaths over and over. After the fifth round, a soft hand wrapped around Tate's where it rested on the center console.

Finally, he started to feel. First, the warmth and softness of Liam's hand, but then a barrage of complicated emotions pummeled him at once. He didn't turn to look at Liam—couldn't without cracking under the weight of his emotions. So, he flipped his palm up and curled it around Liam's, squeezing so hard it surprised him the other man didn't protest.

Only when Liam pulled his car around the back of the dance studio and parked did he let go. Tate followed his lead, climbing out of the car with lead-laden legs. The air felt thick and sticky like he was moving through honey.

Liam hurried around the car and immediately took his hand again. As soon as they were rejoined, Tate exhaled as though he needed Liam's touch to continue breathing. Together, they climbed the long staircase to Liam's small apartment. Each step took ten times more energy than usual. The cotton ball that had replaced his brain allowed Liam to lead him to the door.

A white bakery box with a sticky note sat by the door. Liam bent down and picked it up one-handed. "Sometimes there are benefits to living in a small town," he muttered, speaking for the first time since they left the trailer park.

Tate couldn't muster the energy to ask what he meant.

After unlocking the door, Liam guided him inside. He set the box on the table and then faced Tate. "I ordered an apple pie from the bakery down the street for tonight. I was on my way to pick it up when I ran into your mom, so I never got it. Someone from the bakery dropped it off for me. Why don't you clean off your face and change your shirt? I think I have one of yours in my dresser." His cheeks pinked. "I might have stolen it when you were here last week. While you do that, I'll warm the pie, and then we can sit and eat."

*And talk.*

He didn't say it, but they had to talk about the shit show of the past hour.

There were so many things Tate wanted to say right then. He wanted to thank Liam, apologize, and explain that he'd understand if Liam wanted no part of Tate's life.

Mostly, he wanted to tell Liam he loved him because as he'd watched his brave dancer charge toward Randy with that taser, he'd realized the terrifying and intense emotion welling inside him was love.

But all he was capable of saying was, "Okay." It was the first word he'd uttered since they started driving, and it sounded raw and rough.

Liam nodded, all business, then gave him a gentle nudge toward the bathroom. "There's pain medicine under the sink."

He went, moving through the motions in a robotic, detached manner. The mirror showed a man with a swollen eye, puffy nose, and bruised cheek. Blood had dried in an uncomfortable crust on his chin, neck, and shirt. It wiped off easily with a wet cloth, and within ten minutes, he was clean, medicated, and wearing a fresh shirt, though no less fucked in the head.

When he stepped out of the bathroom, the sight that greeted him had him stopping in his tracks. Two plates with large slices of pie and heaping scoops of ice cream sat waiting on the tiny round table in Liam's kitchen. The lights were dimmed, and a few candles flickered, casting a cozy glow around the room. Soft music played in the background. Liam smiled at him as he walked two bottles of beer to the table.

Tate's favorite brand.

He blinked as a rush of emotion tried to find its way out of his eyes. The last time he could remember crying was when he'd been six and broke his arm falling out of a tree. No one was around to take him to the hospital, so he'd had to wait for hours to get help, crying much of the time. Randy called him a crybaby and laughed. He hadn't cried since. He didn't know how to let his feelings out in that way anymore.

"Come sit." Liam slid into a chair at the table, waiting for him. "The pie is warm, and the ice cream's cold."

"Thank you," he said, his throat tight as he strode across the room to take the other seat. The delicious aroma of cinnamon and sugar floated through the air, making his mouth water. "This, um… this is nice."

No one did things like this for him. Hell, it'd been a few years since anyone even got him a birthday cake.

Liam beamed. "It is, isn't it?" He scooped some pie and ice cream onto his spoon and held it halfway between them. "Cheers."

The playful move made Tate's lips twitch, which hurt more than he'd admit out loud. He followed suit, gathering some pie and tapping his spoon to Liam's. "Cheers."

Liam watched him as Tate ate the first bite. The warm pie, cool vanilla, and sugary goodness mixing in his mouth drew an involuntary groan. "This is so good," he said before swallowing.

"Excellent." Liam gobbled his own bite, moaning a porn-star-worthy hum of appreciation. "Heaven."

No, the pie was delicious, but heaven was the entire moment. Sitting there in the low light with the man he loved. The man who accepted him and hadn't run from an awful situation. Who wasn't making him talk about it yet because he knew Tate and could tell he wasn't ready. Heaven was touching Liam, sleeping beside him, and waking to him in the morning.

Christ, he'd gone sappy.

They ate in comfortable silence, and Tate's tension melted away with each bite. The pain medication kicked in as well. By the time Liam pushed his plate across the table with a groan, "Ugh, I can't eat another bite," Tate was able to smile without more discomfort than a minor ache.

"No worries, I'll take care of that for you." He used his spoon to pull the plate in front of him.

Liam chuckled. "Thank you for your sacrifice. Oh, this is a good song." He hopped up and began to dance to the upbeat pop song playing through a small speaker.

Tate couldn't have named the song or artist for all the money in the world, but he'd never complain about watching Liam dance. After polishing off the rest of Liam's pie, he settled back in the chair and watched the show.

As usual, Liam looked gorgeous as he lost himself in the music. This peppy song was far from his usual style, but movement and dance seemed to come so naturally to him that he could adapt to anything.

After a few moments, the song changed to a slow number. Liam glided over to the table. "This is *Make You Feel My Love* by Adele. It's a beautiful song. Dance with me." He held out a hand.

Tate huffed a laugh. "You know I don't dance, Luxe."

"Come on."

Why did that pout have to be so irresistible? "No fucking way."

"You danced with me at the club the first night we met." If his lip stuck out any farther, it'd hit the table.

"That was different. That was fast. And we mostly just humped each other on the dance floor."

Now Liam was laughing. He grabbed Tate's hand and tugged. "Come on, big guy. I'll lead. All you have to do is hold on to me and sway." He winked. "I think you can manage."

Tate allowed himself to be pulled from the chair and maneuvered into the middle of the den. "Fine, but don't blame me if I break your toes."

"I'm not worried. Now, hold my hand here and put your other arm around my waist," Liam instructed. When he did as ordered, Liam pulled him so close they were basically hugging. "Now, just move with me."

He tried, but he was big and clunky and definitely not built for slow dancing. "I feel stupid, Luxe," he mumbled as an awkward fish-out-of-water sensation claimed him.

"Shh. Listen to the words," Liam whispered.

Tate blew out a breath, shut his eyes, and tried. Liam had said the song was about all the ways Adele would show her man how much she loved him. Within thirty seconds, the poetic words slid beneath his skin and straight to his soul. He relaxed into Liam's hold and could suddenly move without bumbling.

He opened his eyes and found Liam staring deep into him as they swayed to the meaningful song. If this was dancing, he'd dance with Liam all day. The quiet, peace, and closeness to Liam soothed his wounded soul.

Cocooned in an almost dream-like state, Tate tried to convey with his eyes how much Liam meant to him. The rest of the world outside the small apartment could have evaporated for all he knew or cared. Everything he needed to survive was right here in his arms.

The song changed to another gentle tune, and Liam slowed them until they were still. He rose on his toes and kissed the puffy skin under Tate's eye with a tender brush of his lips.

Tate shut his eyes and tried to block another of those damn emotional surges. But this time, it didn't work. When he opened his eyes, he found Liam watching him with so much care in his gaze that he was finally able to speak. "It hurts," he whispered.

Yes, the black eye and busted nose hurt, but that wasn't what he meant.

"I know." Liam didn't need him to explain. He understood the pain Tate referred to came from the rejection and hatred of the people who were supposed to love him. It lived deep inside him, eating away at his heart. "Come here." Liam wrapped his strong dancer's arms around Tate and drew his head into the crook of his neck. "I'm sorry, baby," he whispered. "You deserve so much better. You are worth so much more."

Hot tears stung the inside of his eyelids, and this time, he knew he'd lose the battle to halt them. Liam had to feel the wetness dropping onto his skin, but he didn't comment on it and just tightened his hold. Tate let everything out. Every ounce of frustration, disappointment, fear, and sadness purged out of his soul and soaked onto Liam's shirt.

His man stood silent like the strongest pillar, keeping Tate from crumbling to the dust. How had he ever thought he'd go through life without feeling a connection like this?

When the tears finally dried up, the warm press of Liam's lips coasted up his neck. Goose bumps erupted all over his skin, and a shiver rippled through him. He turned his head and found Liam's mouth, stealing a deep, mind-melting kiss.

He unwound his arms from around Liam and gripped the man's head instead, pouring every ounce of desire and love he had into the kiss. Liam moaned when their tongues met. Tate didn't give him a second to process. He wanted Liam to be a whimpering mess, begging for him.

He kissed him with rough, aggressive strokes of his tongue that demanded a response. His injuries protested the pressure and movement, but Tate ignored it with ease. The pleasure of Liam's lips on his was worth any amount of pain.

"Jesus," Liam whispered against his mouth when he finally let them pause for air.

"I want you so fucking badly, Luxe," Tate said as he kissed him again.

"Take me, Tate. I'm yours."

He swallowed and leaned back a few inches. "Not this time. This time I…" Shit, nerves zinged through his blood. "I want you to fuck me."

Liam gasped, and his eyes widened larger than those plates of pie. "Tate, you're injured, and you don't have to prove anyth—"

"That's not what this is." He kissed Liam, then again, and

one final time, unable to stop sampling his sweetness. "I want to feel you, Luxe. I want to feel you in every way I possibly can. I want you to take me somewhere else. I don't want to think. I just want to feel. I want to feel you inside me."

"Well, fuck, Tate, I want that too. I'm shaking I want that so badly." Liam stretched up and whispered in his ear. "You're going to feel like heaven on earth coming around my cock, and I'm going to make you come harder than you ever have before. By the end of the night, you'll be addicted to my cock in your ass."

Jesus.

His knees shook, and his breath shuttered. "Fuck, Luxe, I'm already addicted to you in every other way."

Liam took his hand and drew him toward the bedroom, blowing candles out along the way.

There were nerves, but they came from the unknown of a new experience. He trusted Liam with everything he had and knew his man would make his first time amazing. And if he had any say in the matter, the first man he allowed in his ass would be the last.

Over and over for the rest of their lives.

## Chapter Twenty-Two

Liam's hand trembled with combined nervous and excited anticipation.

He wanted, needed, to give Tate the best night of his life. To make all the trauma he went through today worth it. To make it so Tate would never, not for a single second, regret choosing to take Liam's hand in front of his family and walk away.

The depth of Tate's agony had been written all over his face and in the stiff way he'd carried himself. Randy confirmed Tate's worst fear, and the aftermath was devastating. The entire goal of bringing him here and feeding him his favorite dessert had been to ease a little of his suffering. When Tate had whispered, "It hurts," Liam's heart cracked in two.

He'd give everything he had to spare Tate that pain.

Liam couldn't travel back in time and erase the toxicity of the afternoon, but he could do his damnedest to replace that memory with one that would make today unforgettable for a fantastic reason.

"Arms up," he said as he stopped Tate before he climbed on the bed.

His man smirked as he raised his arms above his head.

"Mmm." Liam made a show of running his hands all over

Tate's torso as he lifted the shirt, revealing yards of tanned skin. "So many yummy muscles, all for me." Tate had just enough ink to contribute to his gruff image but not so much that it overwhelmed his skin. He had a dragon on his left side, a tribal ring around his upper arm, and an ear of corn on the inside of his right bicep. Apparently, that one had been the result of a lost bet.

He pushed the shirt up and over Tate's head, then off his arms. Once he had the sexy man shirtless, he leaned in and licked those abs he'd just called yummy.

They tasted as good as advertised.

He licked and kissed upward, pausing to drag his tongue over Tate's nipple. The man hissed and gripped the back of his head, holding him in place. "Oh, you're a fan?"

"Fuck. That feels better than I thought it would. Do it again."

"Gladly." He scraped his teeth over the nipple, then laved it with his tongue before moving to give the other the same treatment. Tate cursed and arched his back as though offering himself up to be devoured.

"Luxe…"

Liam straightened, bringing his mouth to Tate's. He kissed his man for a few minutes before saying, "We're going slow tonight, baby. You're hurt, and I'd rather die than make anything worse."

"I-I like that." A light flush turned Tate's cheeks a pale pink as Liam brought his lips to Tate's neck.

"My mouth?"

Tate chuckled. "Yes, when it's on me for sure but also what you said." He shifted his gaze away.

"Oh." Liam shot a sly smile at Tate. "You like it when I call you baby?"

Tate nodded, face serious, still not meeting Liam's eyes.

"Well, then, *baby*," he said as he gripped Tate's chin in a light hold that forced his man to look at him. "Let's get your pants off so I can continue on my mission to drive you insane."

Tate raised his hands, lacing his fingers behind his head. "Have at it, Luxe."

Oh yes. Liam loved bottoming. If Tate had never wanted to try switching things up, Liam would have been more than happy. But this was icing on a decadent cake, and Liam was a huge fan of icing too.

He undid the button and zipper on Tate's jeans, keeping their eyes locked, then pushed them over his trim hips. Once they hit the floor, he hooked his thumbs in Tate's navy boxer briefs and worked them over his ass, making sure to get in a good squeeze on the way.

Tate's cock sprang forward, hard, thick, and ready for some fun.

"You hard too?" Tate asked with a hint of tremor in his tone.

"Are you kidding me?" Laughing, Liam thrust his pelvis against Tate's muscular thigh. He grit his teeth against the urge to shove Tate to the bed and ride that firm quadriceps right to completion. "I get hard when someone says your name, baby. Right now, I'm peeling your clothes off so I can fuck you. Hard doesn't begin to describe how my poor cock is feeling."

He winked, then dropped to his knees and went to work on Tate's sneakers. Once untied, he helped Tate step out of them, as well as his pants and underwear. Instead of returning to a stand, he rose on his knees and wrapped his hand around the base of Tate's impressive cock.

"Damn, you look so pretty down there on your knees."

Yep, it was official. He'd give Tate anything he wanted to continue hearing the guy call him pretty.

"Yeah?" He rubbed the tip of Tate's dick over his lips,

smearing his precum like an erotic gloss.

Tate's eyes darkened. He still had his hands behind his head like some kind of offered-up sacrifice. The way his biceps bulged made Liam want to rise to his feet and take a bite.

"Oh yeah, so damn pretty."

"Thank you." To reward Tate for the compliments, Liam tongued his slit.

"Fuck." He jolted hard. "I need to sit before I fucking fall."

Liam sucked hard on Tate's tip, loving the way his man reacted to his mouth. "By all means," he said after releasing Tate's dick. "Actually, why don't you lie on the bed? On your stomach."

Uncertainty flashed in Tate's eyes, and he swallowed hard but nodded before scooting onto the bed. "You're not naked."

"Ooops," Liam said with a chuckle. "How about I fix that?"

Tate watched him disrobe with hungry eyes. Liam soaked up the attention as he removed his shirt, shoes, shorts, and the tiny pink briefs he'd worn that morning. He'd never grow tired of Tate's eyes on him. Hell, if the man wanted a strip show every day, Liam would be happy to provide it. He was a natural-born performer, after all.

"Christ, those things are sexy."

"Thank you," he said, reaching for his cock.

"Seriously, I'm gonna need you to wear those again soon so I can take them off with my teeth."

*Jesus.* Liam's knees wobbled.

"Anytime. Now, as much as I love the way you look sprawled out on my bed with that gorgeous cock all hard and leaking… roll over."

Tate did, groaning when his erection pressed into the mattress. He folded his arms under his head and stared back at Liam with hot desire.

"God, Tate, your ass is a thing of beauty." He crawled up onto the bed and grabbed the thick cheeks in both hands. Tate's lusty moan made another bead of precum slip from Liam's cock.

He squeezed and kneaded Tate's ass until his man was panting and practically humping the bed.

"Liam…"

He spread his hands and Tate's ass cheeks apart, exposing his tight, pink hole. "Get ready, baby. I'm about to change your life."

"Shit," Tate muttered.

Liam leaned forward and blew a long stream of air on the bared skin.

"Oh fuck," Tate shouted as his entire body spasmed. "Luxe, what the…"

They were only just beginning. If he stayed that responsive, this would blow his mind. "I am going to make this ass feel so fucking good, you'll never want me to leave it."

"God, Luxe, you're fucking killing me. Do something."

A slightly evil grin curled Liam's lips. If his suspicion was right, Tate had no idea how good this could get. But he was about to find out. He leaned in and licked over Tate's rim.

His man bucked and hollered, "Motherfucker," making Liam chuckle against Tate's asshole.

"First time?"

Tate trembled. "Yeah, uh, first time."

"Green light?"

"Fuck, Luxe, yes. Green fucking light to anything you want to do to me."

*Oh, this is going to be fun.*

TATE BRACED FOR what he knew was coming. Quick fucks in a club bathroom didn't lend to such an intimate act. The mere thought of Liam burying his face between his ass cheeks and eating him out nearly had him coming. The puff of air had been enough to make a violent rocket of pleasure coast through him. And his tongue? There were no words.

Liam's warm tongue met his hole again, lingering this time, and the warm, wet pressure awoke neglected nerve endings with a near-violent burst of pleasure.

"Holy shit!" he shouted, jerking his head off the pillow so he could stare back at Liam.

The minx wore an impish smirk. "Too much?"

"Fuck no, that was…"

"Best thing ever, right?"

"Pretty damn close. I'm reserving that title for your cock in my ass." He prayed he could hold out that long.

"Well, aren't you sweet? I think that deserves a reward. Lie back down."

Tate let his head fall onto his folded arms. His ass clenched in anticipation of another tonguing from his lover. He wasn't sure he could survive it, but he'd give it his very best.

Liam wasted no time. He dove in, licking circles around Tate's asshole and occasionally nipping at his crack. Tate tried not to dissolve into a porn-worthy mess of moans and whimpers, but it was damn near impossible, especially when Liam whispered, "Fuck, I love this," into his ass before attacking him again.

His balls ached with the fierce need to come, but at the same time, he wanted to revel in this treatment for hours.

He lost himself in the sinful pleasure of the most intimate act he'd participated in. The discomfort in his face all but disappeared. There wasn't space for pain alongside pleasure this sharp. Words flowed out of his mouth unchecked, though he had no idea what he was saying.

Pleas, praises, whines.

And then Liam breached his hole with his tongue, and Tate

let out a half sob half scream. Liam had softened the tight muscles, so there was no pain, though definitely a foreign feeling of invasion, but at the same time, it felt better than anything he'd experienced before. "Liam," he choked out as he started to fuck the bed. "I need to come. Fuck, I'm dying."

Liam slapped his ass. The sting went straight to his balls, feeling like a hard tug.

"Nuh-uh-uh, no cheating, baby."

"Please, Luxe…" More? Relief? What was he even pleading for?

"Oh shit, if I'd know the sound of you begging would be that hot, I'd have made you do it long before now."

"Luxe…" This time, it was more of a growled command.

He could feel Liam shiver behind him. "That's it. Love me growly, demanding Tate. But I think you're ready for the next step, so let's ramp this up a notch."

Tate groaned when the incredible lips and tongue disappeared, but he didn't have to wait long for the *next notch*. The snick of a lube cap had him tensing, but Liam was right there, crooning in his ear. "Just relax, baby. One finger to start, and it's nice and lubed up. I promise this is going to feel good."

He circled Tate's rim, and like the tongue, it felt new but damn good.

"I wish you could see yourself right now, baby. This beautiful home is already soft and opening up for me. It's beautiful. You're just dying to be full of me, aren't you?"

Pressure came next, and before he had the chance to process the increased sensation or the erotic question fully, Liam's finger slipped inside him.

"I… oh shit… wow."

"So eloquent, baby."

Liam was inside him. A man, the most perfect man, had his finger buried in Tate's ass. And Tate liked it. There was mild discomfort from the unfamiliar invasion, a slight burn and stretch, but nothing he couldn't handle.

"I... I like it."

Warm lips trailed up his spine. "Good. I want you to fucking love it, though, so how about I do this?" Liam circled his finger, probing, testing, and loosening the hole for his cock. Tate breathed and forced himself to relax and feel, not think. "Or this?" Liam curled his finger and hit something that set off an entire firework show in Tate's body.

"Luxe! Fuck!"

Liam chuckled as he kissed along the ridge of Tate's shoulder blade. "Wanna guess what that was?"

His skin buzzed with electricity. Even his body hair felt charged. "Jesus, had I known you guys were dead serious about the prostate, I mighta tried that on my own."

"Trust me, we do not lie about the magic of the prostate." Liam did it again, and Tate's back bowed as he let out a high-pitched whine and bit the inside of his cheek to keep from coming.

"You can't do much more of that, Luxe, or I'll be lying in a puddle of cum and miss the main event."

"No, we definitely can't have that." Liam licked a line up the back of Tate's neck, then sucked where it curved into his shoulder as he sneakily snuck a second finger in him.

It ramped up the intensity for sure, making him feel like he was riding the edge of pleasure and pain, but he fucking loved it. When Liam scissored his fingers, stretching him, he groaned and experimentally pushed back on the fingers.

"That's it," Liam said, still laying a mix of soft and biting kisses all over his back. "You're taking two fingers well, baby. You're gonna take my cock like a champ, but I want one more in you first. Make sure you're ready for me, okay?"

"Yeah, yeah, do it." He panted and rocked back, coming up onto his elbows to get those fingers in deeper.

Liam was really finger-fucking him now, whispering approval and filthy promises as he worked a third finger inside. He hit Tate's prostate a few more times, each accompanied by a dark chuckle when Tate shouted and cursed.

His body shook. Sweat rolled down his back, captured by Liam's searching tongue. His breath came in great heaves and flops. "Oh God, please, Luxe." He was going out of his damn mind. "I'm not gonna last. You gotta fuck me now. I'm ready."

"Mmm, I think you are." Liam pulled his fingers out, and Tate moaned at the loss of fullness. He'd fought this in his mind, but fuck, if he didn't love the feeling of those fingers in his ass. He had a feeling in the future, he'd be fighting Liam for the bottom position, and that they had a lot of flip-fucking on the horizon.

"Roll over, baby," Liam said as he lightly slapped Tate's ass. "I wanna see you when I take you for the first time. Wanna see every single expression on that gorgeous face. Wanna watch those eyes glaze over when I push into you."

"Fuck." Tate rolled over so fast he nearly sent Liam tumbling off the bed.

"Eager?" Liam said with a laugh as he righted himself.

"You fucking know I am. Now get that pretty cock inside me." He hauled his knees up, exposing himself to Liam on his own this time. Any reservations or discomfort over the vulnerable position had passed, replaced by an overwhelming desperation to be filled.

The teasing grin on Liam's face transformed into dark need. He stroked his hands up the backs of Tate's thighs, then shoved two fingers back inside him.

Tate groaned.

"Shit, I almost forgot. Let me get a condom. Jesus, I've never forgotten." Apparently, Liam couldn't resist twisting his fingers one final time.

"No! I'm tested. I'm clean. Fucking promise it. I've never gone without, and I was tested after the last guy many months ago." Had he really just ordered Liam to come bare in his ass? Yes, he had. The thought of Liam's cum flooding his insides had him breathless. "No condom, Luxe."

The other man's eyes widened, and he nodded so fast he looked like a bobblehead doll. "I'm clean too. Never been without one. I might bust before I'm all the way in. This is going to be the hottest thing ever," he mumbled the final part.

The fingers were gone in a second, replaced by the flared head of Liam's dick. He wasn't the thickest, but long and plenty generous enough to make Tate tense as a flicker of nerves returned.

"Relax, baby. Just think about how much you loved my fingers. I promise this is even better. Liam grabbed the lube and drizzled it over his cock before spreading it around.

Their gazes locked, and Tate blew out a slow breath.

Liam nodded. "Bear down on me a little."

Tate did as he asked, and Liam pressed forward with slow, steady determination. "Good, that's so good. You're taking me, Tate. That's the tightest thing ever."

Oh God, he was. He felt so much fuller than when it'd been Liam's fingers. Liam's cock stretched everything at once, causing an intense burn and, yes, a bit of pain, but not enough for Tate to ask him to slow down or stop.

Liam drove forward until his pelvis met Tate's ass as his cock was fully seated. "Jesus." His head fell forward. "I need a minute. I've never felt anything so tight on my dick."

Damn, it felt good to know Liam was struggling with the same intensity of sensations. Tate needed a moment anyway to adjust to the cock splitting him in half. After a few seconds, he was able to relax and let the discomfort melt away. All that remained was that exquisite feeling of being full and connected to Liam in the most primal way.

Suddenly, even that wasn't enough.

"Luxe, please… you gotta fuck me now."

LIAM STARED DOWN at the open pleasure on Tate's face. Had he ever seen anything sexier than the gorgeous man giving up his ass for the first time?

What a gift.

Liam blinked once as though clicking a camera shutter to capture a mental photo of the moment. It would stay locked away in his memory forever.

No matter what happened after, he'd always have this experience.

The clench of Tate's ass surrounding his cock had him seeing stars. As he slid out, the tight walls tugged on the sensitive skin of his dick in exactly the right way. He'd thought sex was fantastic with a condom, but this was another level entirely.

He clutched at Tate's thighs. "Tate, this is… fuck, this is amazing." He thrust back in with a hard snap of his hips. "You're so goddamn hot and tight."

"Oh, fuck yes, Luxe. Do that again."

*Try and stop me.*

He did it again and again with increasing power each time. Within seconds, Tate was moaning and shouting encouragement while Liam fucked him like his life depended on it. The blissed-out expression on Tate's face had Liam fucking him harder and faster just to see him lose himself with each thrust.

Sweat dripped from his forehead down onto Tate, but his man didn't notice. He'd dropped his thighs and planted his feet on the mattress, using them to power his hips and meet each of Liam's wild thrusts.

Liam's orgasm barreled down on him with frightening

intensity and way too much speed. He clenched his teeth and tried to hold off. If it were up to him, this would last all night. He wanted to spend hours inside his man, making him come over and over until they passed out from the pleasure.

But then Tate uttered a savage curse, and his back bowed off the bed. "Again, right fucking there. Fuck, that's it, Luxe."

Liam grabbed his hips and slammed with fast, sharp strokes that hit Tate's prostate each time. His man was a babbling, begging mess in seconds.

"P-please," he said, breathing hard enough to stutter the word. "Luxe, please."

"You're so gorgeous with my cock in you, Tate. I want to fucking live inside you."

"Yes," Tate said as he moaned. "I had no idea…"

But he knew now.

"Luxe, please, I need to come so bad."

"Me, too, baby." Liam grabbed Tate's cock, so slick with rivers of precum he didn't need a drop of lube. He tugged a few times, then Tate shouted and went stiff as a board. Ribbons of white cum spurted from the head of his dick up to his chest. His ass squeezed Liam's cock with the force of a damn vise clamp, making his vision blur.

There was no way in hell Liam could hold on after that.

He cried out as he shook and came with violent spasms into Tate's ass. Before he'd finished coming, his arms gave out, and he collapsed into the mess of spunk on Tate's chest, still twitching.

But he'd never been happier.

## Chapter Twenty-Three

Tate lay beneath Liam, sated and rocked to his core.

"I can feel it." Christ, that had been the most earth-shattering experience of his life on so many levels.

"What?" Liam mumbled against his chest.

"I can feel your cum dripping out of my ass."

Liam groaned. "I'm not sure I can move, but there's no way in hell I'm missing that." He pushed off Tate's chest with an efforted groan.

"Oh fuck, look at you." Tate reached out and ran his hands through the jizz, his jizz, smeared all over Liam's torso. "That is so fucking sexy."

If he hadn't just come like a damn geyser, his cock would be begging for another round.

"Me?" Liam said as he scooted back and encouraged Tate to slide his feet up the bed toward his ass. "Oh, baby, you have no idea how hot this is." He slid two fingers in Tate's ass along with the cum, preventing more from leaving his channel.

"Luxe," he groaned. His ass was tender as hell, but he'd rather die than ask Liam to stop.

"You like feeling it, huh? Part of me left behind inside you."

This time his spent dick did twitch. "Fucking love it,

Luxe."

"Mmm, me too. Can't wait for my turn." His eyes were hot and dark, confirming his words.

"Give me a few minutes, and we can get right on that."

"Perfect." Liam withdrew his hand and then stared at his coated fingers before swirling them through the cum on Tate's chest. Liam moaned as he mixed their cum, then slid his filthy hand up Tate's chest and neck until he gripped his jaw. Then he kissed him, deep and dirty.

Tate grabbed Liam's ass and ground their flaccid cocks together as they made out. It was fucking sloppy as hell, and he loved every second of it. He'd bathe in their combined cum if he could.

They kissed until his lips ached and his lungs screamed for oxygen.

After finally releasing Tate's mouth, Liam kissed his chin once, then said, "How are you? Does your face hurt? Your nose is swollen. Are you having any trouble breathing?" The concern in his expression made Tate's heart flutter.

"Perfect, Luxe. I'm perfect." And he meant it. Inside this little apartment, life was perfect. The outside world might be a clusterfuck, but that didn't have to be dealt with tonight. Other things did, however. "Well, maybe not totally perfect. If we don't clean off, we might end up permanently glued together."

"Worth it," Liam said with a chuckle. "Shower with me?"

It was Tate's turn to laugh. "In your shower?"

"I know," his man said with a grimace. "It's barely big enough for one person, but I think we can manage if we stand really close." He waggled his eyebrows.

The shower was beyond small, but they made it work. Standing chest to chest, they washed each other and played with each other's dicks until both were hard again. When Tate wrapped his hand around both their cocks, Liam rewarded him with a lusty moan. Despite coming less than half an hour ago, they both exploded within minutes and needed a second soaping and rinse.

After drying off in the itty-bitty bathroom, they fell into Liam's bed naked and exhausted. Without words, they sought each other out as though they'd been sleeping together for years. He wrapped his arms around Liam and pulled him close. Liam rested his head on Tate's bicep and snuggled into his chest. Every warm breath wafted across his pecs, proof Liam was real and in his embrace.

It would go down as the best night of Tate's life. The first night he'd been one hundred percent true to himself, and though there'd be hell to pay tomorrow, tonight, he'd fall asleep proud of himself. He shut his eyes and basked in the simple pleasure of holding the man he loved as they drifted off to sleep.

*The man I love…*

Tired as he was, his eyes popped open, and the need to tell Liam how he felt expanded through him until it could not be denied. Restlessness clawed at him. The words bubbled up in his throat and refused to stay in his mouth any longer. "Luxe," he whispered, giving his man a gentle shake.

Liam started. "What? Huh? What's wrong?"

"Nothing. Nothing is wrong. I just gotta tell you something."

Awake now, Liam watched him through wide, concerned eyes. "Oh, my God, did I hurt you?"

"What?" He laughed. "No, not at all. But listen, I have something to say."

"Okay…" Wariness bled through his agreement.

"I—"

He stared at the man he loved. The three words had never left his mouth. Not a single time that he could remember. Randy and he certainly didn't say it to each other, and he couldn't remember ever telling his mother he loved her either. Even worse, he couldn't remember a time anyone had said it to him.

Was this a terrible idea?

Unease he hadn't felt a moment ago washed over him.

What if Liam laughed at him?

What if he didn't care?

What if he didn't feel the same way?

"You what, Tate? You're making me nervous."

"I love you." Peace settled over him as the confession left his mouth.

"You, *what*?" Liam's eyes filled.

"I love you. Only you. You are the only person I have ever loved, Luxe."

"I… oh, Tate." A tear escaped, and Tate swiped it off Liam's cheek with his thumb. "I love you too." He hooked a leg over Tate's hip, pressing them even closer. "I have said the words before. I love my family, and there are friends I love, but this is an entirely new sensation for me as well. What I feel for you exists on a level I'd only heard about but never came close to experiencing."

Even though he'd said the words to Liam seconds before, hearing them repeated back stole his breath. Sad as it was, he'd never told anyone he loved them. What was infinitely sadder was the realization no one had said it to him.

Liam stretched to reach his lips. "I love you," he whispered again before kissing him with a soft, sweet press of his mouth. "I'll say it so many times you'll get sick of hearing it." He seemed to know on instinct that Tate hadn't heard the words throughout his life.

"I don't think that's possible," he said, his throat thick with all the emotions coursing through him.

"What do we do now? Is it safe for you to go home?"

In the dim light, wrapped up in Liam, floating on a couple

of spectacular orgasms, it felt as though nothing bad could touch him. But Tate wasn't stupid enough to believe Randy would wake up tomorrow morning with a changed heart. And once Ducky heard? Well, shit, he'd be on the warpath.

"Probably not right away."

Maybe not ever.

"Stay here," Liam offered without hesitation.

Stay in the apartment with Liam? Fall asleep with him every night, wake to him each morning, and come home to each other after a long day of work? Share their meals and space? God, it sounded like heaven. A granted wish he'd never dared to cast into the universe.

"Luxe, are you sure?"

Liam nodded and kissed his scruffy chin, his cheek, and his lips. "Very sure. I know it's tiny, but I think it'll be nice. And if you need space, I can hang down in the studio."

Snorting, Tate shook his head. "I'm not worried I'll need space, Luxe. More worried I'll annoy the fuck outta you."

"Guess we'll find out," Liam said with a sassy grin that had Tate chuckling.

They kissed for a few minutes, sealing the deal. Tate pulled away when things started to get heated again. Three orgasms in an hour would be a record for him, but Liam needed to sleep. He had a full day of teaching dance classes ahead of him.

"Sleep, Luxe. You'll need a lot of energy if I'm gonna be living with you for a while. I'm a horny motherfucker."

"You better be," Liam said, his voice heavy with exhaustion. He pressed a lingering kiss to Tate's chest and then settled his head against it with a sigh. "I like to listen to your heartbeat when I'm falling asleep."

Well, shit, that was fucking sweet as hell.

Within seconds, Liam's warm body went slack, and his breathing evened out. Tate lay awake long into the night, unable to shut his mind down. Countless questions bombarded him, most of them without a simple answer.

Had Randy spread the news of Tate's sexuality?

Would life in town become difficult for them now?

Were they safe?

What if they weren't?

Could they move? Where would they go? What about Liam's business? What about Tate's job?

Would Liam stay with him if he had to leave?

Eventually, he exhausted himself going around and around without answering a single question. Though he finally slept, it was fitful and plagued by nightmares. Liam woke him once, whispering comforting words in his ear and promising nothing would harm him. He'd shimmied down Tate's sweat-drenched body and swallowed his cock until he came in a near dream-like state. His final memory before passing out again was Liam straddling him and coating him with cum as he stroked himself to completion. After that, Tate didn't stir until the sun came up.

The next morning was one of the brightest, clearest, and warmest of the year so far. As he climbed out of the Uber at the trailer park, Tate couldn't help but feel the universe laughing at him. After the shitshow of the previous day, shouldn't the sky over the trailer park be filled with ominous gray clouds instead of a perfect blue? Didn't his trek to retrieve clothing and toiletries deserve a clap of thunder at the very least?

Or maybe he was a pessimist, and the beautiful day was nature's way of giving him a fresh start.

Either way, he needed some shit from the trailer and had waited until Randy was in the middle of a job before venturing home. His senses were on high alert as he climbed the three steps into the trailer. Every damn noise had him bracing for an attack. He'd refused to fight Randy, but that's where it ended. If Daryl, Ducky, or any other lowlifes who lived there came for him, he'd send them back home, limping and with fewer teeth—though some of his neighbors already had a mouth full of smooth gums.

Thankfully, the trailer park was quiet at nine forty-five in the morning. He pulled the flimsy door open—of course, his mom hadn't bothered to lock it—and strode in, only to come to a dead stop at the sight of his mother sipping coffee at the table.

He didn't have much to say to her, considering she'd offered to blow and shove something up his boyfriend's ass yesterday. He'd finally gotten that little tidbit out of Liam as they sipped their coffee in bed that morning. Tate never would have imagined himself a possessive lover, but the thought of anyone touching Liam had him seeing red. The fact that it was his mother?

Yeah, he walked past her without so much as a good morning. Packing his stuff took less than five minutes. Once satisfied he wouldn't have to come back for a while, he slung his backpack over his shoulder, grabbed his duffle, and made his way back to the kitchen. His mother hadn't moved.

At some point between being rescued off the street by Liam and now, she'd showered and done her hair. The dirty blonde locks hung past her shoulders and needed a trim, but her eyes were clear, her clothes covered all her assets, and she looked the healthiest he'd seen in a while. Amazing what skipping the whiskey in her morning coffee could do.

"I had a feeling, you know," she said as he reached the door.

He turned with a sigh. "What?" Back in the day, before the years of drugs and booze, she'd been a beautiful woman. Years ago, he found a photo album from her early days with his father. She'd been young, happy, and free back before he left her in the lurch with two children and no job skills, education, or money. That was when she started her downward spiral and never stopped.

"I had a feeling you liked dick. Saw the way you looked at our mailman back when you were a teenager."

"Good for you." Well, shit. She sure as hell wasn't known for being attentive, but her observation was spot on. Back when he was eighteen, he'd crushed hard on their very hot mail carrier. Hell, that guy had been the first dick he'd sucked in the very club where he'd met Liam, thanks to a fake ID and raging hormones.

"I don't give a shit, you know," she said, staring into her chipped coffee mug.

"What?"

She shrugged. "Lotta people in the world. All kinds. Some good, some shit. Most fall somewhere in the middle. Who you like to fuck don't matter."

"Yeah?" He turned until he fully faced her and set the duffle down.

His mom nodded. "Don't bother me none. Love is love and all that."

"Wow." He snorted, folding his arms across his chest. "How fucking enlightened of you. You know what mighta been helpful, though? Maybe if you'd taught that to your sons when they were growing up. Maybe if you'd mentioned it, even once, your oldest son wouldn't be a fucking bigot, and your youngest wouldn't have suffered for fucking years, living in the closet because he was terrified to come out."

"Maybe," she said with a shrug, but her voice was devoid of any of the guilt or regret he'd have loved to hear. Something, just a morsel to show him she gave a shit about him. But instead, she plowed on. "Sorry, I offered to peg your boyfriend. Had I known—"

"What?" he asked with a harsh laugh. "Had you known, you'd have stopped at the offer to blow him?"

She shrugged again.

"Un-fucking-believable," he muttered as he gathered his duffle. "I'm staying away for a while. Until Randy simmers the fuck down. If you ever decide you wanna do something maternal, maybe you could help with that."

She didn't respond, so he rolled his eyes and turned to the door. Just as he had it open and stepped through, she called out, "Tate?"

A large part of him wanted to ignore her, but he stilled. "What?"

"Be careful."

It was the first time in his entire backlog of memory that she'd issued a warning like that. The first time, she'd said something to give him a flicker of hope that she maybe, deep down, cared a little bit. "Get yourself some help, Mom," he said before pulling the door shut behind him and jogging to his car.

Now that he had his shit, he could get moving on the long list of stuff he had to take care of.

First, he planned to return a call to the housing developer who left him a message yesterday asking for an in-person meeting to discuss him doing some custom tile work. After one night of living away from the trailer park, things were already looking up.

*Maybe I should have left years ago.*

## Chapter Twenty-Four

"You made it!" Jonah waved Liam over from a table with three other guys in the trendy Culpepper coffee shop. "Come meet everybody."

They all had coffees and welcoming grins. One of the guys dragged an empty chair over from a neighboring table.

"Hey, all, I'm Liam," he said, lifting a hand as he reached the table.

"Sit, sit," Jonah said. "Liam, this is Trevor to my right."

A thin twink with a skintight cropped tank waved. "Hi, sweetie, welcome to our crew." His glossy lips had a natural pout, and the liner around his eyes made them big, bold, and blue as the damn ocean. His hot pink hair was arranged in a tousled style that probably took him an hour to craft. Adorable guy, but not Tate's type. He preferred his men a little scruffier and a little *Tatier*, but he could definitely see them hitting it off as friends. Same with Jonah.

"Next to him is Jimmy Don, but he'll hate you if you call him anything but JD," he said of the man scowling at him. JD lifted a hand. "I prefer people not know I grew up on a thousand-acre corn field in the middle of nowhere. Jimmy Don takes away my mysterious appeal."

Laughing, Liam said, "Makes sense to me. As soon as Jonah said your full name, I imagined you in overalls carrying a basket of corn."

"See," JD said to Jonah as everyone laughed. He certainly didn't have the look of someone who worked on a farm, more like a guy who walked off a cologne ad with tanned skin, perfectly styled light brown hair, and a jawline a sculptor would drool over. Designer sunglasses hung from the collar of his polo. Liam had a feeling that under his clothes, he was muscular, tanned, and hairless.

"Whatever." Jonah waved away JD's complaints. "You haven't even been around corn in ages. Hell, you haven't been in Oklahoma in ages." He turned to Liam. "JD just got off back-to-back European photoshoots with a big-name designer." He pouted. "But he isn't allowed to tell us who it is yet. It's 'in his contract,'" he said, making air quotes.

*Nailed it.*

JD rolled his eyes. "It's not that big of a deal," he said, though his eyes sparkled with excitement. Liam would bet money the designer the guy modeled for was high-end and one they'd all lose their minds over. He'd be lying if he said the prospect of having a connection like that wasn't exciting.

"And last but not least, Murphy."

Liam faced the last and largest of the men. Gigantic was the most accurate description. And a little scary. He wore a scowl that didn't seem to be directed Liam's way, more his natural resting state.

Murphy nodded once in greeting but didn't say anything.

"He's the strong, silent type," Jonah said in a stage whisper that had him earning a glare from Murphy. Instead of cowering under the intensity, Jonah laughed. "He's all bark, well, all glower, and no bite. Murph works security for JD's family's farm. He's a real live cowboy."

"No," Murphy said, speaking for the first time. "Not a cowboy." He had a strong face and a nose with a hint of a bump as though it had been broken in the past. Thick, dark eyebrows arched over his equally dark eyes. His hair was mostly hidden beneath a Jon Deere trucker hat, but it seemed as dark as the rest of his features. The guy had muscles on top of muscles and could probably crack a walnut with one squeeze of his fist.

He was so different from the other three. Liam would love to know how they all became friends.

"Nice to meet you all," Liam said with a smile. "What's everyone drinking?"

"Carmel macchiato," Jonah answered first. "Iced."

"Iced chai latte." Trevor shook his vat of a beverage before taking a sip.

"Skinny vanilla latte with almond milk," JD answered, making the others roll their eyes.

"This one doesn't do sugar," Trevor said, thumbing his hand JD's way. "Heaven forbid he gains an ounce."

"What about you?" Liam turned to Murphy, who had a large to-go cup of something hot.

"Black coffee."

Liam couldn't hold back his grin. "Shoulda guessed that one. Let me grab a drink, and I'll be right back." Thankfully, there wasn't a line, and he was back with his oat milk brown sugar latte in minutes."

"So, Liam," Trevor said when he returned to the table. "What's your story?"

"My story?"

"Yeah." Trevor propped his chin on his hand and batted his thick eyelashes. "Where are you from? What do you do? Why the hell did you move to Swan?"

"Ahh." He sipped his drink and then set it down on the table. "From New York. I grew up about an hour north of the city, but most recently, I lived in New York City. I was a principal dancer in the New York City Ballet Company."

Trevor's eyes widened. "No shit? That's incredible. Now I

really wanna know why you're here in the middle of nowhere."

"I moved here to open a dance studio." He plastered on a smile that felt fake.

"I'm hearing great things about it," Jonah said. "For the first time ever, people are willingly driving from Culpepper to Swan so their kids can dance with a true professional."

His cheeks grew warm. "Oh, wow, that's really nice."

Trevor tilted his head. "Not buying it."

"Huh?"

"Your reason for moving here is bullshit. What's the real reason?"

Snorting, JD shook his head. "You'll have to excuse him. Trev was born without a filter."

"Excuse you," Trevor said as he smacked JD's arm. "Ooh, you've been doing a little extra lifting, haven't you?" His voice turned syrupy as he squeezed JD's bicep with his pink-tipped fingers. The man didn't seem to mind, flexing and winking at Trevor.

"Ain't our business. You don't gotta answer him." Murphy had a deep voice that fit his huge stature.

He considered taking the out Murphy offered, but if anyone would empathize with his reasoning, it'd be these men, right?

"Um, no, it's okay." He fiddled with his straw. "When I was a teenager, I was in a traveling ballet troupe. We, uh, came here and performed at the state fair. Afterward, I was attacked and assaulted, beaten pretty bad."

Trevor gasped and pressed a hand to his lips. JD and Jonah stared at him with wide, enraptured eyes while Murphy's facial expression remained the same scowl.

"After that, I decided that someday I'd come back and give kids like me an opportunity they might not have. I'd give them a chance to be themselves and have a gay male role model." He cleared his throat. "So here I am."

No one said anything for a moment, and he started to squirm under the attention of their stares. Finally, JD spoke. "Well, shit. That's deep for this time of day."

Thank God for him because it broke the thick tension. They all chuckled.

"I remember when that happened," Trevor said. "I was about thirteen and already fabulous." He winked. "My parents forbade me from going to the fair that year. I acted surly the way any teenager who was told they can't do something does, but I was secretly relieved. It was hard enough growing up a gay kid in Culpepper. I can't imagine how horrible it would have been in Swan."

"How'd you get away?" Murphy asked.

"Uh, another kid jumped in and tried to fight off my attackers. Got his ass kicked as well."

Jonah whistled. "Brave guy."

A smile spread across Liam's face. "Yes, very brave. He, uh, he's actually my boyfriend now." And that was the first time he'd said those words. God, it felt good to tell people about Tate and how wonderful he was.

Trevor's jaw dropped. "You lucky bitch."

"Seriously," Jonah said with an exaggerated pout. "All I meet are pieces of shit, and you're with your actual knight in shining armor."

Laughing, Liam shook his head. "I don't know how shiny it is. His style is a little more like Murphy's."

"Oooh." Trevor bounced in his seat and clapped his hands. "We're going clubbing in Tulsa this weekend. You should totally come and bring your stud."

*Tate is a stud, isn't he?*

"Um, yeah, I'll ask him. He isn't exactly the clubbing type." Though, of course, that's where they'd met, but Tate had only been there to scratch an itch, not experience the club.

"That's fine. He can sit at the bar, drink beer, and glare at people with Murph while we dance! This is such a good idea." Trevor seemed so excited Liam couldn't do anything but agree to go.

He stayed way too long, laughing and getting to know the guys who he could see becoming his go-to group of friends. By the time he left, he had three new numbers on his phone, plans for the weekend, and less than one hour until his first class of the day.

As he speed-walked down the street toward the meter where he'd parked his car, he noticed a white pickup truck parked a few spaces behind him. The familiar logo on the back had him grinning and picking up his pace. Had he realized Tate would be in the area, he'd have at least grabbed him a coffee.

He practically threw himself against the open passenger side window. "Hey there, you sexy… oh, shit."

Instead of Tate, Randy sat at the wheel, texting away on his phone. As soon as he heard Liam's voice, he jerked his head up and glared. "The fuck?"

"Sorry. Thought you'd be Tate." He stepped back from the truck, but instead of continuing to his car, he tilted his head and studied Randy.

"The fuck you staring at, perv?"

"What is it?" How many times had he wanted to ask someone those three little words throughout his life? "What is it that you have such a problem with?"

Randy's eyes, the same pretty blue as Tate's, only full of hatred and disgust, narrowed. "My brother's a fag. Do I need more of a reason?"

"Yes." He folded his arms across his chest. "You do. And you need to stop using that word. Why the hell does it matter to you what your brother does with his dick?"

"Because it's fucking gross."

"Fine, you think it's gross. So don't do it. I'm sure there's a lot of kinky shit out there that you find gross. Do you go out of your way to hate people who piss on each other?"

"What?" His nose scrunched. "No. That's nasty, but it ain't my business. Why the fuck would I care—"

Liam smirked. "Keep going. Finish that sentence."

"Fuck you."

"I just don't understand what it is about you uber-straight boys who are so threatened by men like me and Tate."

"I'm not—"

"You are. You are threatened by us." He closed the gap to the car and rested his elbows on the window frame. "News flash, Randy, Tate realized he was gay more than a decade ago. You've lived with him, worked with him, and hung out with him nearly every single day since then. Not a goddamn thing has happened to you because of it."

Randy didn't respond.

"No one is interested in 'turning you gay,' " he said, making air quotes. "That's not even a thing. And if you're afraid he's gonna hit on you, you're just stupid. He's your brother. You wanna screw your mom?"

"What?" Randy reared back, mouth agape. "No, you sick fuck. What the hell?"

Liam shrugged. "Well, you're straight, and she's a woman, so by your thinking, shouldn't you wanna screw her?"

"You're fucking twisted."

"And you're stupid." He stuck his head in the car and pinned Randy with a severe stare. "You're gonna throw away the one brother you have because of some bullshit ideas you have. Tate's sexuality has zero impact on who you are and your life. I'm with him, Randy, and I'm not going anywhere. He doesn't want me to go anywhere. So you have two options. Continue down this path and lose him from your life forever, or grow the fuck up, open your mind, and stop being a bigot."

Randy didn't respond, but a muscle in his jaw twitched with the force of his clenched bite.

"Decide quickly because Tate's getting ready to close the door on you, and once that happens, it won't open back up. I won't let anyone who might hurt him get close enough to do so."

He shoved away from the truck and finished walking to his car. Once behind the wheel, he blew out an unsteady breath and placed his shaky hands on the wheel.

He'd done what he could. Hopefully, Randy had enough brain cells to think about what Liam had said and make some changes.

Tate wasn't the only one who could protect those he loved. Liam would do everything in his power to shield his man from pain.

# Chapter Twenty-Five

Tate hefted a heavy bag of powdered grout onto his shoulder and hopped down from the bed of his truck with a wince. The twinge in his ass reminded him of the previous night's activities. Liam had taught an evening class that ended around eight. Once the last dancer left, he'd come upstairs tired, hungry, and happy.

Tate fed him, ordered him to sit on the couch, and massaged his man's feet until Liam was a mushy puddle of goo on the couch.

He'd been grateful for the attention.

*Very* grateful.

But it would serve Tate well to remember he was new to the ass game and give himself a day or two break before he begged Liam to fuck him again. And he would beg because, at this point, he couldn't decide which he liked better, sticking his dick in Liam or taking Liam in his ass.

Living with Liam the past few weeks had been good. Better than good, it was amazing. He'd never really let himself imagine having a boyfriend, let alone one he lived with, but even if he had, this would exceed his expectations. He'd deny it to his dying day, but one of his new favorite activities was waking Liam with a freshly brewed cup of coffee each morning. The way his man's face lit up at the simple gesture made Tate want to surprise him in a million different ways just to see his expression of adoration.

Liam had made some new friends as well. He'd come home from coffee the other day beaming and unable to stop talking about the amazing guys he'd hung out with. Tate's mild jealousy must have shown on his face because Liam had smirked, dropped to his knees, and shown Tate with very strong suction and tongue action just how uninterested he was in those other men. They begged off the invitation to go clubbing with Liam's new friends, mostly because Tate wasn't ready, but he'd promised Liam he'd meet the new crew soon.

"Been wondering when we'd run into each other." Ducky's voice had him freezing halfway between his truck and the office.

Well, shit. It was bound to happen. He'd managed to keep off Ducky's radar longer than expected. Hell, he'd barely seen Randy or Daryl over the past few weeks, and if he did, he kept communication short and professional.

A few times, he'd caught Randy staring at him with what appeared to be regret and longing, but he'd be damned if he'd make the first move toward reconciliation. That ball was in Randy's court, and he could decide if he was man enough to do something about it.

"Yeah?" He started walking again, heading for the garage, where they kept extra supplies, such as this bag of grout that had been ordered but not used. "It's a real coincidence you showing up at my work and me being here. But I guess life's strange that way."

Ducky snorted. "You always were a smartass."

When he reached the open garage, Tate tossed the grout on the ground next to a few other bags before he turned, hands on his hips, to face Ducky. "Let's get this over with, Duck. Say all the clever slurs and bullshit you think will somehow turn me straight so I can roll my eyes, flip you off, and get on with my day. I'd rather not keep my man waiting at the end of the day."

Damn, he loved being able to say that out loud.

Ducky cocked his head. "Randy gave up too easily. He shoulda put you down."

Unease crawled across Tate's skin. Ducky always was a few cups short of a gallon. The antagonism in his tone had Tate standing tall and preparing for a physical altercation. "You're not my brother, Duck. I'll give back as good as I get with you."

*Come at me, motherfucker.*

"Saw your little bitch this morning," Ducky said with an evil grin.

Now, Tate was on high alert. If Ducky so much as farted in Liam's direction, Tate would tear off his balls and feed them to him. He rolled his shoulders, fighting to keep a casual stance. "Little bitch? That what they call you in prison?"

"Shame about his studio."

*Shit.*

Tate tensed. "What did you do?" He narrowed his eyes. "What the fuck did you do?" he asked with menace in his tone this time.

Smirking, Ducky shrugged. "Didn't do shit."

Tate reached for the phone in his pocket only to remember he'd left it on the dash in the truck. He stormed toward Ducky. "If you even fucking frown his way, I'll—"

"Tate, everything okay out here?"

His boss appeared in the doorway leading from the garage to the inside offices. "All good, boss," he said.

"Hey, Donald, good to see you, man."

Ducky grinned at Larkin. "You too, Mr. Larkin. Swear you get younger and thinner every time I come by."

For someone so goddamn homophobic, Ducky sure

seemed ready, willing, and eager to suck Larkin's dick.

"Well, thank you," Larkin said, rubbing a hand over his protruding stomach. "You looking for a job, son?"

"He's not," Tate said, expression flat. "He's working at the body shop."

"Yeah, but I can always use a few more dollars." Ducky shoved his hands in his jeans pockets and rocked back on his heels. "You need any extra help?"

If Larkin took Ducky on, it'd be the fuel Tate needed to get the fuck out of there and start his own company. No more flirting with the idea. The interview with the developer had gone well, and he refused to work with someone who'd slip a blade between his ribs when he turned his back.

"Yeah," Larkin said. "We got a few big jobs on the horizon."

Big jobs, my ass. Tate had been begging him for months to take on bigger, more complicated jobs, but Larkin was as lazy as a damn sloth.

"Why don't you come on in, and we'll chat, son. And, fuck off with this Mr. Larkin crap. Known you your whole goddamn life. Call me Harry like everybody else does."

"You got it, Harry." Ducky flashed him a yellow-toothed smile.

He might as well have added finger guns to the good-ole-boy routine. Tate clenched his teeth as he counted to ten. It didn't kill his anger, but it kept him from ripping into Ducky in front of his boss.

Larkin disappeared inside with a motion for Ducky to follow.

Ducky back-walked toward the door, tossing Tate a wink.

Hatred flowed through Tate. His hands curled into fists at his sides. How on earth had he ever idolized this asshole? Sure, it was back before he'd hit his teen years, and he was in awe of the older guys who could drive and had the freedom to go wherever they wanted whenever they wanted. He'd followed Randy and Daryl around like a damn puppy, but it'd been Ducky he'd admired the most, probably because Randy and Daryl did as well. Eighteen to Tate's ten, he'd represented everything Tate craved.

It wasn't more than a few years until he'd grown a brain and realized the swagger he'd admired belonged to a bigot and a bully. Ducky had fallen from his pedestal so fast he'd shattered in Tate's mind.

"You know…" Ducky paused in the doorway with a knowing smirk. "There is just something about your little dancer that is so familiar to me." He pursed his lips, snapping his fingers while staring at the ceiling as though he had a brain to think with.

"Don't give a shit," Tate muttered. He turned his back on Ducky. A few more items in the truck required his attention, and they were much more interesting than this conversation.

"Where do I know him from?" Duck continued as though Tate hadn't spoken.

He strode through the garage.

"Oh, shit, I know. He reminds me of this guy I saw at the county fair, oh, fuck maybe a decade ago."

Tate froze mid-stride. Ice replaced the blood in his veins.

"You think it could be him?"

He turned so slowly that it felt like he wasn't moving. Ducky wore a gleeful grin and practically vibrated with excitement. The motherfucker was enjoying every second of this.

"I don't know, man, ten years is a long time, but this guy was memorable. Little fairy dancer prancing around on stage like a fucking girl. I don't know." He shrugged, eyes sparkling. "Maybe it's not him. My buddy and I beat the fuck outta that guy." His voice dropped to a threatening rumble. "Can't imagine he'd be stupid enough to show his face in our town again. You know?"

Atomic rage exploded inside Tate. The knowledge that one of the men who hurt Liam had been within murdering distance all these years drove him to the brink of insanity. Nothing mattered—not the fact he was at work, nor his boss waiting inside for Ducky, or how he could end up in jail. All he could think about was making Ducky hurt as much as he'd hurt Liam all those years ago.

He charged forward with a furious roar, ready to rip the man into a million tiny pieces and stomp all over them. But three strides in, Ducky slipped inside and slammed the door shut. Tate couldn't stop his forward momentum. He slammed into the door with his shoulder, grabbing the handle.

It was locked. "You fucking coward!" he shouted as he slammed his palm against the door. Breathing hard, he lifted his foot, prepared to ram his work boot through it to get to Ducky, but his phone rang with Liam's cheerful ringtone. The pleasant sound from his man's favorite ballet rang through the air in sharp contrast to the harsh thrum of his pulse.

Tate ran to his truck and reached through the passenger side window to grab the phone from a cupholder. "Hey, Luxe," he said, shooting for calm and normal. Instead, he sounded constipated.

"Hey, Tate, I am so sorry to bother you." Liam's voice wavered. "I know you're at work—"

Instantly on alert, Tate ran around to the driver's side and slipped inside. "Fuck my work. What's wrong?"

"Um, I could use your help cleaning something." He sounded beyond dejected. He sounded heartbroken.

As he started the truck, Tate focused on shifting from wanting to wrap his hands around Ducky's throat and squeezing until he stopped breathing to helping the man he loved. "Luxe, tell me what happened. I'm already on my way."

Liam sighed. "Did I mention that I love you today?"

Nothing eased him quite like hearing those words. "Yeah, Luxe, you did. How about me? Did I tell you I love you?"

"Hmm," he said, finally sounding a little more like his happy self. "Pretty sure the last time you said it was when I was pegging your prostate last night.

Christ, this man got to him like no one ever had.

Liam giggled. "You hard now?"

"You know I am, you little shit."

More laughter. Mission accomplished.

"I love you, Luxe."

"Someone smeared shit all over the front windows of my studio."

Tate blinked. "What? Actual shit?"

"Yep. Actual shit. Poop. All over the place. I have a class in an hour, and I refuse to cancel it and give whoever did this the satisfaction of ruining my day. I thought, maybe if you had time to help—"

"I'm on my way. Do you need any supplies?"

"Nah, it was super dirty when I took over the lease here, so I think I have everything I need to clean it. It's just a matter of having the time to get it done."

"Be there in less than ten minutes."

"Thanks. See you soon."

"Hey, Luxe?"

"Yeah."

"You okay?"

Liam sighed. "Yeah, mostly just annoyed. A little sad. I'd started to think maybe the people around here accepted me, but..."

Tate's heart ached. "So many do, baby. And fuck everyone else."

He could practically see Liam's dejected half-smile through the phone. "That's my pet name. No one gave you permission to use it."

"Love you, Luxe."

"Love you, Tate."

He jammed the gas pedal to the floorboard and raced the rest of the way, making it to the studio in a record four and a half minutes.

It'd been easy enough to keep his cool while trying to cheer Liam up, but the second he pulled into the studio's parking lot and the extent of the vandalism came into view, he flipped his shit.

# Chapter Twenty-Six

The smell hit first. Before he'd made it all the way down the stairs to the studio from his apartment, his nose had burned as the putrid stench assaulted him. He'd assumed a plumbing emergency, but when he reached the bottom of the stairs, that notion faded fast.

The lobby and front studio were nearly pitch black, odd for a sunny day at ten thirty in the morning.

"What the hell?" he whispered as he stared at the inside of the filthy windows and tucked his nose into his T-shirt. As soon as he stepped outside, the smell smacked him in the face. As bad as it'd been inside, up close and personal, it was ten times worse.

Someone had covered his entire storefront with shit. It looked disgusting, smelled worse, and would be a nightmare to clean. The sheer volume of mess led him to believe someone had borrowed the *materials* from a nearby farm.

He glanced at his watch with a heavy sigh. In a little over an hour, he'd have ten toddlers and their mothers for a mommy-and-me Intro to Movement class.

*Fantastic.*

What was wrong with people? He didn't have to wonder why someone did it. Their reason was as clear as the reason for the odor.

Bullshit.

He supposed he should consider himself lucky this was the first time someone had openly expressed their hatred. When he'd moved to this town, he fully expected a hostile environment from day one. But when that didn't happen and folks seemed excited about the dance studio, he'd hoped Swan wasn't as backward a town as he'd feared. And that hope led to complacency. Before long, he was living and acting as he'd done in New York, out and proud without an ounce of caution.

Figured that's when the universe decided to knock him down.

After raiding his supply closet for a host of industrial strength cleaning products, sponges, squeegees, and gloves, he'd set about cleaning the windows. Ten minutes into that delightful chore, he realized he needed help and called Tate.

Thank God for that man and his ability to make Liam smile.

He got back to work, scrubbing the windows as he waited for Tate to arrive with all his delicious muscles and work ethic. Hopefully, together, they could knock this out before his class began in an hour. As he scraped the shit off the window into a large trash can, something fell to the ground with a thunk.

He frowned, muttering, "What is that?" If he looked past the mess, it seemed to be something yellow. "A duck?" He grabbed it with gloves and set it on the sidewalk. Why on earth would there be a duck in the—

Oh shit.

A rubber *ducky*.

With that, he knew who had vandalized his shop. Either Ducky was a complete narcissist who couldn't imagine himself going down for this, or he thought Liam would be too scared to report the incident to the police. Well fuck that.

The first break he got today, he'd be making a trip to the police station. He bet Ducky's parole officer would love to hear about this.

The rumble of a truck's engine had Liam peeking over his shoulder. Sure enough, Tate pulled into the lot at the wheel of his work pickup. His eyes immediately went to the soiled windows, and his expression darkened with such intense fury that Liam took a step back on instinct.

Instead of choosing a parking spot, Tate screeched to a halt, his car taking up three spaces. He flung the door open and barreled out of the car like a raging hurricane.

"What the fuck?" he roared, his voice echoing off the building.

Liam winced.

"This is so much worse than you described."

Liam shrugged. "How do you even explain something like this?"

Tate paced, his anger radiating off him in waves. "What kind of sick bastard..." He grabbed the back of his neck and shouted to the sky. "I hate this fucking town!"

When his rage subsided for a moment, Liam pointed to the dirty rubber duck on the sidewalk. "Pretty sure I know which sick bastard did this."

Tate's eyes followed his finger. As soon as he registered the meaning behind the toy duck, an icy chill filled the air.

Oh shit.

If he thought Tate had been furious when he arrived, Liam didn't know his man as well as he thought he did. Tate went eerily calm, his every muscle coiled with lethal intent. His eyes darkened with pure hatred, and his fists clenched. He spun around, heading back to the car with stiff, jerky strides.

"Tate!" Liam called as he flung his bulky cleaning gloves off. "Where are you going?" He grabbed his man's shoulder as he reached the truck, spinning him around. "What are you doing?"

Tate took a menacing step forward, but Liam stood firm. No matter how enraged he became, Tate wouldn't hurt him. Liam knew that with every fiber of his being.

"I'm going to kill him, Luxe."

"Tate..." He placed a hand on each of Tate's shoulders. "Take a breath and—"

"I'm going to fucking kill him!" he roared in Liam's face.

*Holy shit.*

"Tate, shut the hell up!" he shouted right back, glancing around. Thank God, no one happened to be walking by. The last thing they needed was a witness hearing Tate threaten Ducky.

"Luxe, let me go. You don't understand." Tate's eyes were unfocused, and his cheeks flushed with fiery anger. "You don't know everything." He was practically in a trance, consumed by his hatred for Ducky.

Liam shook him. "Tate, snap out of it. Listen to me. We'll get him. He won't get away with this, but we have to play it smart."

Tate didn't refute him, so Liam took that as a green light to continue.

"Ducky did this to intimidate me," he said, loosening his hold on Tate's shoulders. He stroked his thumbs over the thick muscles in soothing circles. "He thinks I'm weak. That I'll be scared and cower because he vandalized my studio, but that idiot has no idea who he's dealing with. This is nothing compared to the hatred I've experienced. As soon as I have a break between classes today, I'll file a police report and make damn sure Ducky's parole officer finds out. He'll go back to jail for violating parole. There's the right way to go about this, and it doesn't involve you going off half-cocked and getting yourself arrested for attacking Ducky."

Shock rocketed through him as he saw Tate's eyes well

with tears. His man blinked rapidly and swallowed before speaking.

"It was him," Tate whispered.

"What? I know. That's why I'll report him."

Tate shook his head and pulled Liam into a bone-crushing hug. "It was him," he repeated. The agony in the words had a shiver running down Liam's spine.

"What? What was him?" Liam's stomach churned with dread. Had something else happened he wasn't aware of?

"Ten years ago…"

"What?" He gasped into Tate's chest.

*No.*

"The fair."

"What?" He ripped out of Tate's arms and staggered two steps back, gagging. Bile burned the back of his throat. "Ducky was one of my attackers?"

Tate nodded with a miserable mix of sadness and anger in his expression.

"Fuck." He slapped a hand over his mouth as he doubled over, dry heaving. He hadn't even had coffee yet, so nothing came up, but his stomach cramped with pain.

Each passing second seemed to push Tate closer to an edge Liam might be unable to pull him back from. He had to keep it together.

He inhaled a long, unsteady breath. "It doesn't matter," he said, the words tasting vile. He straightened and rolled his shoulders back.

Tate's jaw dropped. "What the fuck? It sure as hell does matter. What's wrong with you, Luxe?"

"No." He shook his head and grabbed Tate's arm as he tried to get in the truck again. "It doesn't. The statute of limitations ran out years ago. There's nothing I can do about what happened back then. Reporting this to his parole officer is still our best chance of getting him put behind bars. We have to focus on the present and our future."

"I know the cops won't do shit about it." Tate shook off Liam's hold. "And that's why I need to do this shit myself."

"Tate," Liam pleaded. Would he really go after Ducky? The man was huge and mean as a junkyard dog. He wouldn't hesitate to maim or even kill Tate, leaving Liam to spend the rest of his life drowning in guilt and grief. "Don't go. Please don't go."

Pain twisted Tate's face. "I can't let him hurt you. I *won't* let him hurt you."

"Tate, don't do this. Stay here." He grabbed for his man again, but Tate dodged him. "We'll talk it out. Please. What will happen to us if you go after Ducky?"

"What will happen to us if I don't?"

"We'll be together. We'll clean this mess up, report it to the police, and go about our day. Later, we'll get some dinner, and then I'll show you how flexible I really am."

Tate threw his arms in the air. "And when Ducky comes after you next instead of your building? Did you not hear me say he was one of the guys who hurt you? Did all that therapy you went to make you forget what that fucker did to you?"

Liam reared back as though he'd been struck. "No, Tate, I remember everything about that night. And I remember the nightmares and the fear of being in crowds. I remember the panic attacks and the painful recovery." He snorted. "I wish therapy could have made me forget it, but it did give me the tools to learn how to deal with it. But thanks for throwing it back in my face because it wasn't going to be hard enough to deal with learning who my attacker was."

"Luxe..." The anguish in Tate's voice was almost enough to have Liam backing down.

Instead of giving in, he turned his back on Tate. It hurt more than he would have ever imagined. "I have to get this cleaned up. I could really use your help. Please stay."

"I can't."

Those two words felt like a death sentence. "Well, I can't watch you walk away from me."

"That's not what I'm doing. I'm doing this for you, for us, Luxe."

The nickname had him biting back a sob as he picked up the gloves he'd tossed.

"Why can't you see that?"

He looked over his shoulder, eyes damp. "All I see is you choosing something that could tear us apart."

"I love you, Luxe."

"I love you too."

He swallowed a sob as he bit his lower lip hard. If something happened to Tate, if Ducky did to him what he'd done to Liam or worse, it would destroy him. He was bigger than him, older, and angrier. Hell, he'd done time, and who knew what he'd learned in those months?

"I'll be back tonight, okay?"

Liam sniffed and squeezed his eyes together to keep the tears from falling. "Please be careful." All he wanted was to run to Tate, fall to his knees, and use every dirty trick in the book to make him stay. But it wouldn't work. The conviction in Tate's voice told him all he needed to know, so he stayed put, picked up the sponge, and went back to work cleaning the mess.

Tate's frustrated sigh felt like a battering ram to the heart.

The slam of the truck door, a swift kick to the gut.

And the sound of the engine driving farther away, a door slamming on his happiness.

## Chapter Twenty-Seven

Tate drove straight to the trailer park, blowing two red lights and plowing over three curbs as he turned like a race car driver. Anger bubbled in his veins hot, dark, and deadly. He shoved the fight with Liam to the back of his mind as one thought reigned.

*Ducky hurt Luxe.*

*Ducky hurt Luxe.*

*Ducky hurt Luxe.*

He sped through the trailer park too fast, kicking up dust and gravel. Someone shouted a litany of profanity as he whizzed by like a bullet. He slammed on the brakes outside Ducky and Daryl's trailer, skidding into a ceramic planter with dying flowers. It tipped over, spilling dirt and dead stems onto the ground. Tate didn't bother to right it.

He shoved out of the car, leaving the motor running and the door open as he charged up the three steps to the trailer. He didn't bother knocking, instead kicking the door so hard it flew open with a splintered crack.

"What the fuck?" Daryl leaped up from an old table, splattering a bowl of cereal and milk onto the floor. His chair tipped, and his back hit the refrigerator.

"Where is he?" Tate stormed into the trailer, smacking a kitchen chair out of his way as he lunged for Daryl. He pinned the shocked man against the refrigerator with a forearm across his throat.

Daryl grabbed for his arm with a choked wheeze. His nails scraped Tate's forearms, but Tate barely felt them rip at his skin. "What the hell, T?" Daryl managed in a raspy gurgle of rushed words.

He leaned in, speaking slowly and with a menacing tone. "Where. Is. Ducky?"

This time, he registered Daryl's nails piercing his skin, so he backed off the pressure on the man's throat.

"How would I know? I ain't his keeper. What the hell is this about?"

"Is he here? Hiding in one of the rooms like a chickenshit?"

"What?" Daryl's eyes were wide, face red from lack of oxygen. "N-no. He left hours ago." He shoved at Tate's chest. "Get the hell off me, T."

"Why?" he asked with a smirk. "Afraid you might like it if I get too close?"

The shock in Daryl's eyes vanished instantly, replaced with abject fear. So much fear that Tate's eyebrow arched.

"Fuck you." Daryl began to struggle in earnest, kicking and shoving against Tate with all his strength.

His work boot collided with Tate's shin. "Ow, Jesus, Daryl, calm down." He released the man and stepped back as pain ricocheted up his leg.

"Me calm down?" Daryl rubbed his throat. "You're the one charging in here like some psycho."

He took a breath. The sharp pain in his shin cut through some of his fury, grounding him in the here and now. "I need to know where Ducky is," he said as he ran a hand through his hair. "He met with Larkin this morning about picking up a few jobs. Where would he have gone after?"

Was it Tate's imagination, or did Daryl's face lose about ten shades of color?

"H-he wants to lay tiles with us?"

Could this take any longer? "I don't know what he wants, but he was there talking to Larkin, so I guess." He would have sworn he heard Daryl curse under his breath, but his lips barely moved. "Just tell me where he could be. It's important."

Daryl cocked his head. "Yeah? You gonna go all rage beast on him too?"

Tate didn't respond.

After a few seconds, Daryl shrugged. "You know what? What the fuck do I care?" He dropped his hand from his throat. "Uh, I don't think he's working today, so he's probably at The Nail."

"It's three on a Tuesday."

Daryl shrugged. "Like he gives a shit. Ducky's happy to hit up a bar any timea day or night. You know that."

Of course he was.

Without another word, Tate turned and strode from the trailer.

"You're welcome," Daryl called after him. "Happy to help, asshole. Maybe next time you need something, just, you know, ask insteada tryin' a murder me."

Tate ignored him, jogging down the steps toward his idling truck.

"Don't tell him I gave him up," Daryl called from the doorway.

Tate flipped him off before slipping into the truck and backing out. He could hear Daryl shouting something else, probably about the overturned planter, but he kept driving.

And driving.

And driving.

And driving.

He passed the studio, his office, and the bar where Ducky would be guzzling his fifth beer. It would have been easy to jerk the wheel right, turn into The Nail's parking lot, and go inside. Ducky would be drunk and wobbly, and beating him within an inch of his life would be as easy as singing the ABCs.

But he didn't do it.

Liam's voice echoed in his head, pleading with him to stay and choose their relationship over settling a score.

Tate had chosen to walk away.

"Fuck." He pulled over to the side of the highway and jammed the car into park. *"Fuck!"* he screamed as he beat his open palms against the steering wheel.

How did he do this? How did he look at Liam, touch Liam, love Liam every day, and then look at himself in the mirror, knowing he didn't do shit to avenge him? The thought of his lover suffering any pain worse than a hangnail stirred a homicidal frenzy in him.

Was Liam right? Would it be enough to report the vandalism to the police? How long would he return to jail for a parole violation? These questions came too little too late. He could have asked them an hour ago when he'd been standing outside with Liam instead of losing his cool.

He slumped forward, letting his forehead rest against the steering wheel. Second by second, his fury faded until he was left with a hollow gut and a heavy heart.

"I fucked up," he whispered.

Not the first time. Liam had forgiven him before. Would he again?

He straightened and shifted back into drive, pulling onto the highway with a whirling brain. He drove for hours through the flat countryside, around and around, going nowhere past familiar ranches and landmarks he'd passed hundreds of times before. But he barely saw them.

Eventually, his neck ached from sitting atop tensed shoulders for so long. He took the next right turn, finding himself at a familiar creek—the site of his first date with Liam.

"Jesus," he whispered. Driving there hadn't been a conscious choice. It was as though his mind shut down, letting his body steer him there on autopilot. "I should not be driving."

He killed the engine and climbed down from the truck as he made his way to the creek bank. The air smelled sweet as always, tinged with corn and herbs. He sat then laid back, staring up at the fluffy clouds. Back when he and Randy were kids, they'd stare at the clouds for hours, trying to make out the shapes and characters. They didn't have money for fancy toys, and their mom was either at work or high, so they'd spent a lot of time outside making their own fun. As much as they'd pissed each other off, as often as they'd called each other stupid and drove each other crazy, they'd been brothers. They'd been on each other's teams. They'd had each other's backs.

And now Randy couldn't be near him without wanting to knock him out.

All because Tate was in love with Liam.

Since the day Randy found him with Liam, Tate hadn't taken the time to sit with the encounter and process what had happened. He'd allowed Liam to comfort him, then jumped into the excitement of living with the man he loved.

For over a decade, he'd feared the very thing that happened when Randy discovered he was gay. He'd known how Randy would react. Hell, he'd anticipated the violence, hateful words, and rejection. None of it had been a surprise, yet the pain of losing the one family member who'd given a shit about him was astonishing.

It hurt like hell.

Would Randy go the way of Ducky? Would he take his hatred so far as to go after Liam? Maybe he already had.

Who's to say Ducky acted alone? The motherfucker would love to recruit Randy in his plot to rid the town of Liam, and Randy was just ignorant and hateful enough to do it.

The sun warmed his skin, feeling like a comfortable blanket. The only thing that would feel better would be Liam by his side.

But he'd gone and fucked that up.

He shut his eyes and tried to focus on the warmth of the sun, the prickle of the grass beneath him, and the babbling of the creek.

His phone rang, jolting through him like a cattle prod.

"What? Shit." He sat straight up, blinking and whipping his head in every direction. Darkness surrounded him.

*Where the fuck am I?*

His heart raced faster than a spray of bullets leaving an automatic weapon.

The phone kept ringing.

Finally, the moon and stars overhead registered. The day's events came rushing back to him in a barrage of pain and frustration.

His phone rang again.

Liam.

Shit, he'd passed out. Liam was probably out of his mind with worry.

Tate grabbed the phone and hit the answer button. "Liam?" He shouted into the receiver.

"Tate, get out. You have to get the fuck out of there!"

He blinked. "What?" He yanked the phone from his ear and stared at the caller ID before returning the phone to his ear. "Randy?"

"Tate, don't ask questions. Just listen to me. Get out. Now!"

"Randy, what are you talking about? I'm outside. I'm at the creek."

Silence greeted him for a beat, and then, "Is Liam with

you?"

He gripped the phone so hard his knuckles ached. "No. Randy, what the fuck is going on?"

"Shit, you gotta call him, T. Call him now. It's Ducky."

He hung up without waiting for more and hopped to his feet. He rushed to the truck while calling Liam. The phone rang and rang, eventually going to voicemail. "Luxe, it's me. Call me back as soon as you get this." He ended the call and fired a quick text to Liam.

**911. GET OUT.**

Then he called Randy back, hitting the speaker button so he could drive.

"You get him? Is he out?"

"He didn't answer. Randy, tell me what the fuck is going on." His tires spun on the soft earth as he slammed down on the gas pedal, but a second later, it lurched forward.

"Ducky's gone fucking crazy. He was here tonight when we had a bonfire, ranting and raving about cleansing the town and shit. Think he was on PCP or some shit. I'm telling you, man, he was out of his mind."

"Get to the fucking point, Randy."

He took a turn fast enough to lift the wheels on one side. If he kept up the pace, he could make it to Liam in fifteen minutes. Too fucking long.

"He's planning something. I don't know what. He kept saying he refused to live in a town with fa… uh, gay guys, and it was time to do something about it. Said the problem would be gone by the end of the night. Then he took off. Don't know what he's planning, but if he doesn't slam headfirst into a power pole, I think he's going after Liam."

"Shit, shit, shit. I'm too fucking far away." He slammed his hand against the steering wheel. Fear was so strong it nearly choked him.

"I'll go. I'm getting in the car right now."

Between the heavy pounding of his heart and the blood rushing in his ears, he must have heard wrong. "Randy…"

"I'm fucking sorry, T. I know that don't fix shit, but until that day I always had your back. Trust me to have it now."

What choice did he have?

"Get him, Randy. Whatever the fuck you have to do. Keep him safe. If something happens to him, I'll…" He couldn't even finish the thought.

"Keep calling. Maybe you'll get him. I'm on my way."

"Call me if—"

The line went dead.

"Dammit!" He roared as he threw the phone on the seat with so much force it bounced onto the floor.

He'd never felt like this before. Like he would tear his own skin off if it would get him there faster. Like the panic and fear could drive him literally insane.

He drove as fast as possible, slapping the dashboard as though it could give the truck more horsepower.

Rows and rows of corn whizzed by outside in a seemingly never-ending trail of terror.

He could have prevented this.

If he'd gone after Ducky as he'd intended, he could have prevented whatever horror he was about to unleash.

If something happened to Liam, if he was hurt in any way, he wouldn't have to go after Ducky. He could place that blame right on himself.

He slammed on the brakes, cursing himself for tossing the phone. After wasting precious seconds rifling around the dark floorboard, he finally located it. With one eye paying attention to the road, he called Liam again as he floored the gas pedal.

*Ring.*

*Ring.*

*Ring.*

*Ring.*

*Ring.*

"Hey, it's Liam. Sorry I missed you. I'm probably teaching, so leave me a message…"

He forced even more pressure on the gas pedal.

*Hold on, Luxe. God, please don't let anything happen to him.*

He'd never prayed a day in his life, but he'd pledge his life and loyalty to anyone who'd keep Liam safe.

## Chapter Twenty-Eight

Liam checked his phone for the hundredth time since Tate drove away.

Nothing.

Not a text, not a call, not even a notification.

*Maybe the cell towers are out.*

"And maybe you'll sprout wings in your sleep," he mumbled as he walked into his apartment. It'd been a very long day. He barely managed to get the window cleaned in time for his class. The kids complained about a gross smell in the studio, but it faded as the day went on. Somehow, he'd made it through all his classes without breaking down, but the odds of keeping it together weren't looking good anymore.

He was done teaching and alone in the apartment he and Tate had shared for the past few weeks. At first, he'd worried about living with another man. It was a first for both him and Tate, and he feared it would prove difficult, but the opposite was true. They'd blended seamlessly, and Tate's noticeable absence left a gaping hole in Liam's heart even after only a few hours.

As with lunch, he couldn't eat dinner. But drinking was another story. A few glasses of wine should help lighten the heaviness in his heart. Or, better yet, make him drunk enough not to notice it.

He poured with a generous hand, topping off near the rim of the wine glass. After a few sips to ensure he wouldn't spill, he made his way to the couch. A new episode of his favorite trashy reality TV show was due. Wine and bitchy housewives were exactly what he needed to boost his mood.

Except he couldn't concentrate and was back to obsessing about Tate within minutes. Worry nagged him no matter how many times he reminded himself Tate could handle this and would be fine. But why had he been gone so long? Did he get arrested? Was he hurt? Images of worst-case scenarios wouldn't stop harassing him. Over and over, his mind conjured nightmares of Tate hurt, alone, and suffering, or sitting in Swan's single jail cell. And all of it because he wanted nothing more than to protect Liam.

"Shit," he muttered before taking another sip—guzzle—of wine. "I should have made him stay." Instead of getting pissy and turning his back on Tate, he should have forced the man to stay. "I coulda blown him until he was too stupid in the head to think." He could have done it, but he'd let his hurt feelings take over and turned his back on the man he loved as Tate was to make a dangerous decision.

"What a prize you are."

He sat in silence, stewing in his intrusive thoughts until he couldn't stand himself any longer. Tipping his glass to his lips, he frowned and looked down into the empty glass.

*Whoops, that went fast.*

Nothing remained but a single purple drop of wine. It must be why his head was feeling floaty and his limbs light. He shut his eyes and rested his head back with a sigh, letting the tipsy sensation wash over him. It helped a bit with his misery, sending it to the periphery of his mind instead of the forefront. Sadness lingered, but exhaustion took over the longer the wine had to soak into his bloodstream. He'd keep his eyes closed for a few moments, maybe catch a power nap, then get back to worrying.

Liam's eyes flew open, and he jerked upright with a gasp.

*What was that?*

He blinked, unable to see through the pitch-blackness surrounding him.

*Where am I?*

His heart raced as he tried to take in the dark surroundings.

Home. He was in his home, on his couch, and it was night.

*Where's T?*

The events of the day came rushing back at him with staggering force. "Tate?" he called out, jumping to his feet. "Whoa." He steadied himself against the armrest of the couch. "Guess there was more in that glass than I realized. Tate, you here?"

He ran through the apartment, which took all of three seconds, ending up back in the den.

"He didn't come home."

It hurt. God, it hurt.

But it also made him worry.

"Breathe," he whispered to himself before inhaling a deep breath that had him frowning.

What was that smell? He whipped around, sniffing as he checked the apartment again. A faint scent of smoke tickled his nostrils. Tate smoked on occasion, but this didn't remind him of cigarettes. And what had woken him with such a start? Now that some of the fog had cleared, he'd swear a loud crash had jolted him from sleep.

The smell intensified.

"No," he whispered as an outrageous thought popped into his mind.

Barefoot, he ran to the door leading him down to the studio through the indoor staircase. The acrid odor grew stronger with each step he descended. "No, no, no," he whispered, picking up the pace.

Without thinking, he grabbed the door handle at the bottom of the stairs. Tremendous heat scorched his palm. "Ow, fuck!" he shouted, jerking his hand away. He cradled it to his chest. It hurt like hell, but he couldn't spare the time to assess the damage. Using his uninjured hand, he wrapped the bottom of his T-shirt around the doorknob and opened it as fast as possible. The shirt did little to dull the heat, but it was good enough to keep from searing the other hand while he opened the door.

The second he pushed the door open, oven-hot air blasted into the stairwell. He didn't need to see the flames licking over every surface of his life's dream to know someone had set out to destroy him.

And they'd succeeded.

"Oh my God." The studio was so dark that he couldn't make out a single feature. Orange flames flickered, engulfing almost everything. Thick smoke hovered in the air like black fog. He coughed as the hot, smokey air filled his lungs. Every breath singed his insides and made him hack and choke more. He tucked his face into the crook of his arm, but it did little to purify the filthy air.

*Think. Think.*

What was he supposed to do in the event of a fire?

*Heat rises.*

He pulled the neck of his T-shirt over his nose, then dropped to his hands and knees. Pain exploded through his right palm. He cried out, then bit his lower lip, blinking back tears. The air down there was maybe a fraction of a percent more breathable, but he'd take it. The fire had grown too big, too fast. He'd never be able to contain it himself, but maybe he could save a few things from a blazing death.

He crawled forward a few shuffles, aiming for the front

desk. Smoke and ash stung his eyes, making tears pour down his face. The air was so viscous and dark that he couldn't see a foot in front of his face. With each inch he advanced, the ground grew hotter, his vision decreased, and the coughing worsened.

*Keep going.*

He tried.

Hot fragments fell from above, scorching his neck, arms, and legs. If he could just make it to the desk, he could grab his laptop or some files, something to make it feel like he hadn't lost everything.

A violent cough ripped through him, jolting him so hard he levitated off the ground. Sweat dripped from every pore in his body. Panic clawed at his throat. His brain screamed at him to go back upstairs and call the fire department before it was too late, but he needed to save something. Just one little piece of his dream.

All around him, the flames were closing in. He crawled another few feet forward before a coughing fit made his arms give out. His chest hit the ground with a thump. He shouted, but the sound instantly disappeared into the roar of the fire.

Defeat and despair washed over him. He couldn't do it.

He'd failed.

A sob burst from deep in his gut, turning into another vicious cough. This time, he spit a wad of gunk onto the ground.

The instinct to survive took over, making him nearly desperate for clean, fresh air. Still on all fours, he turned back toward the stairs.

Or did he?

The smoky darkness stole his sense of direction. He didn't have a clue where the stairs were. All he could see was gray fog and flames.

*Get out. Get out.*

Tears blurred what remained of his vision. Every breath felt like spikes driving into his chest. Burning palms and raw, stinging knees kept him moving at a snail's pace.

He crept forward for what felt like hours. Each movement was agonizing and caused more hacking. Dizziness set in. He needed clean oxygen and fast.

For all he knew, he was heading straight into a studio room and to his certain death.

His arms trembled, threatening to give out at any moment. Each movement took a monumental effort. He wasn't going to make it. The exhaustion was too great.

*Where the hell am I going?*

Another coughing fit stopped him dead in his tracks. It zapped what little remained of his strength. He collapsed to the floor, unable to push himself up again.

*Do. It. Get up!*

He tried. His arms shook, and his shoulders ached as he tried to push onto all fours again. But it was a wasted effort.

*I'm sorry, Tate...*

He choked on a sob.

This would destroy Tate.

As Liam lay prone on the burning floor with his eyes drifting shut, a distant shout tried to break through the haze of delirium.

It happened again. Liam couldn't get his brain on board to decipher the noise.

"Liam!"

Oh my God. His name. So far away.

"Liam! Oh, Christ. Liam, are you in here?" The sound grew, still muffled by the flames but closer now.

"Here," he managed in a weak whisper.

"Liam!"

"Tate?" Tate was there?

Oh God, no.

"Don't." He tried to shout, but it was barely audible. "Go back."

A boot crashed into his shoulder, followed by a muffled, "Holy fuck. I found you." Strong arms rolled him onto his back, then hooked under his armpits. His eyes drifted open and shut as he was dragged out of the fire and up the stairs.

"Fuck, what were you thinking?"

"Tate?" he whispered before coughs stole his breath.

"No. But he's on his way."

The air became clearer as his rescuer hauled him up the steps and into the apartment. As soon as they made it inside, his rescuer let him go and slammed the door shut. Liam immediately rolled to his stomach and coughed up a bunch of garbage from his lungs. "I-I can't see yet."

"I got you." He recognized the voice now. "Fire department is two minutes out. We gotta get the fuck outta here. It won't be but a minute before the flames make it up here. Or the fucking floor collapses."

"R-randy?" A wet cloth wiped across his eyes.

"Yeah. Figure the least I owe Tate is to keep you from dying. Maybe then he'll be able to forgive me for being such a piece of shit."

He blinked. The apartment came into view, blurry but clear enough that he wouldn't crash into anything.

Randy coming to his rescue was almost as shocking as the fire itself.

Liam used what little strength he had left to push up to his knees.

"C'mon, lean on me." Randy's arm went around his waist. He hauled Liam to his feet, tucking him close. "You solid?"

"No." A weak chuckle escaped but turned into a coughing fit once again.

"Shit, I can hear it in the stairwell. We gotta move."

Together, they made it out the door and down the outdoor

stairs. Sirens blared in a loud chorus of help coming for them. Randy kept an arm around him as he hobbled around the front of the building, coughing and spitting out black crud the entire way. His vision cleared enough to see well again, but his eyes stung like someone had taken coarse sandpaper to his eyeballs.

Two enormous fire trucks filled the parking lot. A dozen or so firefighters ran around listening to the orders of one barking from near the truck.

"Hey!" Randy shouted, waving his free arm. "We need an EMT over here." He coughed, sounding almost as bad as Liam did.

Two women dressed in uniform ran from an ambulance straight to them, pushing a rolling gurney. Randy stepped away as they reached him.

"Anyone else inside?"

"No," Randy said, shaking his head. "It was just us." He was filthy, covered in black soot, with two white, frazzled eyes peeking through.

The EMTs took over in an instant, professional and efficient in their assessment. Two seconds later, Liam was seated on the gurney with an oxygen mask over his nose and mouth, a blood pressure cuff on his arm, and an IV in his hand.

"Luxe!"

Tate's frantic shout had Liam's spine snapping straight.

"Luxe! Someone tell me where the fuck he is."

Tate. Liam tried to hop off the gurney.

A strong hand clamped down on his shoulder. "Don't even think about it, buddy."

"Please," he rasped, voice like death. "That's my boyfriend. I need to see him."

"We'll get him over to you. You are to do nothing but sit here and breathe all that wonderful pure oxygen."

"Luxe!"

"Over here, T," Randy called back, waving his arms.

Tate tore around the side of a fire truck, appearing like a rough country angel. Liam tried again to jump down but was restrained by a scowling EMT. He paid her no mind, focusing all his attention on the man sprinting toward him.

The man he loved.

"Jesus Christ, Luxe," Tate cried as he slammed into Liam's open arms so hard the gurney wobbled. "Fucking hell, I was so scared."

Liam squeezed Tate as he sobbed against him. Of course, it kicked off a coughing fit, which had Tate releasing him with a gasp. "Shit, sorry."

"Don't go." Liam clung to his forearms.

Tate cupped his face. "I'm not going anywhere. You're stuck with me, Luxe."

They were the best words Tate could have spoken. "I love you, Tate." He coughed and wept at the same time.

"Shh, don't talk, Luxe. Just breathe." Tate kissed his cheek, forehead, then chin, basically anywhere not covered by the mask as he whispered how much he loved Liam and how terrified he'd been. When the EMT finally forced him to release Liam, black soot covered his mouth and nose.

"I got you all messy," Liam croaked as the EMT fussed with his oxygen mask. He reached for Tate's face to wipe away the soot, but the EMT had bandaged both his hands, and he didn't want to dirty up her work.

"I don't give a fuck about that," Tate said as he caught Liam's wrapped hand in his. "How bad is he hurt?" he asked the EMT, scanning the bandages with a frown.

The EMT checked the blood pressure reading and wrote something on her clipboard. "He's got some pretty serious smoke inhalation for sure. BP is a little high, but that's no surprise, considering. There is a nasty burn on his right hand. The left isn't as bad, but it has a few spots that need attention.

We're gonna transport him to the hospital for a more in-depth evaluation." She spoke in a clinical tone devoid of emotion.

Liam shook his head. It felt weird to be talked about while sitting right there. He scowled at the stoic EMT, unlike Tate, who gifted her a winning smile. "He's the most important thing in the world to me, Risa."

Risa might be fooled, but Liam saw the stress and strain beneath Tate's fake smile.

She grinned back. "He's in good hands, Tate. Promise. I'll give you two a minute, but we'll be rolling out of here in five. Tate, you're welcome to ride with us."

"Thanks, Risa."

She nodded before gathering supplies to stow away.

"A friend?" Liam asked.

"We went to high school together." Tate rested his forehead against Liam's, probably smearing more soot on his face. He'd be as dirty as Liam if he wasn't careful. "Luxe…"

"I know." More tears fell. He didn't have the energy to fight them. The only good thing about crying was how it helped clear the smoke residue from his eyes.

"That was too close. I can't lose…"

"I know," he said again. The thought of the reverse, of someone harming Tate, sent a shudder through him. "I can't either."

Tate's arms went around him in the gentlest of holds. "Is this okay?"

Liam rested his chin on Tate's shoulder and his bandaged hands on Tate's back. He'd love to bury them under his man's shirt and feel the warmth of his skin, but it'd be a bit before he could do that again.

"Just let me do this for a few minutes," Tate whispered.

"You can do this forever."

"I'll hold you to that, Luxe."

They stayed like that, with Liam perched on the edge of the

gurney and Tate between his spread legs, wrapped up in each other.

Liam watched as firefighters battled the blaze, blasting it with powerful streams of water. The men and women worked together as a well-trained team, with the leaders directing and others carrying out their orders, no questions asked.

The building was a total loss. Flames engulfed the entire first floor, shooting out of the nonexistent storefront windows and lighting up the night. The sign he'd loved so much hung by one corner, half charred and unusable.

His heart felt much the same, blackened to a crisp and permanently damaged.

Everything he'd worked for, everything he'd built burned into a smoldering pile of ashes. The crushing weight of failure pressed down on him. He'd set out to prove something to himself and the town of Swan. He'd moved there and opened the studio to show the world that homophobic bullies didn't scare him. That the world had changed, and Swan, Oklahoma, needed to wake the hell up and get with the program.

But he'd failed.

One backward bigot wiped out all he'd worked for with nothing more than some accelerant and a spark.

Maybe his plan had been a fool's errand all along.

## Chapter Twenty-Nine

Liam barely spoke after they loaded him into the ambulance, and Tate hated it. It was the quietest he'd ever seen his boyfriend. The silence had Tate worrying hard.

He'd tried to coax a flicker of a smile or laugh, but every attempt had failed. And now, the cops were there asking invasive questions and making Liam describe every terrifying moment he'd endured in great detail.

Tate sat beside the hospital bed, holding Liam's wrist above the bandages. He stroked his thumb back and forth across the delicate bones.

"Can you describe the injuries you sustained?" Officer D'Amico asked. He was the older of the two cops who'd showed up about fifteen minutes ago and could have come straight from filming a Western gunslinger movie. The man was probably in his late forties and had a graying bushy mustache and a large cowboy hat to complement his tan uniform. A chunky silver belt buckle completed the Wild West sheriff vibe. So far, he'd been professional, though his displeased gaze strayed to Tate's hand on Liam's arm more than Tate liked.

"Um, smoke inhalation, obviously," Liam rasped as he gestured to the oxygen tube in his nose. His voice still sounded rough and ragged.

They'd switched out the mask after he'd been assigned a room. They also gave him a little gadget to help keep his lungs open. Liam was supposed to inhale ten times every hour on the hour, trying to make a little blue ball rise to a specific level inside the toy. Every time he did it, Liam ended up coughing so hard, and with so much force it left him weak and shaking until the next time to play the sadistic little game. The doctor promised it was normal, even good, as it helped him cough up the toxins, but every second of watching Liam suffer enraged Tate.

"I have a large burn on my right palm and some burns on all my fingertips," he said, showing his bandaged left hand. "Other than that, I have some minor scrapes, bruises, and small burns pretty much all over my arms and legs. A lot of hot pieces of ash singed my exposed skin."

D'Amico's partner, the much younger Officer Carmichael, scribbled a furious novel of notes on her notepad. She couldn't have been more than a few years out of the police academy, though Tate wouldn't be surprised if he found out she was a rookie. Aside from the rank insignia, her uniform matched D'Amico's. She was shorter than his five-foot-tenish by only a few inches and had her strawberry blonde hair pulled back in a tight bun without a single flyaway.

She peered up from her note-taking when her partner cleared his throat. "Oh, um..." She flipped back a few pages in the notebook. "We spoke with..." She scanned her notes, searching for the name. "Randy at the scene. He stated he was the one to pull you from the fire, Mr. Brady."

"Yes." Liam nodded. His face, now clean of soot and ash, paled. "And please call me Liam. I was being stupid. I thought I could maybe save some things from being destroyed, so I tried to crawl through the fire to the studio's front desk."

"Jesus, Luxe," Tate muttered. What the hell had he been

thinking? They'd been so close to a different ending for this nightmare, and for what? A few dancers' contracts? Once Liam healed, Tate planned to keep him in bed for an entire week, showing him what he'd have missed out on if he'd died in that fire.

Liam leaned over and kissed him right in front of the officers. "I'm sorry," he whispered. "I—"

"I get it. It just messes with my head to think of you in there." Screw the officers watching. He gave Liam a brief kiss before D'Amico cleared his throat again.

Tate shot him a lethal glare. Liam nearly died. That fucker could wait a minute for his damn questions to be answered.

"Sorry." Liam faced them again with pink cheeks. "Uh, it was so dark, I lost my way. I heard someone shouting for me, but by then, I was dizzy and coughing so much I couldn't really crawl around anymore."

Tate's teeth would be ground to nubs if this continued much longer.

"Randy crashed into me. That's how he found me. Pure dumb luck. He dragged me to safety."

Carmichael nodded as she jotted down everything Liam said.

"Randy told us he believes a Donald Hayes, who goes by Ducky, is the responsible party. Does that name mean anything to you?"

Tate snorted.

"Mr. Sutton, is there something you'd like to contribute?" D'Amico asked. He arched a gray eyebrow.

"Yeah, there is." Tate leaned forward. "Randy doesn't believe Ducky is responsible… he fucking knows it. Ducky is a homophobic asshole who beat the spit outta Liam ten years ago and smeared shit all over his studio windows this morning or yesterday morning. Fuck, I don't even know what day it is." He took a breath. "Ducky was pissed his little stunt didn't run us outta town, so he upped his game."

"To arson and attempted murder?" Skepticism bled through D'Amico's question. "Seems like a big leap."

"For fuck's sake," Tate muttered, shaking his head. Damn cops weren't going to do a thing to help.

"I'm just saying there is a big difference between petty vandalism and aggravated arson."

"Petty vandalism," Tate mumbled with a roll of his eyes. "Call it what you want. It doesn't change the facts."

"Could it have been an accident?" D'Amico asked. "You smoke, don't you?" he asked Tate.

Tate stiffened. What the hell was this cop's problem? "What? You think I had a smoke and tossed it in a trash bin full of papers?"

D'Amico shrugged. "You'd be surprised how often people are careless like that."

"Unfucking believable." He flopped back in the seat and crossed his arms over his chest.

Frowning, Liam asked, "Are you saying you don't believe the fire was set intentionally? Is there evidence of it being an accident?"

When D'Amico didn't answer right away, his partner nudged him. "John," she whispered. He still didn't respond, so she stepped forward. "We did, in fact, find evidence of arson, Mr. Brady. It seems someone threw a Molotov cocktail through your front window."

Tate leaped to his feet, fists clenched. "So what the hell is with all the crap about cigarettes and trash cans?"

Carmichael turned to her partner. "John, why don't you check back in with Randy since we have a few more questions for him? He's in the waiting room."

That was news to Tate. He'd assumed Randy would take off as soon as possible.

"I'll finish up in here."

D'Amico's dislike of that suggestion was written all over his scowling face, but he nodded and said, "I'll do that," before he left without another word.

"Sorry," Carmichael said. "He's... old-fashioned."

Liam snorted. "If that's code for homophobic, I'll agree with you."

She sighed. "Yeah, I'm working on him, but he's a bit of a dinosaur, so it's taking a while. My girlfriend thinks I should nail him in the balls with a good swift kick, but I'm saving that as a last resort." Her smile finally had Tate's shoulders unwinding.

"You're gay?" Tate asked.

Liam elbowed him. "You can't just ask that."

Chuckling, Carmichael waved away the concern. "It's fine. I'm pansexual, actually, but I've been with my girlfriend for two years. Trust me when I say I know how challenging it can be living around here. I promise you I will personally oversee every aspect of this investigation and make sure it is handled by the book. I know Ducky and have no doubt he's the type of scumbag who'd do something like this."

Just as Tate began to relax, Liam started coughing. The frequency of the full-body cough attacks had decreased in the past few hours, but the loud, hacking sound still made Tate wince with sympathy. Each episode left Liam exhausted and his chest and throat aching.

"Here, Luxe," he said as he grabbed a small basin and held it under his boyfriend's chin so Liam could spit the crud out as it came up. He rubbed soothing circles on Liam's back as the coughing continued.

When he finally settled, Tate removed the basin and grabbed a cup of icy water, bringing the straw to Liam's lips.

"Thanks," his man whispered after guzzling half the cup in two swallows. Then he faced the lingering officer. "Sorry," he rasped.

She lifted a hand. "Not necessary. I'll go so you two can get some rest, you especially, Mr. Brady... Liam," she added when Liam arched an eyebrow. "We'll be in touch as soon as we have some information for you." She held up a business card before setting it on the rolling table beside the bed. "This is my card in case you think of anything else we should know. Take care."

"Thank you," Liam said.

Tate didn't echo the sentiment. Carmichael might have their back, but he wasn't convinced she could sway the department to give their case the serious attention it deserved.

As soon as she left, Liam turned his head and studied Tate. "You're tense," he said, frowning.

"I'm..." He was too many things to list. "Angry."

"Me too." Liam scooted to the far side of the small bed. "Lay with me."

For the first time since Randy's frantic phone call hours ago, Tate laughed. "We're two grown-ass men, Luxe. I ain't gonna fit in there with you."

Smiling, Liam waggled his eyebrows. "That's the whole point. I want to be close to you."

Tate didn't meet his grin with one of his own. "I don't wanna hurt you."

The pout he could never resist pooched out Liam's lips. "You won't. Please, baby."

Chuckling, he shook his head. "Manipulative little shit." He climbed into the bed with Liam. As expected, they squished in like sardines in a packed can. The bed rail dug into his back, and the head was up at an angle that would have his spine complaining for days, but the second Liam snuggled close and rested his head on Tate's chest, all protests evaporated.

"See? Isn't this better?"

"A million times better." He'd never complain about being this close to Liam.

It was the first time they'd been alone in hours, and it was exactly what Tate needed.

Until he heard a sniff.

"Luxe?" he asked, frowning down at Liam.

"Ignore me," Liam said with a watery chuckle. "Just feeling sorry for myself."

"Pretty sure that's allowed right now." He dropped a kiss on Liam's head. A smokey scent clung to the strands, a potent reminder of what almost happened. He'd help Liam wash it out as soon as they got home. The nurses had cleaned him as best they could, but he'd need a very long shower.

"Wanna talk about it?"

Liam didn't answer for a few moments. He stayed quiet except for the faint wheeze each time he inhaled. The doctor promised that it was temporary and since Liam was young, healthy, and fit, he'd recover without any long-term lung problems.

"It's just… I failed."

Tate tipped Liam's chin up. "What the fuck are you talking about?"

Those honey-colored eyes were full of sadness. "I came here, to Swan, to prove something to myself and this town. I came to prove small towns could change. That places where it wasn't safe for a gay kid to be proud, or a male dancer to perform on stage at the fair, or two men to love each other in the open didn't have to be stuck in the past. My dance studio was supposed to be a haven for kids like me and couples like us. Instead of that happening, I erected a huge target for people like Ducky to take shots at. I failed."

Never in his life had someone come to him for advice. He wasn't the one to impart sage wisdom to anyone because he'd never even left the state of Oklahoma. But he knew what it was like to hate himself, and he refused to let Liam travel that path.

"If I know you, Luxe, and I like to think I do by now, I know damn well that you aren't going to shut your doors forever. You'll rebuild your studio and have it back up and running as soon as humanly possible."

"Well, sure, but—"

"Nu-huh," he said, smooshing Liam's lips between his fingers. His boyfriend scowled, and Tate chuckled. "My turn to talk. You only fail if you let Ducky run you out of town. Rebuilding will show every kid like you and every kid like me whose hiding who they are, that pieces of shit like Ducky do not get to win. No matter what gets thrown at you, you are strong enough to succeed. Sure, you might have some cracks and bruises, and you might be held together with duct tape and chewing gum, but you're there and not going anywhere."

"We," Liam whispered, silent tears rolling down his cheeks. "We're not going anywhere."

"Yeah. We. Ducky's ass is going back to jail. It'll be a long time before they let him out now. You'll be here dancing and showing everyone that the fight is worth it, and I'll be holding your hand every step of the way."

"Thank you," Liam said. He snuggled close and sighed as Tate wrapped his arms around him. "I love you."

"I love you, too, Luxe," he said. He'd never forget how Liam felt in his arms at that moment—warm, soft, alive.

After another moment, Liam mumbled, "Talk to your brother. I think he's ready." Two seconds later, he was breathing evenly, though still wheezing. The hum of the oxygen tank was a comfortable reminder that Liam was getting what he needed for the moment.

Tate shut his eyes. He might have fallen asleep, or maybe not, but sometime later, he popped his eyes open, feeling a steady gaze on them. His first instinct was to roll on top of Liam and shield him from the threat, but he stopped himself when he saw Randy sitting in the chair beside the bed with a remorseful expression.

"I'm not here to cause trouble," Randy said when he noticed Tate had woken up. "I just..." He shrugged and stared at his feet.

A quick glance reassured Tate they hadn't woken Liam. He didn't offer to get up. Randy could get used to seeing them together and touching, or he could fuck right off.

"Thank you," Tate said.

Randy's head popped up, and his eyes widened.

"You put yourself in serious danger to save him." Tate's throat thickened. "Thank you."

Randy shrugged.

No one would claim they were even mediocre communicators, but some things had to be said if they stood a chance at repairing the mess of their relationship.

"He's important to you," Randy said with another shrug. "Couldn't let the guy die."

"I love him, Randy."

His brother met his gaze with a nod. "Sucked not talking to you these past few weeks. I wanna... I wanna fix that. Shouldn'ta punched you."

The punch was the least of it in Tate's eyes. He'd rather take a hundred punches than hear the hateful crap his brother had spewed.

"Shouldn'ta said all that crap either."

Tate grunted. Look at that. Maybe Randy really was sorry.

"I got all these things I thought I knew." Randy tapped the side of his head. "Shit I heard all my life. Shit I believed. But you're my baby brother. I look at you and try to fit you into a box, and it ain't working. Don't know if that makes sense." He picked at a tear in the tan vinyl on the seat between his spread legs.

They'd been so screwed up by their parents and where they grew up. "It does. Hell, I had a lot of those same ideas. It's why I stayed in the closet for so long."

"Yeah."

"Reason you can't fit me in any of those boxes is because those ideas are all bullshit."

Randy lifted his gaze. "Might take me some time to get used to this." He waved a hand in Liam and Tate's direction. "But I wanna try. So, maybe you could help me? Whit said she'd help too, but maybe you could tell me if I say shit that's wrong or offensive so I can fix it. I'd like to see who my real brother is."

Tate glanced out the window before focusing on his brother again. No pigs had flown by. There didn't seem to be an icy chill coming from the underworld either. But something must be off with the universe if Randy was saying all this.

"Not sure you want to see *all* of your real brother."

Randy wrinkled his nose. "Yeah, I ain't ready to see you two sword fight or any shit like that, but maybe we could have a few beers when he's feeling better."

"Sword fight? What the fuck is it you think we get up to?"

Randy shrugged, but he was grinning. "Don't wanna know." He stood. "I'll let you get back to sleep. Want me to bring you two breakfast later?"

"That'd be great, Rand. Thanks."

Randy held out his hand. "No problem."

Instead of slapping his palm the way they normally did, Tate gripped his brother's hand and squeezed. "Thank you, Randy."

His brother squeezed his hand back and then left.

Tate went back to holding Liam.

Liam was safe. They'd rebuild his studio, and he'd be the

best damn dance teacher in the Midwest. Ducky's ass would land back in jail, and Randy just might turn himself into a decent human being.

For the first time in his life, Tate had a bright future to look forward to.

# Epilogue

*Two months later*

Liam's jaw hit the ground. He squeezed Tate's hand so hard his man flinched.

"Sorry," he whispered through a tight throat. "It's just... I didn't expect this."

Tate grinned at him with the same smile he'd worn for the past two months. The new smile. The one that developed the day Liam was released from the hospital and had graced those luscious lips so many times since. It was light, happy, free, and full of love. Liam could live on those smiles for the rest of his life.

And he planned to.

"Shit," he whispered. "I might cry."

Tate moved in behind him. He circled his arm around Liam's waist and rested his chin on Liam's shoulder. "No one will think any less of you if you do," he said before kissing Liam's cheek. "Everyone is here because they love you."

The past two months had been unlike any other time in his life. After a thorough assessment, the fire chief determined the studio building was foundationally unstable, which meant they couldn't safely stay in the apartment until repairs had been made.

They'd been staying in Tate's trailer, which was as

interesting as it sounded. Some of the trailer park residents were open and friendly, while others had dished out some impressive side-eye at him living with Tate. A few were openly hostile, calling slurs and throwing rocks at Liam's car. Tate was aggressive in his defense of Liam and their relationship, going toe-to-toe with anyone who so much as glared in their direction. And wonders of wonders, Randy also came to their defense, standing by Tate's side at every turn.

"Maybe you should say something," Tate whispered.

"Oh, yeah. I can do that." He turned his head and found Tate's lips for a quick kiss. Well, it was meant to be quick, but Tate, the sexy sneak, slipped his tongue into Liam's mouth and upped the ante. "Damn," he said when the kiss finally ended. "You're sexy. Any chance you'd be interested in a date when we're done today?"

Chuckling, Tate shook his head. "Can't, sorry. I already got a man. He's the kinda guy who'll poison my food if I so much as look at another dude."

That had Liam laughing. "And don't you forget it," he said, pinching Tate's buff arms.

Tate released him. "Go speak to your admirers," he said before swatting Liam's ass playfully.

"Hey, hands off the goods, buddy. You think your boyfriend is scary, you should meet mine." He winked, then turned to face the crowd milling around outside his charred studio. Taking a few steps forward, he cleared his throat and peered at the people dressed in work clothes and carrying an assortment of tools. Jonah and their new friends were among the helpers. He'd never seen a pair of pink sparkly work overalls, but Trevor wore them well.

"Um, hey, everyone, I just want to say a few things before we get started."

All eyes turned to him. It seemed as though half the town

had come out to help demo the remains of his studio. With this many hands, a job he'd assumed would take him, Tate, and Randy days of grueling demo work should be done by the end of the day.

"I'm completely shocked by all of you being here to help us today. Shocked and more grateful than I can put into words." His throat thickened again, and he blinked to keep from making a fool of himself and crying in front of all these people. "Uh, so before I start bawling like a baby, I just want to say thank you. Thank you for accepting me and giving up your weekend to help save my dream."

"We love you, Liam!" Trevor shouted, making everyone holler and cheer.

His face heated to a thousand degrees. Being the center of attention didn't bother him. Usually, he lapped it up, but this day was so emotionally charged nothing felt normal. "So, we've already gone through and salvaged what little was savable. Everything else is going. Two dumpsters were dropped off last night. Basically, we just need to fill them up. So, I guess, let's do it."

"Woo-hoo!" Someone shouted, and the crowd broke apart as people went straight to work shoveling ash and burned debris to deposit in the dumpsters.

"Good job, Luxe," Tate said as he hefted a sledgehammer onto his shoulder. A toolbelt hung low on his hips, loaded with various supplies. He wore a white tank, already soaked with sweat thanks to the late August heat. Liam would bet money Tate would lose the shirt in the next ten minutes, completing the work bare-chested.

"Geez, baby, how the hell am I supposed to do anything today when you look like that?" he asked, waving a hand at Tate's general sexiness.

His man's smile turned lascivious. "Oh yeah? You like this construction vibe I have going on?"

"Like it," he whispered. "I'm half hard already. You look like you walked right off the set of half the porn videos out there."

"Really?" Tate arched an eyebrow and stroked a hand up the length of the sledgehammer's handle. "So you like my big tool, do you?"

A loud laugh burst from him. "It's very impressive."

Tate stepped close enough to whisper in Liam's ear. "When we're done here, I'll show you how to use it."

Tate's warm breath tickled Liam's cheek, sending shivers across his skin.

"No need for a lesson. I'm already very skilled with big, thick tools and willing to show you what I know."

"Shit," Tate whispered. He reached down and adjusted himself. "You're fucking dangerous."

"Thank you."

Tate kissed him hard and quickly before walking backward toward the building. "Don't work too hard, Luxe," he said with a wink. "You're going to need some energy for later."

"I don't know," Liam said with a smirk. "We should probably go to bed early tonight, considering you have your first official job tomorrow. You don't want to show up all tired from fucking all night." He bit his lower lip when Tate growled.

"I think I can manage."

"I'm proud of you, Tate."

God, he loved it when Tate's cheeks flushed with embarrassment. But it was the damn truth. He was so proud of his man. He'd left Larkin's company, taking Randy with him, and tomorrow, they had their first job as the Sutton Brothers Tile Company. Daryl stayed behind, but he'd been off since the fire and Ducky's arrest. Liam still hoped he'd come around one day as Randy was, but he wouldn't hold his breath. There was too much good in his life now to let negative people in.

"Stop trying to embarrass me and do some work, Luxe," Tate said with a chuckle before turning and making his way over toward Randy to begin tearing down what remained of the studio.

He watched his man until that gorgeous ass was bent over helping Randy, then he had to tear his gaze away or risk heat stroke. As he glanced around at the fifty or so people who'd volunteered their time without even being asked, a realization washed over him.

He'd done it. This, right here, was the entire reason he'd moved to Swan. There he stood, in the town where he'd once been brutalized, surrounded by members of his community who loved and supported him. Who didn't care that he had a boyfriend or if they kissed in the parking lot for all to see. They accepted him and Tate for who they were.

Was it perfect? No. Swan still had plenty of close-minded residents who hadn't and might never reverse their backward thinking. But he lived in a town where he had amazing friends, a boyfriend he loved to distraction, a business that would be back up and running soon, and more supporters than haters. It was a huge leap in the right direction for Swan, Oklahoma, and exactly what he'd set out to achieve.

"CHRIST, LUXE, WHAT'S gotten into you?" Tate managed as his back hit the wall, and a very sexy dancer rubbed up all over him.

"You," Liam said before he scraped his teeth over Tate's nipple, causing sharp pleasure to shoot down to his balls. "Been stuck watching you work shirtless all damn day. Every time you bent over in these damn jeans, I had to adjust my cock. You knew it too. You've been fucking torturing me all goddamn day."

Tate couldn't help but laugh because Liam hit the nail on

the head, but his humor turned to a lusty moan when Liam's hand slipped into his boxer briefs and wrapped around his dick.

"Luxe…" He thrust into Liam's talented hand. "I fucking love your hands on me, but let me shower first. I'm filthy."

"Mmm, you are," Liam said before licking a path up Tate's neck. "I love you like this." He sucked Tate's earlobe while squeezing his cock.

He should put up a fight. He should insist on a shower, but those hands and that mouth felt too damn good. "Fuck it." He grabbed the back of Liam's head and crushed their mouths together. After a day of hard labor, his back was sore, and his shoulders ached. There'd been a twinge in his hip all afternoon too. But all of it evaporated when Liam's sweet flavor hit his tongue.

"What do you want?" he asked after long minutes of making out and groping against his bedroom's locked door. His mom wasn't home, and Randy knew better than to barge in these days, but they'd been burned before, and he did not want to risk it.

"I want what you promised me." Liam nipped Tate's lower lip as he stroked him and played with his balls. At some point, he'd rid Tate of his pants and shucked his own as well. "I want your big tool. I want you to pound me with it so hard I… oof!"

Tate shoved Liam onto the bed. He landed with a bound and a squeak.

"Roll the fuck over," he barked. His cock was hard enough to rival the sledgehammer he'd spent the day working with.

"Yes," Liam muttered as he flipped onto his stomach in record time. He shoved his silky briefs down and kicked them off before pushing up onto all fours.

Tate wasted no time coating his fingers with lube and working them inside his boyfriend.

Liam cried out, arching his back as Tate scissored his fingers. "Fuck prep. Just give me your cock, baby. Please."

Damn, that was hot. His own cock still drooled with need, so he took a second to work Liam open a bit so as not to hurt him.

"Tate, I'm not kidding. Fuck prep and fuck me."

"So fucking bossy," Tate muttered with a snicker as he withdrew his finger. He smoothed his lubed hand over his cock, transferring the slick moisture, then he notched the tip against Liam's hole. His lover barely sucked in a breath before Tate drove inside.

"Oh, fuck, yes," Liam shouted. "That's what I wanted."

"Really?" he said as he tried to keep his eyes from crossing. Liam's strangling heat did that to him every time. "Why didn't you say anything?"

"Fuck. Off," Liam said around his mixed laughter and moans.

Tate kissed his way up Liam's back as they took a second to adjust to the overwhelming sensations. "Gimme that mouth," he muttered when he reached Liam's face.

Liam turned his head, and they kissed as Tate fucked him. The angle was awkward, and there wasn't an ounce of finesse, but the sloppy, desperate kiss had him drilling into Liam until the bed slammed into the thin wall, rocking the entire trailer.

"God, Tate, so good. Nothing better," Liam practically wailed as Tate nailed his prostate. They'd done it enough times over the past few months that Tate had him memorized inside and out. They'd also done it enough times to be considered addicts, but Tate saw no problem with that. He was happy to give Liam his fix as often as necessary.

"Love you, Luxe," he whispered before sucking on Liam's neck in a way that had him moaning.

"Love you too."

Tate thrust harder, sucked stronger.

"Oh, yes, Tate. Love you, love you, love you."

He grinned as he reached around and took his man in his hand.

This right here—the love, the laughter, the pleasure, the closeness, the acceptance—this was worth every agonizing day he'd spent hiding his true self.

Life wasn't perfect. Tate was nervous as hell about being a business owner. He'd had more than half a dozen meltdowns in the past few weeks, convinced he'd fail before he started, but Liam was there to talk him off the ledge every time. They had the stress of Ducky's impending trial looming over their heads, and neither was deluded enough to think construction on the studio would be without its hiccups, but days like today and moments like this reduced every mountain they faced into a small bump in the road.

Thank you for reading The Duality of
Swans. If you enjoyed this book, please leave
a review on Amazon or Goodreads.

## Other books by Lilly Atlas

### No Prisoners MC
Hook: A No Prisoners Novella
Striker
Jester
Acer
Lucky
Snake

### Trident Ink
Escapades

### Hell's Handlers MC
Zach
Maverick
Jigsaw
Copper
Rocket
Little Jack
Joy
Screw
Viper
Thunder

### Hell's Handlers Florida Chapter

Curly
Spec
Tracker
Frost
Jinx
Lock
Ty

**Mayhem Makers Series**
Solo Rider
Series Page

**Blue Collar Bensons**
First Comes Loathe
Shock and Aww

**Audiobooks**
Audio

Join Lilly's mailing list for a **FREE** No Prisoners short story.
www.lillyatlas.com
Facebook
Instagram
TikTok

Join my Facebook group, **Lilly's Ladies** for book previews, early cover reveals, contests and more!

# About the Author

Lilly Atlas is an award-winning contemporary romance author. She's a proud Navy wife and mother of three spunky girls. Every time Lilly downloads a new eBook she expects her Kindle App to tell her it's exhausted and overworked, and to beg for some rest. Thankfully that hasn't happened yet so she can often be found absorbed in a good book.

www.ingramcontent.com/pod-product-compliance
Lightning Source LLC
Chambersburg PA
CBHW052019240626
47153CB00006B/1873